Thanks

God Bless!
Dennis Patterson
Rom. 8:28

Mississippi *Wind*

"Athletes Church"

706-975-2522

Dennis*Patterson*

Printed by Createspace, an Amazon.com company

Scripture quotations are from the King James Version of the Holy Bible.

Author's note: This novel is a work of fiction. Names, characters, places, and incidents are either products of the author's imagination, or used fictitiously. All characters are fictional, and any similarity of people living or dead is purely coincidental.

ISBN: 1453838724
ISBN-13: 9781453838723

To order additional copies: Go online or request it through your local bookstore.

Printed in the United States of America

Acknowledgments

Tracy…thanks for the freedom you allowed me to write this novel. You were instrumental in more ways than I can list. You helped me tremendously by proofreading this story time and again. I love and cherish you. Let's always keep the Lord at the center of our marriage.

Andrew…you are my first born and I can't imagine life without you. Upon seeing your expression after completing the very first page, it inspired me to write the rest of this novel. I love you more than you'll ever know. Always walk with Christ.

Amanda…you are God's gift to the world. God has put you on this earth as His ambassador of love. You're the most precious child a father could ever dream of having. Study hard and reach for the stars Princess. You are so loved by me.

Hannah…you are the most unique child God has ever created in my humble opinion. I love it when you fall asleep in my arms at night. Words can't describe how special you are to me. Don't stop the entertainment! Your dad loves you very much.

Mama…what can I say? You have always been there for me. Your belief that anything is possible with God has meant a great deal. I am so very proud that you are my mother. Always know that I am thinking of you and loving you.

Church fellowship…thanks for your sincere prayers, love, and understanding. I'm thrilled the Lord has placed me and my family in your midst. We love you and pray you are inspired of God.

Mississippi *Wind*

Prologue

A convicted killer serving *life* without the possibility of parole is common for Mulberry Penitentiary. But what's uncommon and particularly dangerous is a black Mulberry inmate praying for the living white victims of his remorseful crime. Faith wasn't something to be advertised or personally promoted. One of Mulberry's most violent gangs appropriately called *Hell's Chosen* had snuffed out the lives of three openly professing Christians in the past eighteen months, and they'd yet been held accountable. Being labeled one of the *consecrated* would most assuredly fuel the raging flames of the demonic gang who sought their warped excuse to pounce.

Cell inmate number forty-eight rolled off the lumpy mattress and onto the hard floor. Eugene Thompson rarely slept through the night without finding himself on bended knees. With his long skeletal fingers interlocked and pressed firmly against his narrow chin, Eugene purposely prayed to the God who's able to do mighty things if the request was made in faith. His prayers were the means to make his miserable confinement highly profitable for kingdom sake.

The cell was steamy, and sweat streamed down Eugene's bare back. The tall and slender Eugene weighed less than one-seventy. His hair-line had receded significantly since entering prison and beads of perspiration on his forehead and scalp glistened. It'd been *lights-out* for hours, but the tiny dungeon still managed a dim glow resulting from the small viewing window on the locked door. The shatterproof glass kept the lonely dwelling from complete darkness throughout the night.

By day, the inmates lived a much cooler existence, but during sleep hours the air-conditioning was practically shut-down. The current Arizona governor had preached his message of energy conservation during the campaign, and after the landslide victory, he cruelly followed through on that promise.

The summer heat though was a minor factor in Eugene's dramatic weight loss. The primary explanation was his dedication to the twenty-one days of prayer and *fasting*. In all, he'd dropped fifty pounds in two years, and half being the result of the fast. His tongue hadn't touched solid food for twenty days and nights. He flushed the three meals per day in the toilet to prevent the guards from thinking he'd gone suicidal. With one remaining day of fasting, Eugene humbly believed his petition would come to fruition. That belief is what motivated Eugene to stay the course. It's what got him from one day to the next.

Eugene also understood the Biblical principle of reaping what one had sowed. It's an eye for an eye according to the Word. He'd deserved the life sentence which was rendered, and for that matter, even death. Eugene often praised God for allowing him the opportunity to serve his life sentence as an ambassador of intercession. It wouldn't be necessary for Eugene to take the dreadful last walk to the lethal injection room like those of recent months. Number eight was scheduled to take place in three weeks. The average was currently two ruthless murderers put to death each year of his Mulberry residency.

Eugene was grateful he'd been spared the death row list. This saved his children further worry and pain. They'd gone through enough. It was time for them to heal and move into a life of their own. He deeply loved and missed his children, always looking forward to their annual Christmas visit from Mississippi. With each visit and letter, the children mentioned how proud they were their father had come to know Christ. They were convinced his faith was genuine and God had given him a purpose for living. The children were thrilled by his changed life.

Eugene now accepted the life sentence which had been ordered by the Jurors. Eugene, the former lost soul, was the man who stood in the emotional Philadelphia courtroom to receive his punishment. He'd despised the judge, jury and every prosecutor who worked on the case. At the time, Eugene felt they were out to destroy him and his remaining family. He hated them with all his might.

But that was the old man, the lost soul.

Presently, every ounce of pent-up hate and intense bitterness was obsolete and not a trace of it left in his soul. The new man was at peace with his Maker.

Two years after Eugene's conviction his whole world was changed by the awesome power of the Gospel. Eugene, *the convicted murderer,* began to see things differently. Not with limited physical vision, but with boundless spiritual insight, thanks to the ministry of the prison chaplain. It's a rough place for a man to surrender to God's call, but Chaplain Horne was one of those rare soldiers of the Lord. If it hadn't been for the chaplain, Eugene's life would be empty, meaningless and guilt-ridden.

For Eugene, praying was warfare. For two years, he's been waging a spiritual battle against *principalities* and *powers* to unleash the favor of God in the lives of others. Eugene's sole purpose for praying was to discover the providential power of God to be glorified even through a most tragic of incidents.

With his slim six-foot-three-inch sweaty frame bent limply over the sheet-less mattress, the earnest prayers of a blood bought killer penetrated the Throne of Grace. "*Heavenly Father, by the power of your Holy Spirit I make my request in the mighty name of Jesus. Intervene in the lives of those I've hurt with my evil actions. Work a miracle that might bring good out of bad, light out of darkness, hope out of hopelessness, and renewal out of destruction. You alone are worthy of all praise. For you alone have the strong capability to heal brokenness and mend hearts. Hear my prayer from this prison cell, Oh Lord. Consider my petition, Oh Mighty One...*" Continuing to pray, Eugene was cognizant of the geographical distance which separated himself from the hurting families—consequential to his atrocious deed. Mulberry Arizona is a distance from the State of Mississippi. But Eugene understood time and space was obsolete to the Spirit of the Living God. *He is omnipresent*. All the galaxies of creation were within easy reach of the Mighty Hand of God.

It wasn't necessary for Eugene to mentally grasp all of the phenomenal attributes of the One to whom he prayed. Eugene displayed the greatest quality an individual can possess—the necessity of simple child-like faith. After Eugene's conversion, he wrote three words in red bold letters onto a sheet of plain white paper. The Bible phrase was posted above his bed where it remained. It reads: *PRAYER AVAILETH MUCH*

Eugene yielded to the absolute truth of that particular promise of God, no matter the consequence. He'd continue to pray and live out his personal faith despite the pending danger that awaited him outside in the so-called *Blood Yard*. The notorious *Hell's Chosen* prison gang and other hate mongers wouldn't intimidate or frighten him.

Eugene would trust God to the very end.

After more than an hour laboring in prayer, Eugene crawled back onto the lumpy mattress, and repeated the same four words until he eventually fell asleep. *"Thank you Lord Jesus…Thank you Lord Jesus…Thank you Lord Jesus…Thank you Lord Jesus…"*

* * *

The focal epicenter of his every request was specifically directed toward two families who resided nearly a thousand miles from the prison. The two families hadn't the foggiest hint that the horrible monster of their past was now currently asking God's blessings on their lives. Whenever the Patton and Millard families separately thought of Eugene Thompson their hearts immediately flooded with bitterness, fear and hate. These families were trying their best to forget about the murderer, which was an oxymoron to its extreme max.

Of the two families, Susan Patton and her children were of Eugene's most intense prayer. They were the primary target. Susan's face was indelibly painted in Eugene's memory. Her sullen, blank, empty expression was among the anxious courtroom observers. Susan's state of grief and anger was still completely vivid to the day, even though the verdict had been four years ago. It was the Patton family who he'd devastated the most.

Eugene was equally aware he couldn't change the past, not even one second of it. All he could do was look to the future. God had a *purpose* for restoration, and a plan that would bring Himself Glory.

He discerned it from within.

As Eugene slept—the *Mississippi Wind* began to blow.

Chapter 1

The on-deck circle was chalked the shape of a baseball, but after the first batter its white stitches were unrecognizable as young Daniel Patton picked up an orange weighted donut and slid it down his 26-inch, 22-ounce aluminum bat. After a couple of intense swings, the announcer sitting in a small plywood press box behind the backstop of home plate belted loudly into the microphone. "Batting fourth—the shortstop—Daniel Patton."

As Daniel slammed the knob of his bat on the ground sending the donut into the chalky dirt, familiar voices were heard from the spectators sitting on metal bleachers. Some were clappers, others were shouters, some were the stone-faced—*why am I here,* variety. One elderly and completely bald gentleman sat in a tattered lawn chair screaming his encouragement toward every batter who stepped to the plate regardless of the shirt color. "SON, GET YOU A GOOD RIP!"

The harmonious chatter timely resounding from the positioned players sounded like a host of southern crickets singing a rehearsed melody. Little league baseball has as many sounds as sights. That's what contributes to making the game; *America's number one past-time.*

To the average spectator, one would think the Saturday night game was like any other, but on this muggy East Mississippi night, the contest on field four was anything but routine for Daniel.

There was an unexpected lady standing next to the bleachers. She wore a bright yellow dress, white high-healed shoes and a sparkling, pearly looking necklace. She had beautiful, straight blonde hair extending a few inches below the shoulders. Two identical blonde-haired, blue-eyed young girls were tightly gripping each hand.

The presence of Daniel's mother was both exciting and frightening for the shortstop. The sensation of excitement was due to her habitual absence. She never found time to come to a single game to watch her son. The fright was summed into a singe word: *Expectation.*

For the past two summers, Susan had listened to countless after-game stories of heroism on the diamond, stories that were stretched as far as possible without being a complete lie. Daniel wanted his mother to be proud. So he pumped himself as an up-and-coming superstar. He promoted himself as the home run hitting, slick fielding all-star shortstop of the eleven-and-twelve-year-old Mustangs. He was the king of the summer little league establishment in the city of Meridian, but now it was time to backup his self praise and exaggerated stories with real time action.

Daniel began to feel nauseated at the unexpected arrival of his mother. Due of her commitment in raising three children as a single parent, she found it difficult, if not impossible, to squeeze in recreational family time, even little league baseball. Three years earlier Susan opened a ladies shoe store, *Patton's shoes*, located on Meridian's main street. The load of an independent business owner meant frequently working long after the six o'clock closing hour. The bills must be paid and food put on the table, and Susan Patton was determined to survive.

I should've kept my big mouth shut, Daniel thought. *Mama thinks I'm the next Mickey Mantle.*

The pressure was excruciating as he glanced toward Coach Harper standing in his customary spot down the third-base-line. It was the second season Daniel played under the leadership of Coach Harper, who was revered among the locals as a coaching sensation. Five years ago, he'd coached his team to the Southeast Regional Championship in Jackson, en route to the Little League World Series. A huge accomplishment that was still fresh in the memories of the little league faithful.

After receiving the *hit away* signal from Coach Harper, Daniel stepped into the batter's box, secured his right foot by digging a rut with his shoe spike, squatted into his hitting stance, and nervously waited. As Daniel stared from underneath his navy blue batting helmet toward the snarling lefty, his heart began to pound like a jackhammer. He thought he might explode any second.

As the lanky opposing pitcher began his wind-up, Daniel heard the voice of encouragement from *the woman in yellow*, despite the efforts to distract by the chatterers on the field. "YOU CAN DO IT SON, HIT THAT BALL!"

Daniel's countenance was sheepish as he prayed, "*Dear God, please forgive me for bragging to my mom and help me not to make a complete idiot out of myself.*"

Beads of sweat were pouring down both sides of Daniel's face as the lefty released the pitch.

It was an inside fastball, just below the knees.

The right-handed Daniel clenched his jaw and swung with all the fury of a twelve-year-old. Time seemed to stand still as the bat struck the ball solidly. Daniel didn't hear or see the point of contact.

For a couple of seconds everything went blank.

His baseball instincts switched to auto-pilot before his mind had time to process what'd happened. Daniel sprinted to first base and quickly glanced over his left shoulder. Somehow he visually spotted the ball in the corner of his left eye. The white pearl soared high and deep into the night sky, a towering blast over the red and white coca-cola scoreboard in left field.

After rounding second, the pressure of the moment was instantly replaced with exuberance. "I can't believe it! I did it," Daniel whispered under his rapid breath. His sprint toward third slowed to a victory trot. In fact, he experienced an unusual feeling of weightlessness. It was like running in the clouds. It seemed as though he was floating rather than trotting.

After touching third, Coach Harper swatted his moist blue number-8 jersey and yelled, "AD-A-BOY!"

Stepping on home plate, he heard the faithful in the bleachers applauding and verbally expressing their complete approval. Now surrounded by teammates, his ears rang from the pounding slaps upside his helmet. When the swats to his helmet concluded, Daniel proceeded to oblige each with the traditional high-five while jogging to the fenced dugout.

After placing his bat into the rack, he cut his eyes nonchalantly toward the spot his mother and little sisters were standing. Daniel quickly noticed the pleased expression of his mom as she gazed admirably at her first born.

"WAY TO GO SON," Susan proudly shouted. A few parents turned to view yet another over-zealous mother in their midst. Susan didn't care if the next Mustang player was in the batter's box. This moment belonged to her son.

Daniel displayed a smile of relief as he takes the helmet off his sweaty blonde head and placed it gently in the rack. Instinctively, Daniel silently acknowledged the Higher Power. *"Thank you Lord. I know I didn't deserve it. All I can say is; thanks for the help."*

As Daniel turned to sit on the bench along with many of his teammates, a somber thought entered into his mind—*If only my dad could've been standing there too.*

The next Mustang batter struck-out.

Chapter 2

After the 12-5 win, Daniel sat in the front seat of their blue Dodge Caravan. He was dusty and wet. Daniel's face was tilted close to the air-conditioning impatiently wishing it'd quit blowing the warm air. Nevertheless, it made him feel good to be departing from the ball field in the same vehicle with immediate family.

However, Daniel did appreciate his coach.

For the past two seasons, Coach Scotty Harper had been the one shuffling his shortstop back and forth. It was Coach Harper who took on the responsibility to leave his farmhouse located in the Northeastern corner of Lauderdale County, make the loop ten miles to the south, then swing to the Northwestern section of the county, eventually delivering them both with time to spare. The errand was a half-hour out of the way, one of many sacrifices for Coach Sensation.

Daniel wasn't the first pre-teen in his dozen years of coaching who required the extra time, effort and expense—gas was more than two-bucks-per-gallon.

Harper led by example. The coach was determined, devoted and committed, and at times he thought he must be off his rocker, but the Mustang players connected to his '*give it all you got*' philosophy.

He inspired them to reach for the stars and to realize their full potential. His passion for the game was evident to his players, their parents, and the dozens of coaches in Meridian who labored tirelessly in the baking Mississippi sun summer after summer. Harper preached the fundamentals of the game and would, without hesitation, physically demonstrate the correct techniques that were expected from his young players. Often his back hurt, and sometimes he thought his age was creeping up slightly, but Daniel knew nothing about that.

Before each practice and game the coach consistently found Daniel, glove in hand, standing in the driveway of their brick home in the middle-class neighborhood off Highway 39 North. There would normally be a babysitter with the two little blondes. The girls and their sitter would usually stand in the driveway until Daniel's departure and display an enthusiastic farewell with obligatory hand waves as the coach's white Ford truck sped away with purpose. Susan's Caravan would normally be in the carport when they returned.

"Two home runs, that's very impressive Daniel!" Susan enthusiastically exclaimed as she drove away from the baseball complex.

"Thanks," acknowledged Daniel, finally feeling the cool air blow on his steamy face.

"You told me you were a super baseball player but my goodness-gracious-uh-life—wow!"

Instantly Daniel began to feel a mental guilt-trip. He remembered his prayer to God for assistance and it seemed as though God was the one who swung the bat. He sure couldn't take credit for it. After a slight hesitation, he decided it was high time to come clean with his deceived mother or God may never again come to his aid. Daniel sat straight in the seat and gazed out his window. The bright lights from the tall poles of the baseball complex had vanished behind the trees. Daniel swallowed spit, took in a deep breath and said, "Mom, I want to tell you something that's been bothering me."

A perplexed expression appeared on her face. "What on earth could be bothering you after a performance like that?"

"It doesn't have anything to do with tonight's game. It's what I told you about all those other great games," Daniel insisted.

"Well…what is it son?"

"Mom, I've been sort-a, uh, stretching the truth."

"What do you mean by, sort-a—stretching the truth?"

Despite the effort of the manufactured cool breeze, Daniel felt a fresh bead of sweat run down his left temple. He then took in another nervous breath of air and rattled off, "Mom, I just wanted you to be proud of me. You never have time to come to my games. You work all the time and I just wanted you to be proud. So, I uh—made up some of those baseball stories."

After a few seconds to digest his confession, Susan grinned slightly while trying not to laugh. Out of the many challenges of motherhood she began to speak compassionate words of comfort to her conscience-ridden son, "Daniel I am proud of you. It wouldn't change the way I feel about you if you were to strikeout every single time. I'd love you just the same."

"I know that mom," Daniel confirmed.

"Well then Daniel…you won't have to make up one of your whoppers tonight because I saw it first-hand."

"I'm just glad I got lucky tonight," Daniel said.

As the word *luck* rolled off Daniel's tongue, he knew his performance was more than luck. It was divine intervention.

"It appeared to be more than just luck to me Daniel. You got talent son," Susan said nearly reading his mind.

"Well, maybe a little bit," Daniel replied, sounding humble for the first time in the presence of his mother.

"Anyway, your baseball stories are exciting. Don't worry son, I know whose genes you have. Your dad would go fishing and have a blast describing the big one that got away. Nevertheless, it takes a big person to confess their shortcomings and I appreciate your desire to clear the air. I forgive you. Now forget it."

Susan immediately changes the subject by snapping her finger in the air. "I'm starving! Why don't we swing by Dairy Queen and grab some burgers and ice cream."

Daniel, along with his two sisters seated in the back, instantly began chanting, "DQ, DQ, DQ, DQ..."

Daniel was relieved, and felt better than he had in years.

Chapter 3

—

Nothing on planet earth could've prepared Susan for the sudden and tragic death of her husband. After ten wonderful years of marriage, in a flash, everything had changed. Her life was turned upside-down in the twinkling of an eye.

No warning, no sign, no premonition.

The dream of growing old with her soul-mate had vanished in an instant. *"One minute after midnight, wonderful!"* Susan complained, while staring at her constant companion glowing on the dresser. She often wanted to jump out of bed, yank the plug of the digital right out of its socket and throw her own fastball, but the racket would certainly startle her sleeping kids.

Losing her husband in the prime of life was the hardest thing she'd ever dealt with, nothing came remotely close. She'd spent a wonderful evening with the kids—a rarity indeed. The baseball game had been spectacular. Daniel seemed so proud to have played well. Susan recalled the post-game ice cream on Rachael and Rebecca's face and nose. Her three children were healthy, happy and safely tucked away in their beds. Her shoe shop was surprisingly showing good profits after only three years in business, and tomorrow would be a day to rest her tired feet. Yet the attempt to think on the positive side of life would always be suppressed by the haunting of the night.

She was stuck in an endless rut of pain and turmoil.

When the events of the world slowed down, her mind would shift into high gear. Susan squirmed in her queen-size bed staring at that awful digital clock, wishing she'd done something, anything, to have prevented his death.

Four years later, and Susan still blamed herself. When she grew tired of blaming herself, she'd blame God. She hated her husband's killer. She hated him with a purple passion.

Insomnia became a problem.

When sleep did come, there were the dreams. Some were of precious moments with Dan, while others were of the horrific nature of his murder. Each dream, each thought, would cause her grief and bitterness to increase. Wearing the required *brave face* for her kids, customers and friends was beginning to annoy her. She missed him so much that at times it felt as though she might totally come unglued.

Alone in her thoughts, Susan once again returned to the same useless questions. *Why did I demand he go to that stupid store? Why did I need that worthless gallon of milk? Lord, why did it happen? Why did you take him from us? Why didn't he have your protection? Don't you understand how hard it is to raise the children on my own? Are you even listening to me God? This is not fair!* Susan had thousands of questions, but never any answers.

Her tortured mind once again raced back to the event leading up to the tragedy.

The Fourth of July was a hot, crystal clear summer day in the small town of Philadelphia. It was a great place to raise a family despite its reputation as being the little Las Vegas of Mississippi. The entrepreneurial spirit of the Indians brought thousands of gamblers annually to the outskirts of town to try their hand at the casinos. But Dan and Susan overlooked all that commotion.

Philadelphia was their home. They were living the American dream. Dan and Susan had a growing family, steady income and a nice house in the country.

Life was sweet and the future, bright.

They arrived back home around 10:30 P.M. They had spent the holiday eating watermelon and watching the firework show at *Lake Tiak-O'Khata*, located approximately twenty-five miles north of Philadelphia.

A couple of officer buddies from the Philadelphia Police Force, along with their families, had joined them for the Independence Day celebration. Dan was in the *off-duty* mode of rest and relaxation. His socks, shorts and shirt were red, white and blue, but no one seemed to notice.

Dan and Susan thought it was a healthy thing to occasionally spend quality time developing friendships without the presence of relatives. They presumed it was good for their kids to socialize with other children who weren't direct blood. Every Thanksgiving and Christmas was spent traveling to Georgia to spend time with parents, siblings, aunts, uncles and cousins. So the Fourth of July was purposefully appointed: *a day of departure from the norm.*

By 10:45, Susan was walking behind Daniel, Rachael and Rebecca down the short hallway of their 1,900-square-foot-ranch-style home. It was forty-five minutes beyond the children's normal bedding down time. After kissing her tiny girls on their foreheads and tucking them underneath a pink Cinderella comforter, Susan walked across the hallway into Daniel's room.

Dan was relaxing on the living room's recliner, remote control in hand, checking the latest scores of Major League Baseball. He was a huge fan and as a kid dreamed of playing professionally. Unfortunately, a bad throwing arm and the total inability to hit the curve, even a hanger, prevented him from advancing beyond the Junior College level. *"I was one of the greatest third string shortstops in the history of Meridian Junior College,"* he often joked.

Dan didn't have much trouble getting on with life after baseball. He had two years of riding the college pine to form dreams of a more realistic vocation.

Dan's eyes were glued to the scores as they rolled across the bottom of the television screen, totally ignoring an ESPN classic boxing match between Ali and Frazier.

"Yes! Braves 4, Dodgers 3," he verbalized, pumping his fist into the air.

Dan had followed the Braves for as long as he could remember. As a boy, his father made certain they attended at least one Major League game each year. Some years they managed to attend as many as five or six, depending on the standings. Dan's childhood home of Newnan, Georgia was only forty minutes south of Atlanta's Fulton County stadium—a short drive for some Major League action.

Obviously trying to strike the perfect tone, Susan's voice echoed down the hallway from the proximity of Daniel's bedroom, interrupting her husband's undivided attention.

"Honey, do you mind running down to Morton's and grabbing a gallon of milk?"

Dan shot back weakly, as if not really interested, "Don't we have anything in the house to eat besides cereal?"

With persuasive humor Susan tried again, "We sure do, left-over watermelon. How does that sound?"

Dan counterattacked more aggressively, turning his head slightly toward the direction of the incoming fire. "We just passed four hundred convenience stores coming home from the lake. I bet milk was in all of them." Dan snickered slightly—back to the scores.

Susan went for the knockout blow, "Too late to think of that now, don-cha think?" Susan usually won these back-and-forths, she knew it, and so did he.

Dan in defeat, exhaled slowly and asked, "Where are the keys?"

Susan took the sarcasm to the limit by asking, "Where'd you put them last?"

Susan began a slow walk down the hall which emptied into the room where her husband, the defeated opponent, sat. She eased up behind her entrenched spouse and ran fingers through his curly brown hair. Dan rolled his eyes in dread and slowly pulled the handle to the side of his lime-green and ever so comfortable recliner. He stood and grabbed his wife by the waist and said with a serious glare, "You owe me one." He was gazing intently into Susan's bright blue eyes.

"I owe you what?" Susan said, leaning in closer to romantically whisper into his right ear.

"You'll just have to wait until I get back to find out."

"Oh, feeling frisky, are you? The fireworks must've done something...started a fuse of some sort."

"The real fireworks are starting...say...in about fifteen minutes my dear." Dan gently kissed his beautiful wife on her soft lips.

Her penetrating blue eyes got him going every single time.

After slipping on his loafers and throwing on a well-worn Braves cap, Dan spotted the car keys on the kitchen counter, scooped them up and headed for the door. Still dressed in red, white and blue, he opened the door and walked out. Susan momentarily stood in the den, slightly shaking her head and smiling as if to say, *never a boring moment with that man*.

As Susan turned to walk back down the hallway for additional goodnight kisses, Dan opened the door quickly, stuck his head in and asked, "Will you pray with the kids? They might be asleep when I get back."

Prayer time was Dan's nightly routine with the children, so naturally, the very second Dan asked his out of the ordinary request, he thought, *I should take a minute and do it myself*, but decided otherwise.

"I sure will honey. Be careful," Susan said with a reassuring tone.

Dan quickly closed the door and within fifteen minutes, *he would be dead.*

* * *

Glancing at the red numbers of her glowing companion, it rudely indicated 1:13. She was always bewildered at the swiftness of time when in deep thought. Feeling wide awake she jerked the covers from her body, threw her legs off the side of the bed and pulled the cord to a small lamp within arms length. Reaching into the top drawer of her night stand, she gently eased out a yellowed newspaper. The article of Dan's death was beginning to show signs of aging. She'd thought she might do something to preserve the front page report, but why preserve something you despise. Trying to ignore her little friend, *the clock*, Susan began reading the article for the first time in months.

Officer Killed in Attempted Robbery

An off-duty Philadelphia police officer was fatally shot Friday night at a local convenience store in what investigators are calling an apparent attempted robbery. Two witnesses to the crime have stated to police that Daniel R. Patton, a thirteen year veteran of the Philadelphia police force, was apparently gunned down by Eugene Thompson, who was in the process of robbing Morton Brother's convenience store located on the corner of 11th Street and 3rd Avenue.

According to Police, the witnesses, one of which is an employee of the establishment, have been quoted as saying that Officer Patton walked into the store around 11:00 P.M. and surprising the armed Thompson. At some point during the ordeal, Officer Patton attempted to foil the heist by physically disarming the gunman. A single shot was fired into the officer's chest and Patton was pronounced dead by the staff of Memorial Hospital early this morning.

The suspect was unconscious when police arrived on the scene. The unnamed employee who was working at the time of the incident has also informed police that he struck Thompson with a crowbar that was kept underneath the checkout counter, shortly after the gun was fired.

Thompson was also transported by ambulance to Memorial hospital. Charges are still pending but reports suggest he will be charged with numerous crimes including capital murder, assault and attempted robbery. Thompson is listed in fair condition.

Officer Patton is survived by a wife, three young children and many close friends who are calling the officer, 'a hero of incredible courage.' Details concerning Patton's memorial service and funeral will be provided to the public as the information is disclosed. A fund has been established in the memory of the officer at Colony Bank of Philadelphia.

Please make contributions to: The family of our fallen hero.

The family has requested their privacy during this difficult time of loss.

Susan painfully pressed the article to her chest. As tears ran down her pale face, she softly mumbled, "Lord Jesus…why...why?"

Chapter 4

The move thirty miles due-south to the city of Meridian had been an attempt to escape the pain and worry. One month after Dan's death, Susan relocated her family to begin a fresh start. With the help of volunteers from their church, the police station and a few others whom she didn't recognize, the U-haul was eventually loaded and they were on their way. Not even the most intimate of friends could persuade Susan to stick it out in Philadelphia. *What if the same thing were to happen to one of the children?* There was simply too much drinking and gambling in Philadelphia. Even though Meridian was a much larger city, it'd still be a more family friendly environment to raise her kids. Susan's move was motivated by fear, and shared memories with Dan.

The enthusiastic outpouring of goodwill from the citizens of Philadelphia had been nothing short of incredibly inspirational. It seemed everyone in town expressed their last respects. More than three thousand mourners packed Philadelphia's First Baptist Church on the square as Pastor Tim Milton delivered a powerful and compassionate message. It was decided that Dan's own church was too small, so the funeral officials requested the much larger facility.

Dan not only served his community as a dedicated peacekeeper, but was also admired within the Christian community. He had been a faithful member of the historical Hebron Baptist church located ten miles out in the country, near where they once lived. Dan served his Lord as a Deacon and Sunday school teacher. When Pastor Tim needed someone to visit with him on Tuesday evenings, Dan was the one to volunteer, if he wasn't on patrol. He never missed a service with the exception of police duties.

When presented with the opportunity to serve on the mission team to Kenya, Dan had been one of a handful to go, raising the seventeen hundred bucks for his personal expense. Dan's relationship with Christ was deep and personal. He lived his faith by example and there was no doubt that Dan was now dwelling in a much better place.

Likewise, Susan also had been a strong believer, yet not as active as her husband. She and Dan regularly prayed and studied their Bibles together, often staying up late in their discussion of the Holy Scriptures. They'd spent the final months of his life churning through an in-depth study of the Book of Daniel. At the time of Dan's death, the couple had completed all but chapter twelve, the final chapter of the Old Testament Letter. They rationalized that since father and son had been named after the Prophet, it was an essential to thoroughly understand its content.

The couple never got to that final chapter together, and Susan hadn't so much as opened a Bible since.

Now that Dan was gone, Susan was having difficulty putting her spiritual life back together. Instead of drawing closer to God's Word, she drifted away. Deep inside, Susan knew her Christian perspective was on shaky ground. So, out of intentional rebellion, she fought her battle alone.

The last time Susan and her children stepped foot in a church had been the day of Dan's funeral at First Baptist on the Square. Even though there were many invitations from her growing circle of friends in Meridian, she used Sundays as a day to physically rest, forfeiting the sorry state of her spiritual life.

* * *

Daniel walked into his mother's bedroom wearing baseball pajamas. His blond hair was sticking in all directions as he quietly eased to the side of Susan's bed. He gently touched her shoulder and asked, "Mom, you awake?" Daniel knew full-well that his mother was sound asleep.

Susan slowly opened her eyes and asked, "What is it son?"

"Mom, I had a dream last night."

"What time is it?" Susan sluggishly asked.

Daniel looked at the digital. "It's 9:09." It wasn't glowing anymore, but Susan nonetheless still hated the evil little thing.

"Wake me in a couple of hours." Susan knew that it was near four o'clock before she managed to doze-off.

"Mom, I've got to tell you about this dream I had. I think it's real important."

"Can it wait a couple of hours?"

"No it can't mom," Daniel emphatically replied. "Anyways, Rachael and Rebecca are up."

Daniel sat down on the edge of the bed and Susan labored to adjust herself into a sitting position. She tucked a couple of pillows behind her tired back and turned to face her persistent son. Rubbing her eyes vigorously she asked, "Okay son, what is it?"

Again Daniel repeated, "I had a dream."

"What was the dream son?"

"Dad was in it."

Instantly feeling more alert, Susan batted her eyes a couple of times. "What did you say about your father?"

"I think he was in Heaven. At least that's what it looked like to me."

"Sounds like a good dream."

"Mom, it didn't seem like other dreams I've had. It seemed real."

"Well...did he say anything?"

"It wasn't just him—it was them."

"Really...who else was in your dream?"

"He said his name was Jesus. I think he's the Jesus of the Bible because he was glowing. He was standing next to dad. They both were standing next to a beautiful river and the water was different. The water was clapping as it flowed by Jesus and dad. There were all sorts of colorful flowers. And Mom, the flowers sang for Jesus. It sounded something like the choir at the Church we used to go to when dad was alive, only much better. I really can't describe all the things I saw, but it must have been Heaven."

"I like your dream so far. What did Dan and Jesus have to say?"

"They said a bunch. They spoke to me. It was real. Everything seemed so real."

Susan was beginning to enjoy this unusual Sunday morning chat and pressed him for more. "Well, are you going to tell me what they said?"

"That's why I woke you up. Jesus told me to tell you everything."

"You don't say...Go ahead then, tell me everything."

After the request, Susan suddenly recalled Daniel's confession to being a liar the night before.

"First, Dad said that he loves us."

Susan's eyes instantly became moist with the mention of the word *loves*—it was in the present tense.

"Secondly, Jesus said that Dad had to leave us for a reason, and that we'd one day understand why."

Susan was listening intently to her son, even though there was faint laughter coming from the living room. *The girls were probably watching a cartoon.*

"Thirdly, Jesus said that he knows what you're going through and to look to him for comfort. Jesus said He loves us too."

Does he really know what I'm going through? Susan thought.

"The last thing Jesus said was that he has a divine plan for our lives to glorify His Name, but we must first and foremost draw close to him. After that, they just smiled and an Angel suddenly appeared. The Angel walked with Jesus and dad across the flowing river. Mom, they walked on top of the water across to the other side of this river, turned around, smiled again and then I woke up. Dad seemed so happy to be with Jesus. That was the happiest I've ever seen him. He was so perfect."

"Son, you sure have articulated your dream well and have impressed me with an incredibly good memory this morning." Her tone and facial expression was suspicious.

"Mom, you've got to believe what I'm saying," Daniel demanded, also remembering his post-game omission.

"Son, you said that you had this dream and I believe you."

"Do you believe me enough to get out of bed and take your family to church?"

Daniel caught Susan by surprise with the poignant suggestion. "Daniel, it was a dream, a wonderful dream, but it was only a dream. Susan was beginning to feel slightly frustrated while at the same time fighting-off her inner conviction.

"Don't you remember. We never missed church when dad was with us."

"I remember son, but things are different now. Once upon a time I enjoyed going to church, but now..." Susan's voice trailed off. She knew this was a no-win argument. There was no way to logically talk her way out of this conversation with any dignity left.

"Don't you think we still need to go to church?"

Instead of giving Daniel an immediate answer, Susan intently stared into his puppy dog eyes. She knew her son was right. And besides, she didn't want to try and justify her four years of bad spiritual decisions.

Inhaling a deep breath, and then exhaling slowly, a thought was triggered, *what do I have to loose? Church can't make me feel any worse."*

Susan took a pillow out from behind her back and playfully hit Daniel on the head, "Okay, Mister Dreamer of Dreams. What Church did Jesus say we should attend this morning?"

A big smile came across Daniel's face. "Jesus didn't say, but he knew we wouldn't have much trouble picking one. Churches are everywhere out on the highway."

Chapter 5

The door was shut to the Church study as Reverend Jeffery Morrison bent down to his desk chair and got on his knees. People within his congregation called the hefty preacher, Big Jeff. Not so much for his weight, but more for his faith. Pleading for the Holy Spirit's favor upon the worship service was habit for the fifty-nine-year-old preacher. However, the immediate service was beginning to unravel his nervous system, and he was taking the matter to the Lord.

Since awakening at 6:00 A.M., the Lord had been tugging at the Pastor's heart. Reverend Morrison concluded that the Lord was leading him to preach a different message than the one which was prepared, prayed over and ready for delivery. It had been utterly terrifying when the preacher placed his original seven pages of typed sermon material into the bottom drawer of his desk to follow his spiritual instincts. In thirty-two years of preaching, the gray-haired veteran of the pulpit never recalled this happening on a Sunday morning just prior to a service, but obeying the Spirit of the Lord was the central priority of his life and ministry. It still made him nervous, even for an experienced preacher like himself.

The Pastor began to fervently pray: "*Lord Jesus, I don't know why you've led me to this particular passage of scripture this morning, but I will obey the leading of Your Spirit. Take this message and use it to glorify Thy Holy Name. Hide me behind the cross and help the people see Thy Love and Thy Grace. Give me the words to say and make the hearts receptive. I need your help, your strength, and your wisdom. In Jesus precious name I ask these things. Amen...and Amen."*

The preacher worked his way to his feet, grabbed his trusted Bible from his desk and thumbed to the chapter once more. For only the second time that morning he read the words of the final chapter of the Old Testament Book of Daniel. The chapter had only thirteen verses and he read each slowly, methodically and thoughtfully. Gaining some confidence, he closed the Bible and pressed it to his forehead. *"Lord, give me the words you would have me to say this morning."*

* * *

The seats at Oak Grove Church were beginning to fill as Big Jeff entered the sanctuary with a broad smile. He proceeded to mingle among the flock and welcome the worshippers to the service. It was a custom he'd enthusiastically been doing since planting the church thirty-two years prior.

The church fellowship was blessed to have in their midst all three of the original families from that *first service* under the oak tree: one being the good reverend himself, along with his wife and their two grown kids. Secondly, being brother-in-law Charles, with little sis and their three off-springs. Finally, there is the very close friend and spiritual brother of Jeff, Mitchell Harper. Mitchell generously donated the land for Jeff's *Church Vision.* It was the perfect spot, nestled right off the busy Highway 39 North.

The first few services were held under a huge oak tree on the prime fourteen acres of gorgeous country property. Within weeks, a small portable one-room tin structure was moved to the location.

A few years after that, the first building was completed and the church grew at a rapid pace. Within ten years, the Oak Grove congregation blossomed from sixty-five active members, to over one hundred and fifty.

Strategically inserted into the hundreds of messages which covered the span of time, Big Jeff often gave history lessons of Oak Grove's early days and how the Mighty Hand of God had blessed their faith work. Now, with more then five hundred folks assembling in their large and quite modern facility, the leadership of Oak Grove was beginning to prepare for further growth and expansion. The plans included a large, more elaborate sanctuary, new basketball gym, library, and even a small theater for uplifting spirit-filled movies.

There were hundreds of folks now coming from all corners of the county, and beyond, to listen to Big Jeff's inspirational messages of hope and encouragement. The goal of one thousand regulars was now within reach. It was in their spiritual sight.

With Big Jeff's approval, the building committee adopted the popular phrase from the movie, *Field of Dreams.* The phrase was used to spur weekly offerings for the worthy vision. Hundreds of thousands of dollars still had to be raised, but the Oak Grove leadership had faith that God would speak to the hearts and minds of His people. The slogan *'if we build it, they will come'* was seen on posters throughout the church and also heard in every message. Audio and visual repetition is necessary when pumping a vision of this magnitude.

During the past three decades, Oak Grove had become one of the more unique churches in East Mississippi. It was strongly believed that the central reason for its success was the result of a joint decision by those three founding families. At the very first Sunday service in the heat of the morning under that oak tree, a pledge was made. The three families purposely and mutually determined that the Church would never be associated or identified with any particular denomination and/or association. So the Church, in effect, had been blessed in reaching people of all backgrounds, colors and nationalities. Each service displayed a beautiful melting pot of people groups which was a rare sight indeed for the south, and in particular, Meridian.

It was in this worship environment that the blonde-haired, blue-eyed family of four, providentially found their way into the sanctuary of Oak Grove Church.

As Susan entered the opened doors and took a bulletin from an usher, she was noticeably uneasy about her decision to randomly choose to attend the church. Not immediately recognizing a single face, Susan swiftly escorted her children through the spacious foyer, into the sanctuary and quickly scrambled into the back-row. Almost immediately, Big Jeff spotted the visiting family and began walking in their direction. Oak Grove had seekers who tried to sneak in every single Sunday morning, but they were never able to slip passed his radar undetected.

He never missed a new face.

"How are you folks doing this morning?" The preacher said with a robust tone.

"We're doing fine," Susan lied, glancing toward Daniel.

"You folks are as welcome as can be. My friends call me Big Jeff—appropriate name as you can tell. May I ask your names?"

"Sure…this is my son Daniel. These are my girls Rachael and Rebecca. My name is Susan Patton." Susan individually pats the top of each child's head as they are introduced, and they didn't like it.

"I see they have your blond-hair and blue-eyes. You have a beautiful family Ms. Patton."

"I appreciate that."

"Listen, I'm the Pastor here and if I can do anything for you folks, don't hesitate to let me know. I hope you enjoy the service."

"Thanks," Susan replied as the large preacher turned and walked a few feet away to greet a Hispanic couple.

As the sanctuary began filling to near capacity, Susan alternated her attention from reading the church bulletin to gazing at the colorful crowd. There were Blacks, Whites, Indians, Mexicans and a handful of Orientals. This was very different from any Church she'd ever attended. Everyone seemed so joyful.

A sensation she hadn't truly experienced in four years.

When Susan and her children pulled out of their driveway twenty minutes earlier, it was agreed upon that they'd go to the first Church which appeared to have a welcoming building. Fifteen minutes later, they pulled into the parking lot of Oak Grove.

"Mom, it looks like we picked a good one," Daniel said.

Susan shrugged her shoulders slightly but didn't respond.

While mentally processing the colorful flock of people preparing for worship, Daniel noticed a familiar face in the distance. The man was on the stage picking up a guitar. There were a variety of musicians who were already in their respective places. Daniel turned quickly to his mother and pointed his finger to the front of the Church, "Mom, there's my Coach!"

Susan focused her eyes and spotted him, "It sure is son. Did he tell you he attended this Church?"

"No idea. I figured he went to Church because he always prayed for us before and after each game, but that's all."

As Daniel wiggled his body to get in better position, he zeroed-in on the every move of Coach Harper. *My coach plays in the band at Oak Grove Church*, Daniel thought amusingly.

It wasn't long before the band kicked-off the service with upbeat praise music. The people stood and sang every note of the words which were visible on large screens to the left and right of the stage. There were prayers and more praise music which ultimately set the stage for the preaching of none other than, Big Jeff.

Chapter 6

Susan was stunned by what had transpired as she shook hands with Big Jeff who was strategically positioned at the door. Even though there were hundreds of people lined from behind, Susan needed a word or two with the preacher who opened her mind again to the possibility of a powerful and loving God.

"Reverend, do you have a few minutes after you finish here? I have a couple of questions for you."

"Sure. Can you wait around inside the foyer? I'll be with you as soon as possible." Big Jeff motioned to the spot he wanted them to wait.

Susan knew it would take some time for the preacher to shake the hands of the hundreds of people, but it was an essential she stayed as long as necessary.

"Not a problem," Susan confirmed, pulling her children to the side to allow the flow of people to continue. They maneuvered their way into the foyer. Daniel sure didn't mind the wait. This gave him an opportunity to make his presence known to his coach.

After a rather lengthy search, the coach came into Daniel's sight. He was carrying a guitar case in one hand and Bible in the other.

Coach Harper was tanned and in shape.

He wore dark dress pants and a solid blue polo shirt. His light brown hair was perfectly parted, which was much different from a ball cap snuggly gripping his head. Daniel hadn't seen his coach dressed like that. He didn't look like his coach. He looked more like— a guitar player for a praise band.

When Coach Harper came within a reasonable shouting distance, Daniel gave way, "COACH HARPER!" Daniel's squeal was a pitch higher then the rumbling baritone echoes of the departing crowd.

The coach immediately glanced to locate the familiar voice, spotted Daniel, and cheerfully darted through the crowd, heading in his direction. After reaching his shortstop the coach said, "Daniel, what on earth is going on? It is great to see you son!"

"It's great to see you too."

"What brings you to Oak Grove?"

"We decided to go to church this morning and came here."

"I'm glad you did."

Susan and the girls were taking in the encounter as the coach glanced at them and asked, "Daniel, this must be your mother and sisters?" He knew it was Daniel's mother having seen her at their last game. The girls he'd seen numerous occasions standing in their driveway with the babysitter.

"Yes sir, this is my family," Daniel answered.

Coach Harper placed his guitar case down and reached his hand out to Susan. "Hi, I'm Scotty."

Susan smiled, shook his hand and responded, "I'm Susan. It's good to meet you, finally. I've heard your name mentioned many times within the walls of our house."

"I hope it was all good stuff."

"Obviously Daniel has high regards for you and I appreciate all you've been doing for him, picking him up and all."

"Listen, it's been my pleasure. Daniel is my special player." Scotty quickly looked at Daniel and enthusiastically said, "Another great game last night. Are you excited about the big one on Tuesday?"

"Can't wait until Tuesday," Daniel said with a gleam in his eyes.

"It's our final game of the regular season and we need to win in order to go undefeated for the season. In fact, the team hasn't lost a game in two years thanks to you."

When Susan heard the flattering comments, she thought, *I bet Coach Harper tells all his players the same thing, especially when they show up at his church.*

Daniel's demeanor didn't indicate any puff whatsoever, not even a hint of pride. He would never brag on himself again, however, he couldn't stop others.

"Susan, I noticed that you were at last night's game. What'd you think?" Coach Harper asked.

"Oh my goodness, Daniel was great. I guess I came on the right night to see him play."

"Last night was just average for the likes of your son. It's not unusual for him to jack a couple out in a single game. He has smacked twenty-three of them in just eleven games this season alone."

"Is that a fact? I didn't know that," Susan curiously responded while tilting her head suspiciously toward Daniel.

"Daniel doesn't like talking about himself, does he?" The coach asked.

"Not lately," Susan inserted.

"Well, I honestly enjoy talking about your son," the coach continued, and Susan wasn't surprised. "Daniel leads the whole City of Meridian in his age category in home-runs, batting-average, put-outs, fielding, you name it. In all my years of coaching, no player within Meridian's little league level has performed like your son.

Daniel may be the best twelve-year-old ballplayer in Meridian's little league history. I'm absolutely not exaggerating, Big Jeff might slap me," Scotty said with a quick chuckle.

As Coach Harper completed his rather lengthy, statistic-driven exhortation, Susan glanced at Daniel. He seemed to be unimpressed by his coach's comments. Instead, he watched the preacher shake hands with the lively and very diverse congregation as they made their way out of the building.

It was a cultural experience for the boy.

There were only a few more folks to go before Susan could have her more serious conversation with the Pastor. She figured Daniel's startling baseball accomplishments would continue when suddenly the coach directed a question for her. "Ms. Patton, do you think you'll make it to the game on Tuesday?"

"Well, I don't know. I have some inventory coming in and guess who has to work late?"

"Mom, you ought to try and come. It's our last game."

"Well maybe…okay, okay, I'll try. But instead of burgers and ice cream afterward, you and the girls may have to go to the store and help me stock shoes."

"Deal," Daniel said with a satisfied expression.

"Sounds like a winner. We'll look forward to Tuesday's game. Well slick, I guess I better run. I'll see you on field two."

"I think the schedule says we are playing on field one."

"Well anyway, I'm picking you up. Surely we'll manage to find the right field. They're all in the same complex."

Turning again to Susan, Scotty said, "Ms. Patton when you arrive, just look for blue, the same color as this." Coach Harper points to his own blue polo shirt in a failed attempt at mild humor.

"I'll find you, I promise."

"Great...See you folks on Tuesday."

Scotty reaches for his guitar case, walks out of the church foyer and into the congested parking lot. He placed the guitar in the back of his truck, climbs in and slides his Bible to the passenger side. Before starting the engine, his mind begins to wonder. *Susan is absolutely beautiful. Probably wouldn't be interested in me. But who knows. It might be worth a try.*

He cranks the truck, merges with the other vehicles and soon pulls onto the highway, all the while thinking of his shortstop's gorgeous mother.

"Daniel I thought you told me you were stretching the truth about those other games. By what I just heard, it seems to me like you didn't tell me enough." Susan said, after allowing the revelation from Coach Harper to absorb significantly.

"Well, I could've done a better job at being more accurate.

"Accurate?" Susan asked.

"Well…those times I told you I hit one 300-feet, maybe they only traveled around, say, 275-feet."

"How far is the fence from home plate?"

"200-feet down the lines and 225-feet in center."

"Daniel! So you were off a few feet, but you were still telling the truth. Anyway, I know you don't take a measuring tape to your games."

"Yea, but that time I told you that I hit for the cycle, you know; a single, a double, a triple and a homer all in one game. The single was really an error by the third baseman."

"Son what am I going to do with you?"

Just in time to save Daniel, Big Jeff began motioning the Pattons to follow him. It was good to be moving, especially due to the restless nature of Susan's eight-year-old twin girls. But for the most part, Rachael and Rebecca were in a world of their own, entertaining themselves with identical lives.

Chapter 7

Escorting the Pattons through the foyer of Oak Grove, Big Jeff—all three-hundred-plus-pounds, turned to Susan and said, "Why don't we have a seat over here." The preacher pointed to a sitting area equipped with a shiny brown couch and several matching chairs. Worn out from the hour and a half service, and the twenty minute wait, the kids were thrilled to sink down on the cushiony pillowed couch. In fact, the twins were about to lie down until Daniel demonstrated the Oak Grove brotherly love and pinched them.

The twins begrudgingly sat straight.

The preacher sat down in one of the large matching chairs and, in an unorthodox manner, crossed his thick legs. Susan sat in a chair diagonally facing his.

"Sorry for the wait Ms. Patton," the preacher said with a tired puff. He unknowingly impressed Susan with his ability to remember her name. Big Jeff always made a conscious effort to remember the names of every visitor. The downtrodden deserved respect and equality.

"Thanks for taking this time to speak with me," Susan said with an uneasy tone.

"Ms. Patton—"

"Please call me Susan."

"Susan. What can I do for you today?"

"First, I want to say how much I enjoyed being at Oak Grove. It seems like a terrific place."

"Thanks. We strive hard to make it a blessing and I'm pleased you found that to be true."

"Reverend Morrison—"

"Please call me Big Jeff. Everyone else does."

"All right then, Big Jeff. I won't take much of your time. I just had a couple of questions about your message, you know, on Daniel chapter twelve."

"Glad to answer any questions, if I can."

"You said at the very beginning of your sermon that Daniel chapter twelve wasn't your original message and that the Spirit spoke to you early this morning and led you to that particular chapter. My question is this: Did you hear a voice, was it a feeling you had, or what?"

"Susan, it's very rare for this to happen. I have on occasion changed a sermon say, on Thursday or Friday, but this is absolutely the first time it's happened at the last minute so to speak." Big Jeff took a deep breath and continued. "Ms. Patton, I mean Susan. I was simply impressed by the Spirit. God didn't hit me over the head and say, *PREACH DANIEL TWELVE BOY*! It was nothing like that. It's hard to explain other than to say, it was similar to my call to preach many years ago. You just know God is calling you to go in a certain direction. So this morning I did what I thought the Lord was directing me to do…Now may I ask why you want to know?"

Susan's eyes darted toward her curious kids, especially Mister Dreamer of Dreams, and got straight to the point.

"Big Jeff, my husband was killed four years ago. We often studied the Bible together most every night. At the time of his death, we had nearly completed the Book of Daniel. We made it to the end of chapter eleven, and the final chapter was never studied. Pastor, that's the very chapter you just preached. I can understand how coincidences may seem to happen from time to time, but here is the thing, I haven't been to church since my husband's death. Not only that, I wouldn't be here this morning if it wasn't for my son who woke me up to tell of a dream during the night." Susan stopped to catch her breath and discern the preacher's reactions so far. She had his complete attention, so she continued. "You see, my son's name is Daniel and he had a dream of Heaven." She looked at Daniel to make sure the preacher knows that the child on the couch is the one she is referring. Big Jeff darts his eyes quickly to Daniel and then back to Susan. "My late husband, who's name is also Daniel, but everyone called him Dan, was there with Jesus. They had a few things to say which honestly I can't recall."

"I can," Daniel interrupted.

Obviously floored by the morning events thus far, Big Jeff quickly looked over to Daniel again, uncrossed his flabby legs, leaned up in his seat, looked right into his blue eyes and asked, "Do you mind sharing your dream Daniel?"

"I thought you'd never ask."

After Daniel repeated his dream word for word, exactly the way it happened; what he saw, what was said, how he motivated his mother to go to church—Big Jeff knew this was his answer.

"Susan, the Bible tells us to test the Spirit and I think He's been well-tested this morning, and been unquestionably proven reliable and true. Also, the Bible tells us that in the last days young men shall dream dreams. I believe we've witnessed a work of the Holy Spirit. This whole event should give you hope for the future and even great anticipation for the future. This should be your confirmation from God that you've been in the presence of God. I praise the Lord that He's allowed me to play a small part in what he's preparing for your lives. Our God works in mysterious ways to accomplish his purposes and now all you have to do is what He told you. *Draw Close to Him.* He loves you and your children more than a dream can describe. Just draw close to him and He'll bless you in such a way that it will knock your socks off. But the wonderful thing we've witnessed is God's confirmation to you and your children that your husband is with Jesus and is filled with love, and joy, and peace, and happiness."

After Big Jeff articulated his conclusions in a highly engaging fashion, Susan wiped a couple of tears with the back of her hand. She was now ready for question number two, as if the first weren't enough.

"Pastor, that's not all," She said with a sniffle.

Big Jeff was tired from his long day, even though it was only 12:45, but he didn't dare walk away from this. It was too good. "I'm all ears Susan."

"Even though I didn't bring my Bible this morning, I'm a pretty good listener. What verse was it in Daniel 12 that had the two men by the river?" Big Jeff didn't answer, instead he raised his burly gray eyebrows to indicate; *Awesome.* There were deep wrinkles on his forehead, like you might find on a bull-dog.

"And what verse was it which said something about knowledge being increased?" This time Susan helped him out. "In my son's dream, Jesus said that we'd soon understand why Dan was killed."

Big Jeff privately thought, *this is going a bit too far for my comfort level.*

Knowing she'd exceeded her two questions, Susan nonetheless pressed forward. "And what verse was it that said something to the effect that the wise would shine and turn many to Christ? Of course I'm paraphrasing as best as I can recall."

"I hope everyone who attended this morning listened as you have Susan. You are implying that...with Jesus' desire to use you to bring glory to His Name."

"That's exactly right!" Susan zealously snapped, now getting somewhat preachy to her own surprise.

"I have to be upfront with you Susan. The whole book of Daniel relates to Israel and the end-times, as you know from your own studies with your late husband. Don't be offended by my saying that you may be taking liberty with scripture to fit Daniel's dream with those verses. It seems you may be trying too hard, similar to jamming the wrong pieces of a puzzle into the wrong slots."

"But don't you think He can do as He pleases, even if it means taking the true meaning of a chapter and relating it in a creative manner to bring hope to another situation?"

"Susan… you know what I think?"

Susan waited for the large preacher to answer his own question.

"I think God wants to use you, and might I add Daniel, in a wonderful and glorious way. I think our God is showing you that your husband's untimely death is connected to a powerful plan. I also think that God says what he means. When He reveals that you must first draw close to him, then I'd take it with all seriousness. Remember, we are created by God with a free will. You either choose to do things His way and be blessed, or you can choose to ignore Him and forfeit His blessings." After a brief pause the preacher asked, "Now, do you have any other questions?"

"No, I think that about covers it for now." The implication of "for now" suggested that more consultation would likely be needed in the future.

Daniel hadn't missed a single word of the conversation.

The Preacher, Susan and Daniel each eye-balled the sleeping twins leaning against one another. They were prematurely enjoying a Sunday afternoon nap, and the preacher needed one as well. It had been a *draining* day already, in every sense of the word.

After Big Jeff closed the illuminating discussion with prayer, Daniel nudged the twins with his elbow.

It was finally time to go home.

* * *

The Pastor entered his study to grab a couple of books to take home for additional reading. Before doing so, he slowly eased around his desk and bounced his weight into the extra large leather chair—it matched the furniture in the foyer. Leaning forward, Big Jeff put his elbows on the desk, cupping his hands together and thought, *I wonder how Dan was killed.*

She hadn't said, and the preacher didn't ask.

Chapter 8

Coach Scotty Harper had already made up his mind. He knew exactly what he had to do. After twenty-three hours of contemplation, he was ready to take a chance. After all, if he didn't start taking more risks, he would be single for the rest of his life.

Over the years, the hopeless romantic managed a handful of dates with potential marriage prospects from the Oak Grove singles group, but nothing materialized. Finding a compatible partner was much more difficult than he'd ever anticipated. Now thirty-six-years-old, Scotty was sick of the single life. All his old college buddies had been married for years, having children galore.

They aren't any better than I am! Scotty had thought a thousand times in the vain attempt to encourage himself.

He was constantly on the lookout. Whether in the grocery store, at the ball field or Church, he was on an endless search for the perfect match.

This is what made his Monday a miserable experience.

Scotty was sitting in his parked Ford truck on Meridian's busy downtown main street. He was un-fortunate enough to locate a strategic parking spot to monitor the store before entering. He'd hoped there would be no parking, giving him an excuse to back out.

Several times in the past fifteen minutes he'd grabbed the key in the ignition to fire the engine and drive, but instead, hit the steering wheel with his fist, fighting off his coward side.

Is she the one? Scotty had asked himself for the umpteenth time. He would never know unless he made the first move.

Staring through the driver's side window, he began to wonder if it was worth all this effort only to make him into a complete arrowhead in the end.

What the heck, it wouldn't be the first time I made myself look stupid, and probably not the last, Scotty had figured. *After all, she's only a person*, he mentally reminded himself until the stinging reality flooded his brain. *Yea right, she's only a woman of incredible beauty, smarts, cute twins and the mother of the best little leaguer in the universe.*

He knew she was out of his league.

The desperate coach wouldn't know the possibilities unless he forced himself out of the truck, across the busy street into *Patton's Shoe Store,* and asked Susan to accompany him to lunch.

The heat of the morning wasn't helping his 'cold-feet' syndrome. Scotty reluctantly shifted his nervous eyes to the tall matrix sign position in front of the First Citizens Bank just one block away.

He grimaced as it flashed: *11:50 A.M./91 degrees.*

It was time to make his move or his commitment to himself would be down the drain. Once again, he reached for the key, pushed the clutch to the floorboard and this time started the engine. Unable to release the clutch with his *cold* left foot, Scotty instead turned the key again, killing the engine.

He almost said his first curse word in years.

"Get a grip ole boy." He said.

He was determined not to touch that key again until he accomplished the mission, regardless of the outcome.

"I'll never know, if I don't try. Anything good is worth going after. I will not give up the fight," Scotty rambled, giving himself an inspirational pep talk.

He again proceeded to reach for the door handle.

"Here's the plan of action," Scotty said, looking at his own reflection in the rearview mirror while still gripping the door handle.

"I'll simply walk in there and say, 'Susan, just came by to tell you how great it was to see ya'll at church Sunday. Can I take you out to lunch?'" Apparently not satisfied, he shook his head in disgust and practiced another opening line. "Susan, just came by to see if we might go out for lunch and talk some more about Daniel's baseball skills.— Give me a break, that's so lame," Scotty irritatingly whispered.

Cognitively recalling that Susan's business was a public establishment and he had every right to go in there, enabled him to relax enough to open the door.

He timidly exited his truck.

Scotty began stutter-stepping his way across the busy street. For a split second he wished a car would run over his jaywalking self, ending the torment, but the thought didn't last, thankfully.

Scotty nonchalantly walked into the shoe store, but he felt the *casual passer-by thing* probably looked phony. The hundreds of pairs of shoes neatly lining three walls went unnoticed. A professionally dressed gray-haired lady from behind the cash counter broke the ice and asked, "Can I help you with anything?"

"I came by to speak with Susan Patton. Is she here?" Scotty managed to ask even though his bones were in a state of decay.

"Yes sir, she sure is. She's in the back. Give me a minute and I'll get her."

Scotty almost said, *don't worry about it!* But nothing came out of his dry mouth.

The gray-headed lady with a quick first step disappeared through a single door a few feet behind the cash counter. He knew his chance for a last minute retreat was thoroughly destroyed.

Standing alone in dread, he managed to work-up enough spit to swallow uncomfortably, manufacturing a loud "gulp" sound in the process. *This is crazy*, he thought, continuing to question his unorthodox plan.

Within seconds, the old lady appeared with Susan following close behind. Susan wore a solid red dress that made her blonde hair light the room. Susan was even prettier than he remembered from their brief conversation on Sunday.

The instant Susan noticed Scotty she smiled and said, "Coach Harper, what a surprise. How are you doing?"

Scotty just stood there, dumbfounded. He knew his odd looking grin suggested to Susan, *not worth a flip, and you?*

"Ms. Ruby, this is Scotty Harper, my son's baseball coach."

"You don't say. I've heard Daniel speak of you. It's very nice to meet you."

"Nice to meet you too, Ms. Ruby."

"Susan, I'll finish up for you in the back, call if you need me," Ms. Ruby insisted, rolling her eyes in a way to suspect the obvious. The gray-haired Ms. Ruby exited as quickly as before.

"What brings you in this morning Mr. Harper? Can I help you with anything?"

"No...I was just driving by your shop and thought it'd be rude not to stop. I wanted to let you know how good it was to see you and your children at Oak Grove yesterday."

Susan walked to within a two feet of Scotty, "I enjoyed it. That was one dynamic service. I thought Daniel was going into shock when he saw you with guitar in-hand on that stage."

"It sure was a pleasant surprise to see him there as well. You have an incredible son."

"You sure don't mind building up your players. I could tell from just those few minutes after the service. But I guess that's what coaches do." Susan paused to allow the coach an opportunity for further clarity.

"Now you don't think I was just trying to make you feel good when I said those things do you?" Scotty was beginning to feel somewhat at ease, to his own surprise.

"Well, I have to admit. It did cross my mind."

"I can assure you. I wasn't exaggerating at all. Daniel really is that good. He doesn't even know how good he is. The things I've seen him accomplish in just two short seasons have totally blown me away. That goes for everyone else who's watched him play on a regular basis." Scotty felt rather comfortable talking baseball.

"That's interesting. Maybe Daniel will play for the high school team in a few years," Susan was still attempting to play down his comments.

"Susan, he's probably good enough to play for the high school right now, at twelve. I think we can safely shoot higher than that, say.... professionally."

Susan paused to digest the words, "You are really serious, aren't you?"

"Serious as a train wreck," he said, knowing that the professional reference was a bit premature for any little leaguer.

Scotty noticed that Susan glanced at her watch. "I'm sorry. I'm taking up too much of your time?"

"No, No. You're okay. Monday's are our slow day, though I do take a break at noon and grab some lunch."

This was the opening he prayed for and seized the moment by asking, "Where would you like to go?" Immediately Scotty felt a rapid flow of blood into his head. He paused and waited for the rejection. Then, to his astonishment, she said the magic words, "You got a place in mind?"

Without hesitation Scotty said, "There's a veggie bar right around the corner. It's walking distance. I go there from time to time. It's run by a sweet old couple and I just love the fried green tomatoes, sweet potatoes and might I add, good ole southern fried chicken."

"I know the place. I eat there once or twice a week myself. I'll grab my purse and tell Ms. Ruby to tackle any potential customers passing through the store while I'm out. Like I said, Monday is our slow day."

"Great," Scotty responded confidently, for a change.

As Susan walked away, Scotty thought, n*ow that wasn't so difficult, great plan coach*.

Entering the stock room, Susan also had a thought. *This is the first time I've been in the company of a man since Dan's death. I hope it's not a mistake.*

Chapter 9

Serving folks by the hundreds each week, Jergenson's Country Food Buffet had been a popular eating destination for townspeople for many decades. The historical restaurant was a throw back to the past. News was circulating that the owners, Tom and Joyce Jergenson, were preparing for retirement. After fifty-one years in business, the couple was ready to sell and ride off into the sunset. Business was booming in its final days as the locals craved Jergenson's southern style cooking, one more time.

The place was packed as Scotty and Susan picked up their plates, napkins and utensils. They patiently shuffled single file from one end of the buffet to the other, selecting their favorites of the bountiful stockpile. Scotty went for the fried chicken breast, mashed potatoes, greens, fried green tomatoes, sweet potatoes and corn bread. Predictably, Susan chose the low-calorie, no-fat assortment of boiled carrots, turnips and a salad which she topped with a host of rabbit food, carefully positioning it in all the right places. Susan lightly doused the work of art with fat-free ranch dressing. They both filled their glasses with tea, though she opted to sweeten her own.

Over the years, Susan managed to maintain her high school weight, give or take a few pounds. Unlike Scotty, who was thirty pounds heavier, but jogged and worked out regularly. He could afford to eat liberally now and build it into muscle later.

Scotty and Susan were lucky enough to find a seat next to the front window as the nostalgic lunch crowd continued to fill the restaurant.

"I'll ask the blessing, if you don't mind?" Scotty asked.

"Sure," Susan replied.

"Father in Heaven, I ask your blessings on this day. Bless Susan and her children and keep them in your loving care. Thank you for Jesus and what He did for us on the cross. Help us to serve you more fully. Bless the food to the nourishment of our bodies and our bodies to your service. In Jesus precious name we pray, Amen."

They both put a napkin in their lap and Susan began the conversation. "So how long have you been attending Oak Grove Church?"

"All of my life. My father is one of the original founding members. He actually donated the land for the church many years ago. My dad and Big Jeff have been best friends forever."

"The praise band really added to the service. How long have you been playing the guitar?"

"For about eight years. I was looking to do something for the Lord and the guitar seems to be it. Do you play any instruments?"

"Are you kidding? I can barely play the radio," Susan said.

Scotty wasn't expecting Susan to bring up her late husband so soon in the conversation when she said, "My husband loved gospel music: southern, contemporary, traditional, bluegrass, it didn't matter to him as long as it was all about the Lord. Daniel did tell you about his father didn't he?"

"We had a couple of conversations about him during our rides together. Daniel is very proud of his dad. He must have been a great guy. If your son takes after him, I know he was a great guy."

Susan took a couple of bites of salad and Scotty was finishing off his third fried green tomato.

"Daniel told me his dad had passed away, but I could tell that he didn't want to go into it. Of course I didn't push it." Scotty wished he hadn't said that. It sounded as if he was pushing it. *Contradiction,* he thought.

Susan took a couple of sips from her enormous tea glass as if she didn't want to go into the details either. However, since Daniel's dream, the church service, the message and the conversation with the preacher, she was gaining strength. Talking about Dan was beginning to feel natural and comforting. Scotty had a warm, friendly way about him and she was ready to let down her facade and speak openly.

"Dan was shot."

"My word, was it a hunting accident or something?"

"He was a policeman in Philadelphia, just right up the road. He was off-duty at the time. There was a convenience store robbery in progress when he arrived. Dan entered the store to pick up a gallon of milk at my request, got involved...and he got shot. It was the fourth of July." Susan's eyes never left her salad as she gave the brief details. She eased her fork gently through the lettuce, tossing it slightly.

"I'm very sorry that it happened," Scotty said with compassion.

Susan shakes her head up and down slightly. She didn't want to get emotional. Instead she glanced out the restaurant widow at the congested mid-day traffic. Sweaty folks were walking in every direction. Everyone seemed to be in such a hurry. Even for a mid-sized southern town, the people appeared over-worked and over-stressed.

"He's in a much better place," Susan said.

A very short and stout waitress with tea pitchers in both hands instantly swings around to the table and refills their tea glasses to the brim, "Thanks," they both said in unison.

Scotty waited until the waitress had departed and replied, "You are so right Susan. He's in a much better place."

Susan deliberately changes the subject—another sign of progress, "Besides your little league activity, what do you do for a living?"

"I farm. I work with my dad who's been farming all his life."

"Oh really, what do you farm?" Susan asked.

"Mostly cotton. My dad and granddad worked the land together for years, until my granddad died. That's when I started full-time. I had just completed my agricultural degree at Mississippi State and suddenly my granddad dies. Pop was a great man of faith and a hard working farmer. We miss him enormously, but God provides. I was available to begin full-time on the farm. My dad and I harvested twenty-one hundred acres of cotton that first year after Pop's death, and we haven't slowed down to this day. I would imagine that farming is probably similar to selling shoes. I know it's a lot like coaching—it takes awful hard work behind the scenes in preparation for success." Scotty forked a load of greens with a piece of corn bread in the other hand.

"That's the truth," Susan said.

"Did you go to college anywhere?" Scotty asked, hoping she couldn't see the food inside his mouth.

"I went to West Georgia College in Carrollton. After finishing a business degree, I moved to Meridian and married Dan. We both were raised in the West Georgia town of Newnan. We were high school sweethearts. After high school, Dan wanted to play baseball at the next level, but didn't get any offers in Georgia. To make a long story short, he eventually came for a tryout and the coaching staff at Meridian Junior College were impressed enough to sign him to a half scholarship. Dan absolutely fell in love with this area. So after two years at MJC, he applied for several positions as a police officer trainee. He finally landed a job in Philadelphia where we lived until his..." Susan almost said, *murder*, but chose to cut the sentence short.

So engrossed in memories, Susan hadn't noticed that Scotty began choking about halfway through her personal history. *Probably on a piece of corn bread,* she thought. His face was becoming blood red while attempting to wash it down with the huge mug of tea. He sipped the tea, then he gagged, sip, gag, sip, gag, sip, gag.

"Are you choking Scotty?" Susan asked, feeling silly afterwards. Of course he was choking to death. This is all she needed in her life. She could see the headlines, "Woman's First Date Since Her Husband's Funeral, CHOKES TO DEATH."

He held up his free hand to suggest, *give me a minute.*

Regaining his composure, Scotty chokingly asked, "Did…your husband…play…for MJC?"

"That is correct, yes. Why do you ask?" Susan asked puzzled and still plenty concerned about the blockage, but relieved that it appeared the coach would probably live.

"This is absolutely incredible!" Just like that, his throat was clear, so he continued, "Susan, you're not going to believe this. I think I was on the same team with your husband. I haven't put the pieces together until right now. I never had a reason to. Did your husband go by the initials; DP?"

"Only by his teammates—Scotty did you play for MJC with Dan?"

"I played with DP, Dan Patton, I sure did! I attended MJC two years before going to Mississippi State. All this time coaching your son and it never crossed my mind. I never connected the dots. This is astonishing! Your son Daniel is DP's son!"

"I can't believe this!" Susan places both hands on each side of her face.

"You are really not going to believe what I'm about to tell you. DP is the one who led me to the Lord. He was a strong believer as I'm sure you are well aware. He was an awesome Christian example for all the players. He helped start the Fellowship of Christian

Athletes on campus. I was going through the motions of religion for many years. I was born into the Oak Grove vision, but it wasn't until DP came along that I viewed Christianity as being something personal, more than just religion. It's what I saw in DP's life that inspired me to give my heart to Christ."

"Dan would talk for hours on the phone about that FCA group. He loved baseball, but he was much more excited about how the Lord was moving on campus, especially in his teammates lives."

Susan and Scotty were flabbergasted. Neither was eating. Scotty for sure had taken his last bite.

After a couple of minutes, Susan added, "Scotty I feel like I need to tell you what's been going on."

After Susan described the events of the past two days, they both sensed something supernatural was taking place. They didn't know exactly what, but they knew God was at work.

They further discussed Daniel's dream, Big Jeff's message on the final chapter of the Book of Daniel, the meeting with Big Jeff in which he disclosed the Holy Spirit mysteriously instructing him what to preach—and now this.

They both concluded that the events obviously were more than just coincidence. It must be the work of an unexplainable force. It had to be the doings of an unseen hand. It was a God-thing.

They could've elaborated all day, but Susan had to get back to her shop. She was already thirty-five minutes late. Ms. Ruby might become even more suspicious of the two.

Chapter 10

The prison in Mulberry Arizona housed the most ruthless of convicts. The facility was surrounded by doubled steel chain-link fencing, intertwined with barbed wire which stretched fifty feet into the air. Mulberry was no regular hunky dory America town. The prison was the town in itself.

Mulberry was as secure as any prison in the country, and any attempt to escape would certainly result in death. If the razor-sharp fencing didn't slice you to death, certainly the sharp-shooting prison guards would. Positioned atop its four towers, the guards wouldn't miss their intended target. Rumor had it: They could nail a gnat right off a tick's back from one hundred yards. They wore dark sunglasses to shade their eyes which made their presence ominous.

Mulberry prison is where America's most violent of criminals are incarcerated. It's where the murderers eventually rot in their cells, if they're fortunate enough to escape an early death. Each year, numerous deaths occurred in the *blood yard,* it's affectionately called. For an hour a day, the prisoners are allowed to spend time in the *blood yard* to play with their hidden weapons used for the purpose of gang rivalry wars. For one hour under Arizona's burning rays, every loner inmate must constantly watch his own back. Approximately half of the play hour is spent with every face in the dirt due to some unseen stabbing. That's better than getting your head blown off, courtesy of the dark shaded ones.

Eugene Thompson sat on a wooden bench in the *blood yard* gazing east toward his home State of Mississippi. After being sentenced to life without the possibility for parole, he spent most of his time waging the good fight of faith instead of the gang-related, *flesh and blood* wars. If it weren't for his 'unintentional' defense, Thompson would've been scheduled for lethal injection in a few years.

During his trial for the murder of Officer Dan Patton, Thompson's Public Defense Attorney was successful in delivering Thompson from the death penalty on the grounds that Thompson had no pre-meditated plan to shoot the off-duty police officer. The defense argued that the gun never would have been fired if the wrestling match between the two could have been avoided. It was argued that during the scuffle, the wielded .38 was accidentally fired when Patton attempted to pry the gun from the hand of Thompson.

Another bit of crucial evidence brought just enough sympathy for Thompson to save his life. The defense proved with clear evidence from Thompson's blood which was examined by the fine medical staff at Philadelphia's Regional Hospital; the man was highly intoxicated during the robbery. Thus the testimony of Eugene having no memory of the incident was plausible—if not probable.

Additionally, it was brought to the court's attention the verified evidence concerning Thompson's wife of twenty-seven years. Mrs. Eloise Thompson was notified by her doctor of a late stage of cancer which had already spread throughout her body. According to the testimony of Dr. Kramer, the notification came just seven hours prior to Thompson's violent episode. The final decision of the jury was *life,* without the possibility for parole.

The death penalty was dismissed, unanimously.

The prosecution's weapon for convicting Thompson of first degree murder was the two witnesses who saw everything, the added bonus being the surveillance which recorded the fatal shooting. One of the two witnesses; an eleven-year-old girl who'd been dropped off by a relative to share the remaining hour of her father's shift to enjoy some *on the job* bonding time. The Morton Brother's employee, Keith Millard and his young daughter testified that it was definitely Eugene Thompson who was on the surveillance tape pulling the trigger which ended the life of Officer Patton.

A rather lengthy contest between the Defense and Prosecution ensued concerning the mental and emotional maturity of Mr. Millard's daughter to testify. The Federal judge ultimately rejected the argument of the Defense. Judge Mathis made his final decision on the grounds of "*relevance*"—"*she was there and her life was in danger. Surely she was 'relevant' to the case against the suspect. All unusually brave young girls of her stature should never be denied an opportunity to be heard in a court of law in the United States of America*," the Prosecution dramatically had emphasized to the Judge.

Millard's young daughter testified that Thompson held her in a headlock with one arm, while pressing the barrel of his firearm firmly against her temple. Thompson threatened to shoot the innocent little girls head off if Millard didn't cooperate by opening the cash register and emptying the contents into a bag which was placed on the counter. Millard testified that he was so shaken by Thompson's violent involvement of his daughter that he nervously hit the wrong combination of keys and somehow jammed the register. Thompson then became so agitated at Millard that he shouted, *"I'LL GIVE YOU TO THREE OR SHE'S DEAD!"*

Just as Thompson began his countdown, Officer Patton entered the store and froze.

Mr. Patton spoke with professional calmness, "Sir, put the gun down and release that girl immediately."

Thompson refused.

Patton's only obvious options were: Stand there and risk the girl's demise, run away and risk the girl's demise, or make his best move to save the girl, also risking the girl's demise. He chose the latter which resulted in his own demise, while saving the life of the young girl.

* * *

Eugene heard the deafening siren blast from the intercom system located a-top the guard towers. It was time to merge into a single line with the other murderers and march back to his dungeon. In over two years, he'd never made any eye contact whatsoever with the other prisoners while in the *blood yard*. He was committed never to be involved with a prison gang. Eugene Thompson was now in the gang with Jesus, but it was a lonely gang of one. The other Christians were either dead, or hiding their faith.

His violent rage began on that mindless Fourth of July, and it ended when he asked Jesus Christ to be his Lord and Savior. If a prison gang ended his life in the *blood yard*, better for him.

He'd made his peace with God. He wasn't afraid of death.

If physical death is what God wanted, he was more than ready to blast out of Mulberry and into an eternity with his Lord and Master.

Since becoming a Christian, Eugene had interceded for his victim's families wherever they might be, though he assumed they still lived in East Mississippi. He continually pleaded for God to work a miracle in their lives, and cause something good to come out of his recklessness. Every waking hour was filled with prayers for Jesus' name to be ultimately glorified through the tragedy. Prayer had become his new life's ambition.

If it weren't for the dedicated and sincere ministry of Phil Horner, Mulberry's only prison chaplain, he may not have discovered the love and forgiveness of God through His powerful Son, the Lord Jesus. If only the Pattons and Millards knew of his changed life and his desire to ask for their forgiveness. Pleading for forgiveness was something he was too bitter to ask at pre-sentencing. At Mulberry, Eugene Thompson patiently waited for God to answer his petitioning, in a strong and powerful manner.

After the door slammed behind him, he sat on the bed in his cell and immediately picked up his tattered Bible which was resting on the pillow. He turned to a passage he'd read hundreds of times in the two years of being free. A single tear fell from his right eye onto the passage. He began reading Ephesians 6:10-18, once again—

Finally, my brethren, be strong in the Lord, and in the power of His might. Put on the whole armour of God, that ye may be able to stand against the wiles of the devil. For we wrestle not against flesh and blood, but against principalities, against powers, against the rulers of darkness of this world, against spiritual wickedness in high places. Wherefore take unto you the whole armour of God, that ye may be able to withstand in the evil day, and having done all, to stand. Stand therefore, having your loins girt about with truth, and having on the breastplate of righteousness; And your feet shod with the preparation of the gospel of peace; Above all, taking the shield of faith, wherewith ye shall be able to quench all the fiery darts of the wicked. And take the helmet of salvation, and the sword of the Spirit, which is the Word of God: Praying always with all prayer and supplication in the Spirit, and watching thereunto with all perseverance and supplication for all saints.

Eugene closed the Bible, got on his knees—and began to pray.

Chapter 11

Fully dressed in Mustang blue, Daniel sat on the edge of his bed sadly looking out the bedroom window. Since stepping off the school bus at 3:45, the dark foreboding clouds hadn't cooperated with his wishes. He was excited it was the final week of school before summer break, but the rain had destroyed his immediate plans.

It was now 5:30 and the bottom had dropped out.

With his hand snuggly inside his glove, Daniel pounded a baseball into its web while monitoring the liquid stuff falling to the ground in sheets. The rain was so heavy he almost didn't bother putting on his uniform. Instead he figured: *this will be the last chance to look at myself in the mirror as a Mustang, better make the most of it.* He was preparing for Coach Harper's call at any minute to inform him their final game of the season was a wash.

Daniel stood, walked to door of the closet and kicked the rubber bottom spikes from his feet, sending them bouncing off the back wall. It was only a matter of minutes before the phone would ring and *Charlotte the babysitter* would pass along the bad news.

He hated when this happened.

He would rather play and lose than not play at all. This Tuesday evening would be a rainout for sure, but Daniel held out hopes for a miracle. Why not, he'd seen a couple recently.

Just as expected, as soon as shoeless Daniel walked out of his room and into the den, the phone rang. Charlotte was on the couch watching cartoons with the twins. "Daniel, why don't you get it, it's probably your coach," Charlotte said.

"I know. I'll get it," Daniel said in dread.

He picked the receiver off the kitchen wall, "Hello."

"Daniel, this is you-know-who. I guess you know why I'm calling don't you?"

"No game, right?"

"How'd you guess? The mud puddles forming in your yard must have given it away."

Daniel didn't respond.

"Well, we can't do anything about the rain, can we?" Coach Harper said while sensing Daniel's depressed tone.

"I know it."

"Listen, I want you to know that it's been a real treat coaching you these past two seasons. As far as little league goes, you have graduated. You'll have much better competition next year in the thirteen-fourteen-year-old pony league. I think you'll do very well. I know a few coaches who are already maneuvering to get you. Daniel, I know you'll go a long way in the game of baseball…if you keep at it."

"Thanks Coach. Too bad it's raining, but maybe I'll see you on Sunday. I think Mom liked your Church."

"You may see me before Sunday, unless you are planning on going somewhere."

"I'm not going anywhere. Where are you going?"

"Listen…Daniel," The coach began while sniggering slightly, "I just called your Mom right before I called you. I told her about the game cancellation, as if she couldn't figure it out on her own.

Anyway, she invited me over for dinner tonight...at your place. Does that sound okay by you?"

"That sounds great by me!"

"And by the way, I have something that I want all of you to see."

"What is it?"

"You'll have to wait until I get there to find that out."

"Alright, I'll see you later...Coach."

"See you sport."

Daniel hung up the phone and wondered why his mom had invited the coach for dinner. He wondered what he had that was so important for them to see. He also wondered why his coach had called his mom before calling him. "What's up with this?" Daniel said, scratching under his cap.

Daniel had no knowledge concerning the connection between his Dad and Coach Harper. Scotty and Susan had initially planned to tell Daniel after the game, and show him some startling pictures.

With the rainout their plan had changed. They mutually agreed that a *rainout* dinner was the perfect opportunity to have a little fun with Daniel and the girls. Their lunch at Jergenson's buffet wasn't public information either.

In a couple of hours, the children would know more.

Chapter 12

Susan opened the carport door and Scotty entered the house carrying a folded umbrella. It was dripping wet, but he was dry. Though the rain hadn't let up, Scotty wasn't about to let the weather dampen his good mood. He was actually more excited about spending time with Susan than playing that final game. *Sometimes rainouts can work in one's favor*, Scotty had thought. *There would be more games in the future, Lord willing.*

Although quite tired from another long day at her shop, Susan was energetic and cheerful when welcoming Scotty to her home. She still wore the light blue dress which she put on at dawn. However, she did manage to slip on decent looking, and much more comfortable shoes.

Charlotte Morgan, the babysitter/housekeeper, had departed just prior to Scotty's arrival time. The twenty-four-year-old part-time college student was employed by Susan to help with her children and do light house cleaning. She was flexible during the week and available every Saturday. On occasion, Susan even used her at the shop to ease the workload. Charlotte was a kind, well-spoken, trusted young woman who conveniently lived with her parents only two blocks away. She was a valuable asset to Susan and considered an extended part of the family.

Susan was pleased when she returned home to find the house and children in ship-shape. All Susan had to worry about was preparing a good dinner for Scotty.

Scotty looked like the country boy that he was as he entered the house. He wore a brown button down shirt, blue jeans and cowboy boots. Immediately, he un-tucked the front of his shirt just enough to carefully slide out a manila envelope. "We wouldn't want them to get wet," Scotty said.

Susan smiled and whispered, "Are those the pictures?"

"They are right in here, safe and sound," Scotty whispered in return.

"Great, why don't you set them over on the counter until after we've eaten," Susan said, pointing to the spot.

"Perfect."

Scotty walked into the small dining room off from the kitchen area. Daniel and the girls were already seated. The dinner was conveniently prepared and perfectly placed on the table. Upon entering, Scotty noticed several family photos on the wall, opposite the window. Every picture was a suggestion of love and appreciation for the husband and father they all so dearly missed.

Dan was front and center in each of the pictures.

Scotty unfortunately found himself fighting the temptation to visualize his own face in the place of his late-pal, DP. Right then and there, Scotty privately determined to embrace the pictures. He would never let his imagination get the best of him again.

Daniel suggested that his coach sit next to him, so Scotty gladly pulled out a seat next to his shortstop, giving him a high-five in the process. Susan and the girls filled in the remaining chairs.

"Scotty, would you mind saying grace?" Susan asked.

"My pleasure...*Dear Lord, I give you thanks for this family and ask you to bless each of them. Thank you for the rain as the farmers and all others are dependent on it. I now ask you to bless this time that we have together. Bless this food we are about to receive. And Lord, please bless the hands that prepared it. In the precious name of Jesus we pray these things, Amen."*

"Now don't be shy. We have plenty to go around," Susan said.

Scotty boldly had a little of everything. He piled his plate with mashed potatoes, country fried steak covered in white gravy, corn on the cob, and yes, fried green tomatoes. After noticing the half dozen or so that Scotty devoured at Jergensons, Susan picked several of the greenest at the produce section of Winn Dixie. She went into her speed shopping mode after she detoured into the parking lot of the shopping center on her way home.

They were still warm—not long out of the frying pan.

As the metal forks tinged against their plates, the coach noticed that Daniel's demeanor had improved with each bite. No longer depressed about the untimely rain, Daniel said, "So Coach, why don't you move up to pony league and coach me again next summer?"

"Well sport, I've been in the little league division for so long, and you know the saying; it's hard to teach an old dog, new tricks."

For fifteen minutes, it seemed the whole conversation centered on baseball: Scotty's coaching career, a diving game-saving play by Daniel, some kid's 80-mile-an-hour fast ball, on and on. If it wasn't for Susan interrupting and asking Scotty what it was like being a farmer, the baseball stories would've continued into eternity, which would have been fine with Scotty and Daniel.

All in all, the dinner was going well and there were other topics of conversation. Susan recalled the time Ms. Ruby accidentally sold a pair of shoes she'd kicked off because of sore feet. Susan placed her own shoes in a corner of the store and figured they'd be safe. Later, Susan asked Ms. Ruby if she'd seen her shoes, Ms. Ruby responded, *"My goodness Susan. I think I just sold them to Ms. Rosenburg."*

The twins humored everyone with stories of occasionally deceiving folks into thinking that one was the other. The biggest laugh came when it was told of Rachael being invited to spend the night with a friend, the only thing being, it wasn't Rachael who went, it was Rebecca. The friend never knew, and to this day, still has no clue.

Susan was enjoying herself. Scotty not only was a good conversationalist, but was an equal opportunity listener. She could tell he took great delight in being with her family. He especially connected well with the children. He laughed no matter how corny their jokes.

After only three times in his presence, Susan was beginning to think she might be developing a liking to Scotty—maybe a friendship, maybe something more. Even though she'd been out of fellowship with God since the death of her husband, she was beginning to feel God's presence once again. After only one Sunday back in church; the Lord was speaking, she'd slept better, and there wasn't the usual fake smile. Susan was opening her heart to all the possibilities of what God might be doing.

That wouldn't have been true a few days earlier.

After Susan cleared the table and everyone's tummies were bulging, Scotty raised his eyebrows and gave Susan a look to signal the upcoming surprise. After clearing his throat, Scotty turned and faced Daniel. "Hey sport, did you happen to notice the envelope that I brought in with me?"

Rachael beat Daniel to the punch, "That's it over on the kitchen counter."

"Is that what you wanted us to see?" Daniel asked.

"That's right...Susan, do you want to tell them what's inside the envelope?" Scotty asked.

"Why don't we play the guessing game? Daniel, why don't you go first?" Susan asked.

"My guess is pictures," Daniel said.

Scotty and Susan both began choking this time. When they stopped choking, they started laughing. "You hit it out of the park slugger. How'd you know?"

"Is it pictures?" Daniel asked his mother.

"You hit the nail on the head," Susan replied.

"Well, what kind of pictures?"

"There are only three and I think you'll be interested in each of them," Scotty said after picking up his tea glass still remaining on the table. He takes a sip with a silly grin on his face.

Susan motions for Scotty to get the envelope and he eagerly does so, casually bringing it back to the table. Before opening it, Scotty looks into Daniel's eyes and begins to ask questions that even surprised Susan.

"Daniel, do you believe God will often do things to let us know that he loves us and has a purpose for our lives?"

"Sure."

"Do you believe God had a reason for putting you on my team for the past two seasons?"

"I guess so."

"Do you believe that God gave you that dream last Saturday night?"

"I sure do," Albeit, he thought, *how does he know about the dream?*

"And do you believe it was no accident that you and your family attended Oak Grove on Sunday."

"I sure don't believe it was an accident."

"Neither do I, and when I show you these pictures, I want you to know that we serve an awesome God, a miracle working God. He has done an incredible thing by allowing us to be friends. When you see the pictures, just know that God has done this to let us know He loves us and desires that we trust Him with our lives."

Scotty opened the envelope and carefully pulls out three pictures, spreading them out on the table in front of Daniel. The twins rise from their chairs and look over Daniel's shoulders. Susan likewise stands to view them, opposite-side of Scotty. Having only heard about the specifics, Susan was as curious as her children.

Daniel's eyes darted at each picture and asked, "Who are the baseball players?"

"Do they look familiar to you?" Scotty asked.

"I'm not sure."

First, Scotty points to the one on the left of Daniel, "That one was taken after a game several years ago when I played at Meridian Junior College." The picture had two players standing side by side.

"Neat, so that one must be you right there," Daniel replied, correctly putting down his finger on Scotty's image.

Scotty turns and looks for Susan's reaction. He noticed her eyes were becoming red with moisture. Susan managed to ask, "Who do you think that is standing next to Scotty?"

Suddenly Daniel realized it was his dad and grabbed the picture up and shouted, "MY DAD!"

Then Daniel looked closely at the remaining two photos and shouted, "THESE ARE PICTURES OF YOU AND MY DAD!"

"Daniel, your father and I were very close friends. We played two years together at MJC."

"You've got to be kidding me!"

Daniel expressed his shock—the twins just stood there. They didn't know the relevance of anything. It would take more than that to impress eight-year-olds.

Scotty was now connected to the family by a bazaar set of circumstances. The supernatural events of the past three days had impacted their world in a thrilling way. Scotty went on to explain each photo in detail. Daniel hardly blinked an eye as he viewed each picture carefully and heard stories of his Dad's college days—as a ballplayer, a friend, especially as a Christian witness.

Susan was still astonished to think that the one who'd coached, and even picked up her son for two solid summers, was a good friend to Dan.

Chapter 13

The landscape draped in color indicated that autumn had arrived. With the changing of the season, Scotty and Susan's friendship became more colorful as well. After three months of so-called courting, Scotty finally gave Susan an appropriate hug in the parking lot of Oak Grove Church following a Sunday morning service. Daniel noticed the friendship between his mom and former coach was beginning to appear, *different.*

Scotty began conveniently dropping by the house to eat dinner three or four evenings a week. The two routinely spoke of their lunch dates to various eateries in town. Scotty twice loaded his riding lawn mower on a trailer and pulled it behind his truck to Susan's place. He spent hours mulching leaves, and hauled the load to his family farm to be burned. That alone would certainly indicate more than just friendship.

* * *

By Christmas, the entire Patton family had made three trips to Scotty's farmhouse, a couple of times touring the spacious countryside on his John Deer tractor. Daniel managed not to stare, but he could see it from the corner of his eye. Scotty's arm was securely wrapped around his mom's shoulders, making sure she didn't tumble-off the tractor during the bumpy joy ride.

They exchanged several gifts on a chilly Christmas Eve night. Scotty split some oak from his property, delivering half a truck load to Susan's house and building a cozy fire in the fireplace. Then the gifts were opened. Scotty bought Daniel a bucket of pearly white baseballs, a bat, and a new Wilson infielder's glove. He presented the girls with an assortment of clothing, Susan helping to pick them out. When Susan received a beautiful gold necklace with the Cross of Christ, she gave Scotty a quick kiss of appreciation. The kiss left Christmas-red lipstick imprinted on the side of his face.

Things were changing at a rapid pace and Daniel loved every minute of it. The genuine joy of life had obviously returned to Susan. Daniel easily observed it by the glow of her countenance.

* * *

The following summer, Daniel signed up for pony league and immediately got off to an eye-popping start. After just four games, he connected for seven homers and fielded everything within reach. It wasn't long before news of Daniel's accomplishments reached the Meridian High School Baseball Coach. By mid-season, Coach Terry O'Neal was scouting Daniel as an *up and comer,* which was very rare for a thirteen-year-old in his first year of pony league.

Coach O'Neal had posed an opportunity for the young slugger by the end of the pony league season. Daniel was offered the chance to practice with the Junior Varsity when fall practice began. Daniel suggested the coach give his mom a call to ask her for permission, which he did. After Susan discussed it with Scotty, they came to the quick conclusion that it was an honor, and accepted the invitation.

Scotty then nominated himself to take on the responsibility of making sure Daniel made every practice. *Some things never change*, Scotty said to himself many times during the fall practices. But Scotty was more than happy to help. He relished the JV workouts usually staying the entire two hours to observe Daniel's continuous growth into a sensational talent.

At the youthful age of just thirteen, he was hitting with such tremendous authority, the JV coach made a flattering comment which Scotty overheard, "*Half the guys on the Varsity aren't hitting the ball as hard as Daniel.*" Scotty knew this to be true, and so did anyone with reasonable baseball insight. Although Daniel wasn't eligible to play in regular JV games yet, he was making waves within the high school ranks, and still had one more year of pony league.

* * *

At fourteen, Daniel received the '*superstar award*' for outstanding play for his final year in pony league. The award is given to the city's best overall baseball player in the thirteen-fourteen-year-old category. His picture was photographed and placed on the front page of the Meridian Star along with a lengthy article highlighting Daniel's remarkable statistics. That year Daniel's batting average was an astonishing .632, with 21 homers in only 19 games. The article also mentioned his outstanding fielding performance, making only two errors in seventy-four chances. His team, *the Cardinals*, went a near-perfect eighteen and one, winning the league championship. Also written in the article were three answers Daniel had given in response to the writer. When asked, "*What do you want to be when you grow up?*"

Daniel replied, "*A Major League Baseball Player.*"

Secondly, the writer asked, "*What do you think your chances are of making the big leagues one day?*"

His answer was, *"I really don't know, but I do believe God wants me to give it a try."*

Lastly, the writer asked, *"Why do you believe that?"*

To which Daniel responded, *"I had a dream one night when I was twelve...that's why."*

* * *

The following Christmas was one to be remembered. Scotty gave Susan a humongous, neatly wrapped present. She opened it, only to find another wrapped present. She proceeded to open that one and found yet another wrapped present. Seven boxes were unwrapped until finally, there was this very small, perfectly wrapped little box. When Susan opened it, she began to cry.

It was a ring!

She accepted his marriage proposal and the wedding was set to take place in the spring. They both had fallen deeply in love with one another having a strong spiritual sense their union was the will of the Lord, and witnessing first hand the Lord's miraculous providence.

On a beautiful Saturday afternoon, with a hint of spring fragrance in the air, *Susan Patton became Susan Harper*. They stood under the same oak tree the three founding families gathered so many years ago to launch Oak Grove Church. The oak had to be more than a hundred years old. It was huge three decades ago, but had grown even more, with its trunk thicker and limbs fuller. Its shadow, courtesy of the oak's protruding limbs, provided perfect shading for the bride and groom.

To the west, Oak Grove Church sparkled in the bright sunlight as a testimony of what was possible with an inspired vision of God. Before and after the wedding ceremony, Scotty's Dad and Big Jeff would gaze at the beautiful church in the distance and give one another an enthusiastic thumbs-up. They were still impressed with what the Lord had accomplished through a couple of back-wood country boys.

Big Jeff stood before the bride and groom as the couple repeated their wedding promises. Susan wore a beautiful flowing white-laced wedding dress. Daniel's comment was, "M*om looks just like an angel.*"

Susan's smile beamed love for Scotty as her blonde hair gently blew with the fresh breeze. Scotty wore a black tuxedo and appeared to be relieved that the loneliness of bachelorhood was behind him.

Even though there were no official invitations mailed, more than seventy-five family members and friends were in attendance. Susan was particularly blessed to the point of tears by the unexpected arrival of Dan's mom and dad. They rode from Georgia with her parents. Mr. and Ms. Patton were extremely supportive and grateful at how the Lord had worked in this mysterious way, making a point to express nothing but their blessings.

Susan had always been an independent person. Although she dearly loved her parents, they had played a very small role in her life since she turned eighteen—much to their chagrin. They averaged talking on the phone about twice a month, and she'd traveled to Georgia only four or five times since Dan's death. Susan appreciated their trip to the wedding, and in return, promised more frequent visits to Georgia. Scotty was thoughtful in offering lodging to the in-laws anytime they wished to visit. The invitation was also granted to the Pattons. Everyone promised to make a better effort to stay in closer contact, especially for the sake of their grandchildren.

Mitchell Harper, Scotty's dad, was a thoughtful, hard working, well-intentioned man. After it was determined that the family of five would live in the remodeled eighty-year-old farmhouse, Mr. Harper asked his best friend and pastor to advertise Susan's house *for-sale* in the church bulletin. Within the month, the house sold to a young dentist who had also recently married.

God was certainly opening up windows of Heaven's blessings upon their lives.

* * *

Adjusting to country living wasn't hard for Susan. She'd become accustomed to changes in her life. Susan and the children were embracing the new adventure of farm life with vigor. With a touch of class, but not to overdo it, she worked diligently to convert the bachelor farmhouse into an appropriate home for the family, and Scotty didn't protest for a second.

After Scotty's granddad died, the main farmhouse along with twenty-five acres had been willed to Scotty. His parents built their home years ago, and willed the remaining farm—hundreds of acres of prime Mississippi land. Oak Grove Church was just through the woods, but wasn't visible from either house. However, seasonably the families were able to clearly view each other's residence. There was a patch of woods separating the old farmhouse from where Scotty's parents lived. When the trees were bare in fall and winter, each could faintly see the other house. But father and son treated both homes as their own.

That's the way Papa Harper would've wanted it.

* * *

By the time Daniel entered his first year of high school, Scotty became so involved with Daniel's Major League dream that he gave up coaching little league altogether. He wanted to devote as much spare time as possible to help Daniel achieve his goal. Scotty, and fifteen-year-old Daniel, methodically designed and constructed a rather modest baseball field on the Westside of the farmhouse. A batting cage, equipped with a pitching machine was assembled near the right-side of the field, up on a slight embankment.

Every day except Sundays, Scotty and Daniel worked on the fundamentals of hitting, fielding, throwing and base-running.

Long after the sun had gone down and all the chores of farming had ended, Scotty often fed balls into the pitching machine. The echo of contact resounded throughout the farm, disturbing the wildlife for a country square mile.

Scotty wouldn't let nightfall prevent him from his commitment to Daniel's pursuit, even if it meant the inconvenience of occasionally running down the battery of his truck or tractor while using their headlights to shine sufficiently on a batting practice session.

Susan, on the other hand, continued to build her business. Thanks to the contributions from the fine people of Philadelphia following Dan's death, she was able to have enough capital in the infancy years of Patton's shoes to pump most of the profits back into her business. Susan also felt blessed to live in a country with financial benefits for families of police officers killed in the line of duty. Even though Dan was off-duty at the time, benefits were rewarded, due largely to the lobbying efforts of one particular East Mississippi congressman. Susan had never asked for a dime from anyone, but God had blessed despite her rebellion at the time.

Susan possessed an excellent business mind, and to her credit, saw an incredible opportunity to purchase the former Jergenson's buffet storefront just around the corner from her shoe shop. She transformed it into a women's retail clothing store. Charlotte, the housekeeper/babysitter, graduated from college and became the full-time manager of *Patton's Dress Shop*.

Susan was busier than ever, and truly much happier.

After turning fourteen-years-of-age, the girls were slowly maturing, thank goodness. They no longer needed to be constantly watched. However, most of their after-school hours, and every Saturday were spent at one shop or the other. They mostly chatted with customers, but sometimes were given menial jobs to occupy their time.

With *two* retail stores on the same block, Susan had correctly assumed it would bring more lady shoppers to the area. Since the grand opening of her new dress shop, the shoe shop nearly doubled its revenues. In her thoughtful evaluation, each store would successfully complement the other.

She was right.

Scotty continued to work diligently on the farm with his dad harvesting a quality crop each year. Susan's businesses were taking off. The twins were becoming beautiful young little ladies. And as for Daniel, he was excelling in his high school baseball career, and was fairly consistent academically. His grades stayed steady initially, despite the constant pressures and demands of high school athletics. Daniel was making all A's and B's until the ever increasing attention from the college and professional ranks resulted in an occasional lack of focus in the classroom.

He knew that his solid grade-point-average would tank.

On or off the baseball diamond, Daniel never once put on a cocky air, thinking he was better than others. He knew God had blessed him with a talent and never desired personal glorification. On one occasion, in front of hundreds of Oak Grove worshippers, Daniel courageously delivered a heart-felt testimony of how God had put him in a position to point people to the love of Christ.

That was his purpose, and that's what he intended to do.

As the Senior Captain of the Meridian Wildcat Varsity Baseball Squad, Daniel was the first player to maintain a batting average over .500—according to the record books dating back more then fifty years. Daniel also became Meridian High's career all-time hits leader and home run king, with one hundred ninety-six, and fifty-seven, respectively. He'd started all four years and never rode the pine. His junior back-up was thrilled that Daniel Patton was finally graduating. Just seven more games and he'd be numero-uno.

Daniel had the same struggles and temptations as any other Christian, and many times failed, especially after his mother bought his first ride: A used black Ford truck—over one hundred-twenty on the odometer. He never drank, smoked or cursed, but he loved an occasional joy-ride. One late night, with a few baseball buddies in the back clinging on for dear life, Daniel lost control on a curvy dirt road doing sixty-five. He plowed over a mailbox owned by a deacon of Oak Grove Church. Somehow the crash didn't put any additional scratches on his truck, but thoroughly destroyed the deacon's mailbox. Ten days later, Daniel finally owned-up to the property damage and offered to do yard work to repay the man of God. The joy-riding stopped and he was glad no one was killed. After the incident, Daniel was grounded for a month from so much as touching the keys to the truck.

It was during that time Daniel found himself examining his life and the direction he must follow. Daniel didn't want anything to come between himself and God, and was driven to his knees under the Holy Spirit's conviction in order to get himself back on track for God—a rare Christian trait for a popular senior still in high school.

As Daniel's senior year was rapidly coming to a close, it seemed everyone in the community were on pins and needles, wondering which direction Daniel would choose. *Would he choose to sign with a major college? Would he be drafted professionally, right out of High School? If Daniel was drafted, would it be in an advantageous round which would encourage him to forgo a college scholarship?* As the newspapers and baseball fanatics in East Mississippi made their predictions, Daniel and his parents quietly prayed for the Lord's direction.

Susan and Scotty knew the decision would ultimately have to be made by Daniel himself.

Chapter 14

Robert Walker had scouted for the Atlanta Braves organization for seventeen years. For the past two years, he'd been a regular among *Meridian Wildcat* fans, transparently monitoring Daniel's potential as a future Major Leaguer.

The successful scout is one who has a keen instinct. He views players on the merits of future development and their current ability to excel in the minor leagues. Over the years, Walker had submitted hundreds of players to be drafted with only three being called up to the Atlanta Braves club. All three had been selected in Atlanta's top two rounds. For scouts and their prospects, the startling statistic was obvious; it's extremely advantageous for a player to be drafted in the early rounds.

Top prospects will be given every opportunity to make the big club, but the journey is still long and difficult.

After a prospect is drafted, he typically starts out in rookie ball, moves to the Single-A level, hopefully Double-A will follow, and finally the Triple-A level. Often a talented player will bypass Triple-A, getting the call up to the Majors straight from the Double-A farm team.

Every scout is aware of the overwhelming odds for most kids who are assigned to one of their minor league clubs. Even if a player is successful in making it to the big leagues, it becomes more difficult after their arrival. If one doesn't perform, they'll be packing for a return trip to the minors. The stakes are high, and winning is everything for each organization.

So based on the obvious, all top high school and college prospects hope to be drafted early, thus enhancing their chance to move up the ladder quickly.

Robert 'Bob' Walker had a notebook scribbled with loads of information concerning Daniel. Over the past two years, he wrote and rewrote *player evaluation forms* on the Mississippi prospect. He rated critical details such as; foot speed, throwing arm strength, bat speed, fielding range, quickness, instincts, maturity, strengths, weaknesses, and the like. From all his combined years of experience as a scout for the Braves, he was confident Daniel Patton was ready for the jump from high school baseball to the professional level. The only question the Braves organization had to answer was; *in what round to draft the power hitting shortstop of the Meridian High Wildcat*s. They were aware of the numerous college programs and professional organizations who'd like nothing better than to capture Daniel. But the Braves felt they had the upper-hand in the process. Walker discovered through unidentified sources that Daniel and his family had been big Braves fans all their life.

That bit of information was a huge plus.

They also assumed that by selecting him in the early rounds of the draft—top three picks in the country, their chances of signing him were excellent. They also hoped that an appropriate signing bonus would encourage Daniel to by-pass a college scholarship and immediately turn pro.

The conference table was littered with papers, sketch pads, pencils, computerized statistical information and photographs. Bob Walker, the Braves Regional Scout of the Southeast States, discussed player selection with Farm Director, Matthew Townsend. Stuart Bennett, the General Manager of the Braves was also in the room to make critical decisions concerning a ton of high school and college prospects. There were two dozen other scouts seated at the table who separately covered territories in and out of the States, including the Dominican Republic, Puerto Rico, Central and South America, China and other regions around the globe.

Every year these same veteran scouts assembled themselves in Atlanta's Stadium Duplex Suite to sort through hundreds of kids. The conference room in which they sat had a full-window-view of the field below. The Braves were on the road, but a few members of the grounds crew were on the infield doing their art work. Hardly anyone in the room took notice to the movement out on the field. It was game-time within the walls of the conference room. Their ultimate goal was to draft the best of the best.

They fully understood their duty to maintain a solid organization top to bottom. The goal was to develop the strongest professional talent in the baseball world, being aware that all thirty Major League organizations had the same ambition as well.

Baseball was all about competing.

"Bob, do you really believe Daniel Patton is a future Atlanta Braves shortstop?" Matthew Townsend asked while sipping a diet coke. He'd gained a few pounds since his pro career. He was known as *Matt the Cat* during his playing days of patrolling second base for the Atlanta Club. Nobody pounced around the infield like *the Cat.* At fifty five, he still had that cat-like intensity in his eyes.

"Matt, I'm totally confident in my assessments. Daniel Patton should go no later than the second round, if not first. This kid has it all, and I mean '*all*' the tools to make it to Atlanta within two or three years."

General Manager Stuart Bennett glanced down at the photograph of Daniel lying on the table and asked, "Bob, have you met with his parents yet?"

"Not yet…I do know that his mother recently married and the family lives on a cotton farm in East Mississippi. They're very religious from what I've heard. Stu, I would be shocked if this kid has ever been in trouble. He's just a solid kid altogether. His father was a police officer but was unfortunately shot and killed during a convenience store robbery. Daniel was eight-years-old at the time. His mother owns a couple of women apparel businesses and his step-father spends his days on the farm. He has a couple of twin sisters, cute as can be. Stu, he's unusually strong for his size. He's proportionately as strong as any eighteen-year-old I've ever scouted. He's a well-spoken, humble kid. He is idolized by the people in that area. And what's so unique, he doesn't seem to realize how talented he really is. He's so different from others I've seen with half his talent…strutting around like peacocks with their feathers in full-bloom. Daniel is a breath of fresh air, and it's been a privilege scouting him."

"That's sad about his father, but Daniel and his family sound like super folks. I like what I hear. He looks tremendous on paper too," Matt said while guzzling the last of the diet coke.

Stuart shuffled a few more pages of printed material and said, "I haven't seen stats like this in a while from a high school kid."

One of the other scouts inserted, "We need pitchers. My USC boy is ready. I've consistently clocked him at 93 on the radar, and with excellent control I might add. He should go number one, no question about it. He is a number one all the way. That's my humble opinion."

Everyone at the table shot their eyes toward Stuart's reaction to the strong opinion. However, Stuart was the decision maker, and looked the part with his perfectly tailored suit. Stuart was the youngest General Manager in the Majors. At forty-one, he was becoming the most talked about GM in the country for his professionalism and good looks. He even made it on the cover of GQ magazine six months ago. The ladies often remarked that he looked like Brad Pitt.

After a few seconds of personal deliberation, Stuart calmly said, "We've basically decided on the order of three-through-twenty, so let's make a solid decision based on the facts concerning number one and two. I don't want to make any assumptions here, not yet. We just need to look at this before jumping the gun on who should go first, and who should go second. We've made great progress and I appreciate all the work each of you have been doing, but let's think the matter through before we make the final decision on our overall number one pick. We have narrowed it down to Daniel Patton, the high school standout from Meridian, Mississippi, and Willey Emerson, the hard throwing pitcher out of the University of Southern California. Both of these young men have a great future in baseball. Both will either go first or second in Atlanta's draft. Let's do this; Bob, why don't you fly out to Mississippi in the next couple of days, go out to that farm and have a little sit-down with the Patton's. Tell them we're planning to draft Daniel number one. See what their reaction is to a signing bonus of 1.5 Million. If they like the offer, then I think we should go with Daniel. Willey will probably take less. His next step is obviously the professional level. Daniel and his parents on the other hand have other options. We have to convince him to sign and turn down the college route. I think it's wise to pursue Daniel Patton for the number one slot."

"Sounds like a solid strategy to me," Matt *the Cat* said, as he tosses the emptied coke can into a trash container over in the corner. He pumped his fist as it went in. *Still got it,* he thought to himself with pride.

Bob stared at Stuart with a pleased expression. "I'll be on a flight in the morning."

"Good, now let's finish our thirty-through-fifty picks. We'll make our final decision on Daniel and Willey depending upon Bob's upcoming meeting," Stuart insisted.

The scouts began grabbing additional papers off the table, but Bob's mind began to drift. He was meditating on the winning approach to Daniel and his parents. He hoped it'd spell *victory* for the Atlanta Braves organization. Bob Walker had been anxiously awaiting this possible scenario for months. Finally, the scout will meet the player in which he'd already become a fan. The veteran scout was about to rock Daniel Patton's world—for a change. *This was the best part about scouting. This is what makes the thousands of miles of travel and time spent away from family, worthwhile.* He thought.

Chapter 15

The Meridian Star already had made its prediction. Their hometown sports hero would be drafted in the top five in the country. By the final game of the regular season, no one really knew the intentions of Daniel, but understood something rather interesting was taking place.

Attending Daniel's last few high school games were an increasing swarm of scouts. But even his closest of teammates were not privy to the avenue Daniel would choose. Would he sign a scholarship with a major university or immediately go pro. Opinions tilted heavily in favor of Patton going straight to the professional level. They had followed his remarkable high school career and knew their local boy would doubtless be drafted early.

Coach O'Neal couldn't go out in public without being inundated with the usual question. Whether in the grocery store, at a movie, or with family at a restaurant, he was constantly asked, *"Coach, where do you think Daniel will play next?"* The coach would give his stock answer, *"You'll have to ask him."*

With Daniel's senior year ending and the June draft nearing, Daniel was beginning to feel the pressure. He wasn't the same twelve-year-old boy who his mother frightened by showing up to watch him play, but privately he was beginning to feel a similar overwhelmed feeling. He was no doubt in a pressure cooker. Daniel's focus had always been on the next game, the next pitch, the next grounder, and now there was, *the next giant-leap in life.*

Baseball wasn't supposed to make him feel twisted on the inside. It was a dream, a passion, a game played with friends. Baseball was supposed to be played for fun. The competition was a challenge Daniel relished in. That part of the game he enjoyed, but the hype he didn't care for. It wasn't compatible with his shy personality to successfully absorb the talk and attention. He didn't want to disappoint anyone—not his family, not his friends, not his coaches, and especially, not his Lord.

* * *

Daniel figured everyone was in bed sound asleep, so he decided to unwind by taking a walk under the bright full moon. His six-foot-one-inch frame cast a shadow onto the shortstop area of the homemade baseball field he and Scotty labored to build. The suppressed anxiety was too much to hold back any longer. Daniel was like a dam ready to crack.

He suddenly and uncontrollably burst into tears.

With the end of his high school playing days having concluded just four hours earlier, Daniel lifted his head toward Heaven and sobbingly cried to God: "*Lord, I don't know what to do. You gave me the ability to play baseball and I wish you would show me the way? I want to feel your presence, but I don't have peace right now. Lord, I don't care about any potential offers. I don't care about all the attention. I just want to be in your will. If you don't even want me to play baseball, I won't. If you want me to work on this farm the rest of my life, I'll do that. I feel you have a purpose for my life, but I'm scared Lord. I'm terrified. I know you desire your children to have joy and peace. But I don't feel so great right now God. Please help me Lord."*

The tears streamed down the tanned face of Daniel. He ran fingers through his sandy blond hair, and then wiped the tears away with the sleeve of his blue Wildcat tee-shirt. Glancing toward the ground, he noticed a small shiny pebble in the dirt. He was impressed at how it glowed only by the light of the moon. Picking it up, he studied it. It was tiny in his leathered hand. Daniel suddenly remembered a family vacation at the beach in Panama City Florida when he was just a small child. His dad was helping him build a sand castle, and from the recesses of his mind he recalled a father-son conversation. How it came to him at that particular moment was unknown, having never once thought of it at any point in his life. He could even hear the sound of the sea gulls and visually see the white capped waves break toward the ocean shoreline. It all seemed as though it was happening at that precise moment: "Son, do you realize God knows the exact number of grains of sand there are on this whole earth?" Daniel's father said, picking up a handful of the white powdery stuff.

"He can sure count high," six-year-old Daniel said.

"He sure can son. Do you realize that God also knows the number of hairs on your head?"

"Does He know how much sand is in my hair?"

"I'm pretty sure he knows that too son. God knows everything, that's what makes Him the great God He is."

"What else do you know that God knows?" asked little Daniel.

"Well I know that the Bible says He loves us, and He will never leave nor forsake us. See that ocean Danny-boy? See that sail-boat out there riding those waves? Our lives are a lot like that sail-boat. All we have to do is let the wind determine our direction. You see son, let's say the wind is God and the sail-boat is you and me. We are never in control of the wind. The wind is in control of us."

"I get it Dad. God is in control and not the sail-boat, I mean us."

"I think you got it son," Daniel recalled his dad saying as the vision quickly faded.

As Daniel contemplated its meaning, he took the shiny pebble and put it in the pocket of his shorts. He eased his head upward, stared once more at the full moon. Daniel spoke again to its Creator: "*Well Lord, I think you have given me your answer. I will let you be in control and do according to your will. I surrender my life, my baseball and my entire future to you,*" Daniel prayed with a reminiscent smile.

* * *

Daniel was at peace with himself and God as he walked off the field, when out of the shadows he heard a familiar voice, over by the barn. "Nice night."

Focusing on the nearby tractor, Daniel clearly saw the outline of Scotty. He was slumping on the seat of the tractor. His feet were kicked up on the steering wheel, so Daniel strode to the John Deer.

"How long you been sitting there?" Daniel asked suspiciously.

"A few minutes…give or take. How long you been standing at shortstop?" Scotty was staring at the moon, suggesting his preoccupation with its beauty, and not so much with Daniel. His hands were linked together to support his head and a twig of straw hung out the side of his mouth. Scotty was in a laying position, seat to steering wheel.

"I just came out to get some fresh air," replied Daniel.

"Yea, I know what you mean. It can get stuffy in that old farmhouse sometimes. I been meaning to get a central cooling system installed…maybe one day."

After several seconds of silence, Scotty removed his feet from the steering wheel and sat up. He took the twig from his mouth and threw it on the ground. "I can't imagine the kind of pressure you must be under Daniel."

"It's not that bad," Daniel said in an unconvincing manner.

"Not many young men wrestle with a decision the magnitude of the one you may be tackling very shortly."

"Scotty, I've decided to leave it entirely in God's Hand. That's the only way I can deal with it. He put me in this position and He will move me when and where He chooses."

"Amen to that. God is in control, is He not?"

"Yes sir, He sure is. I know He is."

"Daniel, walking out here praying like you did is the best thing you could ever do. I'm so proud of your personal relationship with Christ."

"Scotty, I want to thank you for everything you've done for me. You gave up coaching for me. You built this field—"

"Wait just a minute, we built this field," Scotty demanded as they both glance toward the field to admire their handy work. With the brightness of the full moon, they separately thought the lighting was sufficient for a round of midnight batting practice.

"Okay, we built this field, but you've sacrificed for me. I don't know how to say—"

"Listen Daniel, it's been a joy. You know what I remember about your dad. He dreamed of being in the position you're in right now. It's an honor to help his son to achieve what he wished for himself. Your dad helped me to realize I needed my own personal relationship with Christ. In an indirect way, he's the one who should get the credit, not me. He definitely had a big part to play in both our lives in ways we can't even comprehend. I just praise God for him. That's the miracle that is unfolding before our very eyes. The miracle of God's providence just blows me away." Daniel caught the phrase "*blows me away*" but didn't say a word about the flashback minutes earlier. That would stay between himself and the Lord.

Scotty climbed down from the tractor and places his arm around Daniel's shoulders. "You just keep praying and everything will work according to His will," Scotty exhorted while squeezing Daniel's shoulder blade firmly.

"I plan on it."

"Why don't we go in and get some rest."

"That sounds good to me."

As the two walked toward the house, Scotty teasingly said, "You sure went out with a bang tonight with your last plate appearance as a Meridian Wildcat—a check-swing, right back to the pitcher."

Daniel started laughing, "Well, as the saying goes; you are as good as your last at-bat. What a blunder!"

"I know how you can atone for that blunder in the morning."

"You don't say...You got a pick-up game taking place on the farm?" Daniel replied.

"Sure do, you know...*pick-up that shovel and dig, game*. You got a few hours to spare in the morning?"

"Absolutely," Daniel said, obviously enjoying their back-and-forth as they approached the house.

"I realize Saturday mornings' are normally the time you catch up on your beauty sleep. I wouldn't want to interfere with that."

"Don't worry about me. Anyway, I've been meaning to help you more. Now that the season is over maybe I can lend you a hand from time to time. Consider it room and board."

Scotty opened the back door and held it wide for Daniel to enter first, "After you, Mr. Check-Swing."

"Thanks, Mr. Cotton-Picker," Daniel responded with equal sarcasm.

Scotty entered the house last and closes the door.

Chapter 16

Bob Walker's shuttle flight into Meridian's small airport was bumpy and unpleasant. He almost wished he'd simply driven the five hours down I-20. Nevertheless, Bob was satisfied with the efficiency of his morning flight. He arrived in Meridian the same hour, so to speak, as his departure from Atlanta. The small aircraft had departed at 10:15 eastern standard time and arrived at 10:17 central standard time.

Carrying only a briefcase, which had been at his side the entire flight, Bob walked through the automatic glass doors of the airport dressed in neither a black nor dark blue suit. He sported a white shirt and favorite blue Braves' tie. The tie had a red tomahawk centered perfectly down toward the bottom-end. After a quick survey of the few vehicles positioned out front, he walked directly to his prearranged rental waiting by the curb. He was immediately impressed at how remarkably easy it was exiting out of the smaller airport, as opposed to entering the hustle and bustle of maybe the world's busiest.

The clouds were puffy straight up and Bob was happy the weather was fair, but the morning humidity made him regret wearing his favorite suit and tie.

"You must be Mr. Walker?" asked the very short and stubby rental agent standing in front of a shiny grayish Dodge Durango. Bob requested something sturdy in the event the directions thrust him onto a Mississippi dirt road, or two.

A good scout always plans for things like that.

"That's me, I appreciate it. I'll meet you back here at three sharp," he said, barely glancing into his eyes. Bob was at least two feet taller than the short rental agent.

Grabbing the key, Bob hardly broke a stride before taking a seat behind the wheel. Obviously, he'd gone through the same routine many times before; with a shuttle flight here, a rental vehicle there, a draft pick here, there and everywhere.

"Do you need any directions?" The short agent said before Bob had time to slam the door.

"No, thanks to the internet, I've got all the directions I need. Thanks anyway," Bob said just before slamming his door shut.

Bob drives north-bound out of the airport and onto Industrial road, hops on the busy by-pass heading east. He looks to his left momentarily and views the splay of Meridian's buildings. After five miles on the by-pass, he exits onto Highway 39 North. After driving 12.4 additional miles, he notices the huge sign advertising Oak Grove Church. He takes the next right onto a narrow dirt road. The name on the sign read: *Harper Farm Road*—the computer printout was perfect, leading him precisely to the Harper's address.

As the scout drives slowly, steering along the red clay narrow road, he views the freshly plowed fields. From his travels as a Southeastern Regional Scout, he knew the white cotton wouldn't be visible until late summer and into the fall. Looking to his right he notices a fat bass jump into the air from a small pond. Instinctively, he begins to visualize himself on the bank, yanking the bass to high heaven with his favorite fishing rod in hand. He wished he'd brought it along for the trip. He might have celebrated signing Daniel to a contract with a little fishing detour. Sadly, all the fishing equipment was collecting dust in the storage room back home in the mountains of North Georgia.

All good scouts must also plan for impromptu fishing expeditions. This time he fell short on the planning.

In a daydream of reeling in the monster bass onto the pond's bank, he was suddenly startled back to reality. Coming directly toward him was an ambulance screaming around the curve just ahead. He pulled to the side, almost into a ditch, and said audibly, "What in the name of blue blazes is this?"

The lights flashed and the siren sounded as the red and white emergency rescue vehicle came much too close to his rental.

Catching a breath, he looked into the side rearview mirror as the ambulance sped out of sight. Bob hesitatingly eased his way forward, hoping it didn't involve the ones to whom he was about to pay a surprise visit. *Think positive. This has nothing to do with*— Bob refused to think the worse. *It's going to be okay. I'm going to find Daniel and his family safe and sound. No problem.* He was trying to convince himself, but his gut told him something different.

In less than thirty seconds a white pickup appeared, spinning around the same curve. Once again, Bob frantically steered his rental off to the side, avoiding yet another head-on collision. He'd caught the faces of the man and woman in the white dusty truck. Though he couldn't be absolutely sure, it appeared to be Daniel's mom and stepdad. He'd seen them on a few occasions, but had never spoken to them. The blurred faces which sped passed looked exactly like the parents of Daniel, only their expressions at the games where much different. From the ever-so-brief glimpse, Bob was able to visually gather in his sight the faces of absolute panic and terror.

The curve was sharp and he wondered how the rescue vehicle and white truck could've taken it at such a high speed. Beyond the curve, the narrow road led to an old farmhouse. The house had tremendous oak trees standing in the yard and beyond. It had an impressive looking baseball field and batting cage off to the left. He knew he had arrived at the Harper's residence.

Who else would have a baseball field on a cotton farm?

The Durango slowly crept onto a long circular dirt driveway which led to the front of the house. There wasn't a person in sight, but the door of the house was open, like someone had left in a mad rush. Bob naturally thought the open door may be connected with his two near head-on collisions. *They didn't even take time to close the door—another bad sign.*

Stopping within a few yards of the porch, Bob apprehensively crawled out of the rental, walked up the steps and onto the porch. He knocked softly on the side of the facing right beside the opened door and gazed into the house, listening for movement. Bob could see the kitchen and living room, but tried not to be too nosey in case someone was watching from the distance.

"Is anyone home?" the scout shouted appropriately.

After there was no response from within the house, he walked off the porch to get a better view of the surroundings. *Maybe there is someone in the barn, or out working the field.*

He spotted a tiny glimmer of a structure through a patch of woods and noticed a narrow road winding in its direction. He wouldn't have noticed it on a typical day, but this was no typical day. He decided to go and investigate. *If those folks are home, maybe they'll be able to tell me what's going on.* His thought continued. *It might even be where I'll find Daniel and his family, safe.*

Bob returned to the vehicle and proceeded down the pig trail road, steering around its many pot holes. After emerging to the opposite side of the woods and into the opening, Bob saw a much larger, more modern house. Bob immediately saw movement. Four people were standing in front of the house curiously looking in his direction. The two young girls were familiar—they were the twin sisters of Daniel. The older man and woman who stood alongside the girls were unfamiliar. The man wore overalls and the woman had on an apron. Bob drove to where the group was assembled and before he could get out of the car, he knew something was seriously wrong. Except for the man in overalls, all were in tears. The older couple had arms wrapped tightly around the girls in an apparent effort to bring comfort.

Bob put the Durango in park, killed the engine and slowly climbed out, dreading the forthcoming horrible news.

"Hi, my name is Bob Walker," he said softly as he approached the weeping group.

The man in the overalls asked with a trembling voice, "Are you from the hospital?"

"No sir, I came to pay a visit to Daniel Patton and his family."

"They've gone to the hospital," he said, attempting to keep his composure.

"Is someone sick or something? I just passed the ambulance as I entered the property."

"We've just had an accident. Our grandson was badly injured."

"My word, what happened?" Bob asked, knowing that the injured was likely Daniel.

Gripping the weeping girls tighter the man said, "Could you come back at another time? I'm sorry sir. This isn't a good time."

"Sure, no problem Mr.—"

"Name is Harper. This is my wife and granddaughters."

"You must be Daniel's grandparents."

"Yes we are…by marriage."

"May I ask if he's the one who is being rushed to the hospital?"

"Yes sir, unfortunately he is."

"I just flew out here from Atlanta. I'm with the Atlanta Braves organization."

"You came here to talk with Daniel about baseball didn't you?"

"Yes sir, I did."

"Well in that case, maybe you should come on in the house and we'll explain what's happened."

Bob nodded affirmatively and followed the four into the house. He knew this wasn't good, not good at all.

Chapter 17

The emergency vehicle wheeled into the emergency section of Piedmont hospital and the rapid response team was prepared and waiting. The call to 911 came to the dispatcher by way of Scotty's cell at exactly 9:47. Forty minutes later Daniel's unconscious body was being taken from the back of the ambulance and rolled into Piedmont's trauma ward. After a team of medical professionals gently picked Daniel's limp body off the cot and slid him onto the appointed bed, the lead Doctor shouted, "Listen folks, this boy of ours has lost significant blood. Let's get it under control."

A portion of the medical team concentrated on the lower extremities of Daniel, while the others efficiently connected all the necessary monitors. The same Doctor said, "He's going to need some help to steady the heart…get the life support going immediately. Let's put a tube into his lung and get a drip going—"

Susan and Scotty jogged frantically through the same emergency doors which Daniel was wheeled. There was a substantial amount of blood on the front of their clothes. Susan had streaks of dried blood on the side of her face and forehead. Very seldom had she ever taken Saturday off from her shops, but on this fateful day, she was home when the accident happened. She planned to check on things that afternoon, but now the two shops were a million miles from her mind.

Susan spotted the first person and frantically asked, “My son, where is he?”

The overweight colored lady dressed in a blue nursing outfit places both hands on Susan’s shoulders and sympathetically said, “Sweetie, my name is Rosy. They’re doing everything they can for your boy. I’m sure someone will be with you shortly. Can I get you anything, some water or something?”

“Please, I just need to know how my son is doing.”

“If you’ll come with me, we have a place for you to wait. The Doctors will look for you there.”

A much younger white woman walked toward them and asked, “Ms. Rosy are these the parents of the young man who just came in?”

“They sure are. This is Mr. and Mrs.—”

“Harper…Susan and Scotty Harper,” Scotty promptly said.

“It’s nice to meet you Mr. and Mrs. Harper. My name is Heather.” Turning to Rosy, Heather says, “I need to take the Harper’s to my office to complete some patient information.” Heather directed her attention back to Susan and Scotty, “You folks come right along with me and then we’ll get you an update on your son.”

Scotty held Susan close to his side, assisting her as they followed behind the emergency room worker into a small room located around the corner from the main waiting area.

* * *

“Mr. Walker, may I get you some coffee?” asked Mrs. Harper, soon after entering the den of their home.

“No. But thank you,” Bob said, surprised by the offer in the midst of an apparent sudden family tragedy.

The girls sat with their grandparents on the couch. Bob was relieved the sobbing had subsided.

"So you came to Meridian to speak with Daniel?" asked Mr. Harper.

"Yes sir, ten o'clock, I just got here…Mr. Harper, tell me what happened to Daniel?" Bob wanted to put fingers in both ears.

"My son Scotty, Daniel and myself were in the barn right next to the ball field. I guess you noticed it coming in. Well…we got up fairly early this morning to do some mechanical work on one of the tractors. You know, we stagger the cotton almost year round. Even though three-quarters of the land has been planted, we still needed to plant that final-quarter for the fall harvest. You know, we harvest the cotton through the fall and into early winter. Well…it was rather urgent that we get the tractor conditioned so we could plant that final quarter. Scotty and I were under the tractor with the grease gun doing some lubing and such. This was around 7:30 this morning. Daniel shows up to help around 8:00. For the most part, he stood around, mainly watching. It takes quite awhile to do all the necessary things we do to keep our equipment going properly. I think it was around 9 o'clock when we heard a loud slam on the ground. Scotty and I were still under the tractor. We looked and saw Daniel lying on the ground. He apparently had climbed up into the loft and somehow fell. His left leg was completely folded under his body. The leg and head were bleeding profusely." As Mr. Harper recalled the tragic event of the morning, the twins began sobbing again, pressing their faces onto both shoulders of Mrs. Harper.

"My Lord," Bob whispered.

"He was unconscious the whole time. I think he hit his head very hard on the ground. Obviously, his leg is shattered. A bone had penetrated the skin, just below the knee. There was an awful gash to his head. He was bleeding something terrible from the back of the head. We did our best to stop the bleeding with towels that we got from Scotty's place, but I know the kid lost a ton of blood."

"Did he ever gain consciousness?" Bob asked.

"Not even the slightest movement. His breathing was erratic. I have no idea of the internal injuries he may have suffered. All I know is; we need a miracle from God today."

Bob looked down at the floor and sat in silence. He knew they weren't interested in baseball, or the opportunity he came to offer. In fact, the tomahawk that dangled on the end of his tie made him sick.

Everything had changed.

"Sir, we're a praying family. I think it's time for us to get on our knees. You are welcome to join us, if you like."

The girls joined their grandparents and got down on their knees in the center of the room. They huddled close to one another.

Bob Walker sat, and bowed his head reverently.

Chapter 18

Big Jeff arrived at Piedmont Hospital before noon. He was escorted to a small room, separate from the miserable folks still waiting for medical assistance in the much larger waiting area. Scotty and Susan sat beside each other with blank expressions, then Big Jeff slowly entered and the couple immediately rose to their feet and hugged the preacher. His over-sized arms easily wrapped the both of them. The pastor began to pray: *"Dear Lord Jesus, help your people dear Lord. In the Powerful name of Jesus have mercy on this family. Lord, fill them with your Spirit of comfort and peace in the midst of tribulation. We trust you with Daniel Oh God. Take control Lord Jesus...Take control."*

"Thanks for coming Big Jeff. How'd you get the news so fast?" Scotty asked while still in the arms of his pastor.

"Your dad called right after you and Susan left the farm. He told me what happened. Listen, I've been on the phone with all the deacons and we have started our prayer chain. By now, there are literally hundreds of people praying for Daniel."

"Why did this happen? Why now? This doesn't make sense. This wasn't supposed to happen...not to Daniel," Susan said in tears.

"Listen Susan, in my many years of serving the Lord, I have learned personal crisis are *no respect of persons,* even for those who are serving the Lord. I totally understand you asking those questions. Just know this doesn't mean God isn't still in control. He's with Daniel. He always has been, and He always will be."

"I can't think of the possibility of—" Susan said, not able to finish.

"Listen Susan, we both believe that God has a special plan for Daniel's life and this doesn't change that. I don't know if the accident was God's plan, but I do know God is still on His Throne."

Within a few minutes of Big Jeff's entrance into the room, another man walked in and introduces himself. He was obviously a Doctor. "Hi, my name is Dr. Dillon."

"How's my son?" Susan anxiously asked the Doctor as everyone in the room stood to their feet.

"Ms. Harper, we have Daniel stable. His vital signs are close to normal. He is still unconscious however. We have him in x-ray now, and we should know more about the extent of his injuries shortly."

"Thank God," Susan replied in relief.

"The information I have is that Daniel fell from the loft of a barn. What did he strike his head on?" Dr. Dillon asked.

"I was there at the time. My father and I were working on a tractor in the barn. We didn't see it, but we heard the impact. We have all kinds of farm equipment laying everywhere. Daniel fell right in the middle of a bunch of old engine components. Listen, it'd be hard to fall from that loft and not hit something. He must've fallen about fifty feet. We're talking about a high loft area from a rather tall barn."

"Well, we have stitched his head and the bleeding has stopped. There was a substantial amount of blood-loss from the head and leg. We have called a specialist, Dr. Moreland, and he'll perform the surgery on the leg after we have the opportunity to view his CAT scan. We've given Daniel several pints of blood. The thing of most concern is possible swelling to the brain. The CAT results will tell us more about the cerebral region shortly."

"When can we see him?" Susan asked.

"You can come back when the x-ray and scan are complete. I'll have one of the nurses to get you as soon as possible. Do you have any questions before I leave?"

Scotty and Susan shook their heads slightly.

"I'm sorry this happened and we'll do everything in our power to help Daniel get through this."

"Thanks Doctor," Scotty said, as Susan pressed her face in her hands.

The Doctor hurries out of the room.

"The good news is; Daniel's vital signs are steady. Praise the Lord for that," Big Jeff encouragingly replies.

"That's right. All we can do right now is pray," Scotty said.

Scotty, Susan and the preacher take a seat and all three bow their heads in silent prayer.

* * *

His flight wasn't scheduled to depart back to Atlanta until later in the afternoon, so the scout decided to go by the hospital. Bob approached the receptionist of the emergency room and said, "I'm looking for the family of Daniel Patton," Bob informed through a little round hole in the glass.

"You aren't the only one," the lady replies, pointing to the folks seated in the chairs against the wall.

Bob knew the media when he saw them.

There were three groups: The group he knew to be the newspaper folks were the ones with the note pads and their cameras hanging from the neck. The other group was assembled around a man holding a news camera with channel 11 written on the side. Lastly, a small cohort sat in the far corner with a microphone and taping device with a large WARL 930 sticker. It only took Bob five seconds to visually gather the newspaper, television and radio folks as each waited patiently for any shred of information concerning Daniel.

"You can take a seat and our hospital spokespeople will be with *all* of you before too long."

"But I'm not the media. I'm from Atlanta."

"How'd you get here so fast?"

"No, No, I didn't know that the one I was coming to visit would be at the hospital, Daniel's accident happened right after I got here."

"Are you family?"

"No, I'm not family, and I don't have long before catching my flight back to Atlanta. Do you think it's possible to visit briefly with Daniel's parents?"

"Have a seat and I'll ask."

The receptionist leaves her little space of authority, walks to the family waiting room and sticks her neck and fake-black-wig around the corner. "There's a man who insists on speaking with you, says he's from Atlanta."

"Atlanta? Who could possibly be here from Atlanta?" Scotty asked Susan in bewilderment.

"You can ask him to come on back"

Soon after the gruff receptionist with the high-pitched voice departs, Bob reverently walked into the room and introduced himself. "My name is Bob Walker and I'm with the Atlanta Braves organization."

The second Bob mentioned *Atlanta Braves*, all three instantly notice the Braves tomahawk emblem on his tie.

Scotty stood, shakes his hand and introduces himself, Susan, and Big Jeff. He invited the visiting Bob to have a seat. Bob takes a seat on the opposite side of the room of the three. The family room was no bigger than an extra large closet.

"What brings you to Meridian?" Scotty didn't have to ask, but he did anyway.

"First I want to say how very sorry I am that Daniel was hurt. How's your boy?"

"He has a head injury and a badly broken leg. That's all we know at this time. They say he's stable, but still unconscious," Scotty said.

"I just wanted to drop by for a minute to find out the latest. I came here to talk about Daniel's baseball future. Geez, I hope for the best. He's a terrific kid and a sensational talent. I've been watching him for two years. I passed your truck on Harper Farm Road as you were leaving."

"I remember. You were the one in the ditch," Susan said with a half-hearted grin.

"That was me," the scout said turning his attention more toward Scotty, "Listen, I met your father, mother and the girls. They invited me in their house and told me what happened and we had prayer. I just didn't want to go back to the airport without coming by and meeting you."

"Are the Braves interested in Daniel?" Scotty knew that answer before asking too.

"All I can say at this time is; I hope Daniel will recover with flying colors. That's the main thing. We can talk in the future," Bob said, knowing the accident sadly changed everything.

"Daniel's baseball career doesn't seem important to us right now Mr. Walker. We aren't thinking about that," Susan said.

"Mrs. Harper, I have children and I know exactly what you mean...changing the subject, I wanted to inform you there is quite a crowd assembling in the front waiting area."

"Media?" asked Scotty.

Bob shakes his head affirmatively.

"We've given the hospital permission to keep them updated through one of their spokespersons. I'm sure this is going to be a shock to the people in the community. Everyone had such high hopes for—" Susan's voice broke with emotion.

"Listen, I unfortunately must be on my way. I just didn't want to get back on that plane without coming by to tell you folks that the Braves organization will be pulling for Daniel. Here's my card, please call me soon and let me know how Daniel is doing." Bob reached into his wallet and hands Susan a card which clearly identified his position—*Southeast Regional Scout, Atlanta Braves*.

The tomahawk on the card matched the one on his tie.

"I know this is disappointing for you to travel to Mississippi and for this to happen," Susan said.

"My concern is for Daniel. I'll be fine. I'm just as sorry as can be this happened. You folks are in my thoughts. Give me a call soon, and I will most certainly be in contact with you folks. I hope and pray for Daniel's speedy recovery."

Before Bob left, Susan, Scotty, and Big Jeff thanked him for taking the time to come by the hospital, and wished him a safe flight back to Atlanta.

Just as Bob disappears out the door, a nurse pokes her head in. "You can come back now to visit with your son."

Scotty and Susan nervously followed the nurse down a short hallway and took a right through double revolving doors. Big Jeff was trailing from behind quietly. Daniel was lying in a room with two medical personnel busily punching buttons and taking notes. A white sheet covered Daniel's body, exposing only his shoulders and head. Susan's knees almost buckled so Scotty steadied his wife from behind. A large tube extended into his mouth and the wires connected to his body ran to various beeping devices. Susan could see that the left side of Daniel's head was shaved and sewed up. Dried blood still matted his remaining hair. Scotty looked toward the direction of a monitor to study Daniel's heart rate. He couldn't tell whether the darting lines looked normal or not.

"My precious boy," Susan sobbed bending down to kiss Daniel on his forehead. All the dried blood on her face had been washed off, but she was surprised at the amount still in Daniel's unshaved hair. The blood had bleached his sandy-blonde hair, orange.

"Dear Lord Jesus, help him," Scotty said pressing his hand gently on Susan's back. Big Jeff had a hand on both their backs. He silently prayed.

"Scotty, he looks horrible…He looks so pale…He's not going to make it without a miracle."

"He's going to make it…His vital signs are good. Listen to me…Daniel is a fighter...He's strong."

Not saying a word, Susan placed her hand on Daniel's stiff hair, bent over again and whispered softly into his ear, "Daniel, I know you can hear me. Jesus is with you son. He loves you...We love you."

Dr. Dillon enters the room and without hesitation said, "We have looked at the scan and in fact Daniel does have some swelling of the brain, but nothing that should require surgery. However, if there's additional swelling, we may have to open the skull slightly to relieve some of the pressure. He's taken a serious blow to the head…we'll monitor everything closely."

"Is this good news?" Scotty asked the Doctor.

"Let's just say we're cautiously optimistic."

"How about the leg? Is there going to be a surgery?"

"The bone has to be set with a few screws. It's broken in three places. One piece penetrated the skin. It was an awfully bad break, but we have a surgeon who specializes in putting bones back together. He's en route to the hospital as we speak."

"So Daniel is about to go into surgery on the leg."

"I think you have some papers to sign. When that's all completed, it's all systems go."

"What's your prognosis on the leg? Scotty asked, accidentally using a medical word in the process.

"Well, there are three fractures of the shin bone. They were all rather jagged breaks. After they're screwed back together, and Daniel wakes up, he's going to experience pain in that leg for sometime. He's going to need to be medicated…but with some intense rehab, he should be able to walk fairly normal."

"Doctor, when do you think he'll wake up?" Susan asked while staring at her son.

"That's the million dollar question. I have no idea. Just look at it like this. The coma is a gift from God to allow the brain to rest. It also prevents him from feeling the pain for now. Just look at it like a heavy sleep. He won't remember any of this. When the swelling goes down, he'll start coming out of it."

"Where do we go to sign those papers?"

"I'll have someone come in shortly. You folks try to take it easy. Hopefully things will look much better in a few days."

They thanked the Doctor before he left the room.

During their wait for whomever, Big Jeff said a powerful prayer. But Daniel never moved a muscle.

Chapter 19

Bob Walker had a few minutes to spare before departure, so he decided it was as good a time as any to make the dreaded phone call to Atlanta. During the drive to the airport, his mind bounced around from Daniel's condition, to the grieving family, to how in the world he would explain the situation to the front office of the Braves. This was the most incredible set of circumstances he'd faced as a scout. He decided that all he could do was simply tell Stuart what he saw, and everything he knew to be true.

He pressed the send button already programmed into his cell phone. "Stu, this is Bob."

"Good afternoon, Bob. How are things going in cotton country today? I've been anxiously waiting for your call."

"Stu, are you sitting down? Something terrible has happened," Bob said, breathing erratically while slumping further into the airport chair as he waited to board his flight. He had an excellent window view of the Delta shuttle plane being stuffed with luggage by a couple of airport employees.

"What do you mean by terrible? Were they not satisfied with the 1.5 Million?" Stuart's voice had dramatically changed.

"Daniel Patton has been badly injured. It happened this morning, right before I got to their house."

"You've got to be kidding me? Tell me you're kidding Bob."

"I wish I were. It's like a nightmare."

"What happened?"

"This morning Daniel fell from the loft of a barn. He broke his leg to the point where a bone came through his skin. Stu, he hit his head on something upon impact and was taken to the hospital by ambulance. He was unconscious upon arrival at the emergency room and the last I heard, is still unconscious."

"Dear Lord, it sounds serious. Is the kid going to make it?"

"Don't know. I actually passed the ambulance as it was leaving the property. After discovering what had happened from Daniel's step-granddad, I went to the hospital and visited with the parents. They are totally devastated."

"Did you tell them we planned to draft Daniel number one?"

"Stu, I didn't go into all that. I didn't tell them about the signing bonus. I figured everything had changed now."

"Sometimes the business of baseball takes a toll on me. I certainly hope the best for the kid and his family, but unfortunately we can't take a gamble on a young man who may not be able to do the job. It's hard enough to compete at a sufficient level at one-hundred-percent. All we can do is keep in touch with the family and monitor his progress. We've got to move forward without Daniel, and I can't believe I just said that," Stuart said with a puff. His voice indicated to Bob that he was in disbelief.

"Stu, I've got an idea. I know we have a two week deadline on the draft. Why don't we stick Daniel somewhere in the middle selections and see what happens with his recovery."

"Bob, I sympathize with the situation. It breaks my heart, but we can't. That would bump players down a notch in the draft. No professional organization, college or otherwise will want to offer him anything with those sorts of injuries. If Patton does somehow, someway completely recovers, he'll be on crutches for no telling how long. We're drafting young men who are ready to go this summer. That's just the way it has to be. I'm sorry Bob."

"I understand Stu...and I suppose you're right. This is a wait and see scenario. But I don't want anyone in the Braves front office to give up on this kid. If he pulls through this thing, he could still turn out to be something special."

"No one in this office will give up Bob. That's not in the Braves vocabulary."

"Guess I better go." Bob had sorrow in his voice.

"Let's do lunch in a couple of days. Have a good flight, and thanks for all you do for the organization. I know how discouraging this must be...with all the time you've put into Daniel, but this is beyond your control."

"See you soon Stu," Bob said clicking his phone shut.

Bob stands to his feet and picked up the briefcase which he had hoped to open, but didn't have the opportunity. He noticed a small speck of dried blood on the index finger of his right hand. It was the blood of Daniel, transferred from the hand of the distraught. He walked toward the restroom to wash it off before boarding.

* * *

The televised evening edition of the local news had a picture of Daniel decked out in his Meridian Wildcat uniform. It was graphically positioned just above the sportscaster's right shoulder.

"The entire sporting community and beyond will be in a state of shock," Sportscaster Ken Sparks of TV33 News told an associate just before going live. He knew his audience was limited to the county and a couple of minor surrounding outlets. He also felt this was the biggest story of his short broadcasting career. The freak accident of local high school star on the verge of something big in the baseball

world would be of intense interest. Daniel wasn't only at the very brink of making a name for himself, but the city of Meridian was so close to producing a nationally recognized athlete. The locals were excited about the prospects of Daniel's baseball talent propelling their city into the national limelight. Meridian would finally be on the map, but all that would soon turn sour, flushed in an instant.

Ken Sparks would dedicate the entire ten minutes allowed for his sports report on the bombshell news. Sparks understood the name Daniel Patton wasn't much known outside of Meridian, but for the sports enthusiasts who'd be watching his short segment, he was already a household name.

After Sparks presented the essential history of Daniel's four years as a Wildcat, including all the broken records, he gave a brief summation of the accident. He was able to burn three minutes of live TV before switching to previously recorded testimony: The Piedmont Hospital spokesperson reported all the facts; the time of the 911, location of the accident, fall from loft, type of injuries, planned surgery, and chances for recovery. After the initial statement, two rapid fire questions were asked by Sparks himself who was in attendance for the hospital news conference just three hours prior: "Was Daniel conscious when he arrived at the hospital? And did the accident appear to have ended his bright future in baseball?"

The spokesman's answer to the first questions was; "Yes he was," as for the second question, Sparks was given; "It's way too early to make that judgment. Time will tell."

Sparks spent the last half of his sports report with additional interviews with teammates in the parking lot, and Coach O'Neal, who got out of his car just in time for a few impromptu questions.

Sparks chose to conclude the report with footage of Daniel hitting several home runs and making three spectacular plays at shortstop. Luckily, the small network had plenty of highlights from Daniel's four years of excellence.

The final seconds showed Sparks standing strategically in front of the emergency door of the hospital. He simply repeated the hospital spokesperson, "Time will tell for young Daniel Patton... Ken Sparks...reporting for TV33 sports."

* * *

By 7:00 P.M., there were no parking spaces remaining outside the hospital. The news was definitely out. There were more than fifty teenagers gathered in the rear section of the hospital parking facility. Many of those were teammates. The three Wildcat coaches were huddled on the sidewalk just outside the emergency room door, one of which was Coach O'Neal. Pete Bowden, the athletic director stood in the midst.

At least twenty members of Oak Grove Church stood inside the main waiting area. Big Jeff was among the group, providing them with all the information that would be relevant for effective prayer.

These were the Oak Grove prayer warriors.

The phone was constantly ringing. An unidentified man was heard giving the latest on Daniel's condition. An elderly lady, probably in her eighties, walked person to person, hugging everyone in sight. A few members of the youth group sat in the corner consoling each other. Every now and then, a security guard had to clear the emergency entrance which was blocked most of the time. The convention of the concerned had officially camped at Meridian's Piedmont Hospital.

The Georgia connection was en route to Mississippi having received the emotional call from Susan at some point earlier in the afternoon. Scotty's parents and the twins arrived after Daniel was taken into surgery. They now sat with Scotty and Susan in the family waiting room.

The specialist, Dr. Ted Moreland arrived eager and confident. He had courteously informed Susan and Scotty that the procedure was rather complicated due to the multiple breaks. He surmised that the surgery would last up to five hours. Surgery began approximately at six o'clock.

The rumor circulating among the crowd outside was negative. The same comment, spoken in different ways, was heard several times by various people. *"They are saying Daniel will never be able walk, much-less run."*

The inside crowd was more positive. One plump lady with a silver bee-hive-hair-do proudly held a Billy Graham size Bible and repeatedly proclaimed, "We know that all things are possible with God, the ole devil is not going to get the victory." To which her Oak Grove prayer warriors would respond, "Amen." These same warriors showed up for every tragedy associated with their church, and a few tragedies that weren't associated with Oak Grove at all.

The group was as culturally diverse as on Sundays'.

A reporter for a local radio station walked up to Coach O'Neal and asked a few questions. The deep voice of O'Neal echoed throughout the parking lot to the listening ears of his players. They couldn't hear the questions, but easily heard the answers. "Daniel Patton is one the finest young men I've ever coached. This is truly a shock. My prayers are with him and his family."

After pausing for another question, the teens heard the coach's reply again, "Listen, if anyone can come back from this sort of injury, it's Daniel. But the game of baseball isn't on our mind right now. We're here at this hospital because of Daniel, and the fine young man he is. You know...what he stands for, his faith and all that. There's certainly more to Daniel than just baseball." The radio interview lasted only two or three minutes, but long enough to potentially be aired ten times a day for the next week.

Back inside, Big Jeff glanced at his watch. It was time to go check on the family. His best friend Mitchell Harper was back there.

Big Jeff wouldn't be so big, if not for him. Mitchell had invested much time, effort, resources, land, prayers and encouragement for the preacher's life, and dreams. No one on earth meant more to him than Daniel's step-granddad.

The pastor was well known by all the hospital staff and had free access to the family waiting room beyond the electronic doors. Every thirty minutes, Big Jeff walked to the same security guard seated beside the large double doors, and the guard would promptly punch the secret five digit code on the wall. The doors would swing open and Big Jeff would lumber in.

No questions asked. All others had to wait it out.

"How are you folks doing?" Big Jeff reverently asked, scanning each face.

"We're hanging-in. How are things going out there?" Scotty asked with a drained appearance.

"They're hanging in as well. The crowd is as big right now as any time during the day. The hospital parking lot has turned into the Saturday night *hangout of choice.* I don't know how long it'll be before security will have to break that up."

"Is anyone being rowdy?" Susan asked with a concerned tone.

"Not at all, it's just a mighty big crowd for a hospital parking lot, and limited waiting room. I noticed an elderly couple driving around in search for a space to no avail. They looked fairly perturbed from my viewpoint," the Pastor stated truthfully.

"Oh, my word, we still have a couple of hours before Daniel's surgery is complete," Susan said glancing at the clock on the wall. "I may have to go out there in a few minutes, thank everyone for coming, ask everyone to keep Daniel in their prayers, and tell them it's best they go home in order to free-up some room."

"If you do, you'll get surrounded by the media. They are like vultures out there," Big Jeff said.

Susan nodded in agreement—a bad suggestion at best.

"Can I get anyone coffee or water?" The preacher offered.

Mitchell was the only one interested and joined his friend in a walk down the short hall. Mitchell and the preacher caught an elevator and descended underground.

They sat in a small snack room with vending machines lining one wall. For an hour, the two men who, over the years had been through so many trials, tribulations and tests of faith, bowed their heads—once again.

They forgot about the coffee. Prayer was the only item on their menu.

Chapter 20

Chaplain Horne made it his priority to individually visit prisoners on Saturday evening. He knew the ones who were open to counsel and prayer. In his fifteen years of prison chaplain ministry, he had discovered Saturday evenings to be the most depressing time for the inmates—reason unknown. He'd never entered a single cell. This was against the rules listed in the *Ministry Protocol Handbook for Prison Chaplains*. All spiritual counseling had certain non-flexible guidelines and was strictly enforced by the State of Arizona and the appointed Warden.

In the middle of each cell door, there was a small feeding hole, or hatch. The hatch was approximately eight-inches-by-six-inches and not very intimate, but Horne had learned the art of making the most of it.

Two hours into his visits, the chaplain saw the face of his seventeenth inmate. It was the face of Eugene Thompson. "How's it going friend?" Chaplain Horne asked as if Eugene was the only prisoner on his agenda.

"I'm glad to see you Chap," Eugene stated, in a manner to suggest something of great importance was forthcoming.

"Got something on your mind Eugene?" Horne asked through the little hatch, while noticing Eugene's sweaty forehead and bloodshot eyes.

"My Spirit's been troubling me all day. Something is happening. I don't know what, but something is definitely happening," Eugene said almost in a panic.

"Take a breath Eugene and try to relax...Now what's troubling you friend?" The chaplain asked with a tone of compassion.

"Chap, I've been in continuous prayer for days. This is a critical time. They're in trouble. I just know it."

"Who's in trouble?"

"The families I've been praying for since getting saved. My heart's been burdened. I'm feeling a great heaviness within my spirit. They need a miracle. I just know it."

"Maybe the Holy Spirit has revealed something to you," the chaplain interjected, knowing beforehand Eugene was the most spiritually conscious of all his subjects.

"I think we have reached the critical hour. This is the critical hour. The devil can't have the victory," Eugene emotionally said.

"You are referring to the Patton and Millard families in Mississippi I assume?" Horne had heard Eugene speak of these families many times since leading him to faith in Christ.

"Yes sir."

"Well, what do you think the Lord is revealing to you?"

"Not sure."

"Is there anything I can help you pray for?"

"I've been waiting for you all day. You may be able to help me. I don't know if you want to, but I'm going to ask anyway."

"What can I help you with?" Horne knew that most prisoners ask him for favors beyond his control and calling.

"I need you to find out what's going on."

"Going on with what Eugene?"

"In Mississippi," he informed.

"Eugene, I can't get involved with the families associated with your past. That's against the ethics of the chaplain program. I would be fired for sure. I'd get busted for harassment. If they want to talk to someone from this prison facility, they must make the first move. That's not only common sense, but it's the procedure I'm ordered to follow."

"You don't have to tell anyone who you are. You don't have to tell anyone who I am."

"Eugene, even if I were allowed to get information for you, I wouldn't know where to start. What am I suppose to do, call a private investigator?" Horne responded, but thought, *I could go on-line.* The crime had been big news at the time. Even though he wasn't close to the State of Mississippi at present, the internet would certainly yield information about the murder of a cop in a small town. It really wouldn't be too difficult. A couple of internet searches of articles and addresses would do the trick. He privately felt he could have some detailed information in less than thirty minutes, but it would probably be limited and not satisfactory to Eugene.

"Chaplain, you don't understand where I'm coming from. I think the Lord has revealed to me that a life is in danger. I've been in this hell hole for two years praying for my victims. I know they hate me. They don't have to hate me. I love them. I want their forgiveness. They must know how I feel. They must know how God feels. He wants to set them free. *Dear God, I hope it's not too late.*" Eugene was emotional, and tears ran down his cheeks.

"What kind of information do you want to know?" The chaplain asked, regretting the question as soon as it left his lips.

"I just want to know about their well-being. Is it so wrong to want to know how I should be praying for someone?"

Horne didn't answer. He didn't have a good answer. Instead, he remembered times in his own life when God had laid someone on his heart to pray for, only to find out later of a car wreck, a sickness, a serious problem of some sort. He had personally witnessed the powerful work of the Spirit in revealing certain situations. The chaplain could relate with Eugene and began to sympathize with his plea. He had been there, done that, got the t-shirt.

"Please Chap, will you help me?"

The chaplain paused for several seconds, looking down toward the flood on his side of the cage. He inhaled and exhaled slowly. "Listen Eugene, I might be able to help you. I have my doubts just how much, but I'll see what I can uncover. In the meantime, you need to try and relax. Keep on with your prayer life, but relax. Remember, God is a God of peace."

"Yea, but I'm in here fighting the good fight of faith. This is warfare as far as I'm concerned."

"All that is fine Eugene, you go right ahead with the spiritual warfare. But remember, all you can do is pray and leave the rest to God."

"You said you might be able to help me. What are you planning Chap?"

"Don't ask too many questions Eugene. Remember what I told you. We've got to keep this above reproach," the chaplain whispered, quickly glancing to the right and left.

"Above reproach is the only way to go. I appreciate it Chap."

"I appreciate and admire your willingness to seek forgiveness from those families. I hope we'll find them doing just fine."

"Thanks, I believe their willingness to forgive me is connected to a blessing. It's connected with God being glorified in their lives. That's all I have to live for now—God being glorified."

"I'll come by tomorrow. Get some rest Eugene."

After a brief visit with several other lifers, Horne walked to his office located down the hall from the Warden's office. Warden Pendergrass was long gone for the day. He drove from his appointed parking space at five sharp every day. Now 7:15, the hall was quiet except for the occasional sound of footsteps of the guards outside his small window just above his computer. Within twenty-five minutes, Horne was startled by what he had discovered.

It was all there.

First the Chaplain had typed in a search for: *Information on the murder of Officer Dan Patton, July 4th, Philadelphia, Mississippi.* The information was endless. Horne had several articles to choose from; the funeral service, trial, sentencing phase, names, places, events, and more. In one small article posted after the trial, the Philadelphia newspaper gave some interesting facts. Susan Patton and her children had moved to Meridian where she planned to start a business of her own. She had thanked the people of Philadelphia for their memorial gift of love. Not much was mentioned about the Millards. They were more on the witness side of Eugene's crime. The Pattons received the bulk of the attention as being the family affected the most by the crime—for obvious reasons.

Horne was astonished by what he uncovered next. He typed in: *Susan Patton, Meridian Mississippi.* The news of Daniel Patton, son of Susan Patton, was a current post. Horne knew he had the right family on the monitor in front of him. Not only did the family story match, but the picture of Susan matched the one in the Philadelphia article. The story was late breaking news: *Baseball standout Daniel Patton in serious but stable condition following fall.* The whole story was there and Horne read every word. Overwhelmed by the powerful and supernatural working of the Spirit of God, Horne put his head on his desk and prayed: "*You are God and there is no other. Lord what is your purpose behind this? Your child Eugene Thompson was led by your Spirit. Lord, I am your servant. I am available to you. Use me in whatever manner you choose, according to your will, to help the Patton family, and Eugene.*"

Eugene would now have the information he needed. Though it might be against official ethics, Horne understood what he must do. It was doubtless the will of God. He felt Eugene deserved to know the truth. If not, God wouldn't have spoken with such clarity. If a leak resulted in his firing, then so be it. He was willing to take that risk—all for the One he served.

* * *

The next morning, the chaplain walked into the prison earlier than usual. He walked through several steel doors which only opened by the manipulation of a guard stationed in a control room who monitored everything by video. The chaplain barely broke a stride as several steel doors opened in front of him and then shut behind him.

Upon reaching the center of the prison, Horne walked up some stairs and then took a left onto the second deck. He came to inmate number 48—the cell assigned to Eugene. Horne opened the hatch with his personal key and gave all the details of Daniel's accident to Eugene.

"Daniel was still in a coma as of last night, but the surgery on the leg was successfully completed." Horne whispered, following his brief oratory detailing all that he discovered on-line. The chaplain was constantly glancing in both directions to make sure a guard wasn't approaching.

Eugene was glad to know, but felt burdened and concerned. His troubled spirit made sense now. After thanking the chaplain profusely, the hatch closed, and Eugene bent down next to his bed.

Praying for the Pattons was all he could do.

Chapter 21

Horne exited the building, and drove away from the fortified prison in his moody yellow Toyota Corolla wagon. He'd driven the car since graduating from Southwestern Baptist Theological Seminary in Fort Worth Texas twenty-four years earlier. The vehicle was on its last leg, and third engine. The current motor had started to rattle about three weeks prior, and Horne was all too familiar with that sound. Mr. Corolla was due for another overhaul. Besides the rattle, it still handled fairly well, was paid for, looked okay, but he was beginning to despise the piece of junk. At the next service station, he'd be sure to satisfy the clunker with a fresh quart of cheap oil.

Coupled with the sound of rattling, and to further agitate his raw nerves, his cell phone was beeping. He checked the bar count and noticed the lone bar blinking for his prompt attention, which competed wonderfully with the red light on the other side of his steering wheel which read: *check oil.* He wrestled briefly with the charging cord and finally stuck the correct end into the cigarette lighter sufficiently enough. It was all systems go for his cell, but he wasn't sure about the third motor. With those minor matters in life to deal with, he was glad to speak with an understanding wife who'd be more cooperative.

He called his wife and informed her they'd be taking a little vacation. The kids were grown and out of the house, so twice a year they had the freedom to travel and explore. The Disneyland adventures were over, though they still enjoyed going to Florida's Eastern Coastline for some deep sea fishing. Horne had yet to take a single, solitary vacation day, and he was entitled three weeks per year. He needed a restful week of relaxation, but this upcoming get-away wouldn't be it.

When Mrs. Horne asked her chaplain husband w*hat he had in mind this year.*"

He responded, "Mississippi."

There were several seconds of silence before she asked, "The gulf?"

"No...Meridian."

"What's in Meridian?"

"A shortstop—goes by the name of Daniel Patton."

"I don't follow you honey, we must be breaking up," Mrs. Horne heard every word perfectly.

"I have something important to take care of. You'll have to trust me on this one."

"When do you want to go?" She asked.

"In a few days...maybe a couple of weeks, I have to put in my notice to the warden."

"Do you mind sharing with me the business that has all of a sudden sprouted in Meridian, Mississippi?"

"Let's just say that I have a divine confrontation. I'll tell you more when I get home darling."

After her bewildered *bye-bye, drive careful honey*, he snapped his cell shut and laid the phone on the passenger's seat to his side. The cell cord stretched from the cigarette lighter to the seat. Under his cell there was a picture of Daniel, downloaded and printed from his office computer. Next to the picture was his Bible, which always remained in his office.

Until now...

Chapter 22

The two weeks following the accident were touch-and-go for Daniel. The Doctors were getting concerned due to the number of days in which Daniel had been in the coma. Time was of the essence. The swelling of the brain had subsided. The bone in his leg had been surgically repaired, and the healing process had begun. His *vitals* remained stable throughout, although he'd lost fifteen pounds. The Harper's were notified that Daniel would stay in ICU until there was some sign of physical consciousness. No one could predict when Daniel might come out of it. Concussions were serious, and in rare cases, life threatening.

It was essential for the family to keep a positive attitude despite the facts. There were many cases on record of comatose patients who remained in the condition for years. Everyone involved understood the historical facts surrounding the head traumatized. It was one day at a time, and hope for an awakening. Family and friends gathered and prayed that this would be the day Daniel came back to them. It was now Friday, thirteen days and counting.

Susan had left the hospital on two occasions, both times to make a quick trip home to take a shower and pack fresh clothes. Each day Scotty stayed with Susan from noon until 9:00 P.M. The twins would come everyday for a couple of hours, accompanied by Scotty's parents.

The Georgia families had come and gone. During their four days in Meridian, they lodged at the comfort Inn out on the by-pass. They hated the idea of returning to Georgia when things were still so uncertain. Susan and Scotty thought it was impressive for them to stay as long as they did, helping with anything and everything.

Ms. Ruby and Charlotte managed the stores as best as they knew how. Once or twice each day, Susan would check in with the two, passing along expert advice, while at the same time trying not to sound overwhelmed and out of control. Her mind was on Daniel and she'd pledge not to return to her business until Daniel's condition had dramatically improved. Until then, she'd be by his side. Susan would give the shops up in a minute for just one bat of an eye, one move of a finger, one...*Mom I love you.*

Everyday updates where provided to the community by the local big three: TV, Radio and Newspaper. The crush of the crowd outside the hospital had all but gone, and *routine* had somewhat taken over. Everyone stayed informed from the efforts of the media. Close friends of the family would contact Scotty or his dad by phone.

On two consecutive Tuesday nights, Big Jeff called prayer meetings for Daniel. The place, time and date were put in the church bulletin and the Meridian star. More than one hundred people participated both nights, pleading for God's mercy.

Susan had a long list of people who she hadn't returned phone calls—at least she figured. Her cell had been turned off for thirteen days, except for her calls to Ms. Ruby and Charlotte.

Daniel was in the final month of his senior year of high school. He'd already missed the end of the year sports banquet at the school. Coach O'Neal had come to the hospital and presented five trophies to Scotty and Susan, who humbly accepted them on behalf of Daniel. A photographer was there who snapped a picture of

Scotty and Susan holding the trophies outside Piedmont hospital. A rather detailed story, along with their picture, was on the front page of the sports section the following day. Daniel received the MVP, Team Captain, Best Defensive Player, Best Offensive Player and Sportsmanship Awards.

Graduation was only two weeks away. Susan and Scotty had briefly discussed the lost opportunity for Daniel to attend the graduation ceremony. It would be months before he could make up the work in order to receive his diploma. They mutually hoped and prayed he got that opportunity.

Thankfully, Susan and Scotty had previously purchased a family *health and medical policy* from an insurance agent who attended Oak Grove. The premiums were high and burdensome, but now they were plenty relieved that all but a $1000 deductable would have to be paid on their end. It was one of the smartest financial decisions they'd ever made as a couple.

* * *

Chaplain Horne was on the short side, no more than five-feet-eight-inches-tall. He wore narrow rimmed glasses. He was thick, but not fat. His crewed brown hair was spiked. Horne's appearance was a cross between a drill sergeant and a mild mannered scientist.

Susan was seated in the ICU waiting area along with Scotty. They'd just finished eating noodles down in the cafeteria. Susan's head was resting on Scotty's shoulder, when Horne appeared in the doorway.

In a soft, reverent voice Horne asked, "I'm looking for the family of Daniel Patton." Horne immediately recognized them from his research. They sat in chairs facing the door he'd just walked through.

They slowly sat up straight. "That would be us."

Horne slowly walked into the room toward the very tired looking couple with a heart about to jump out of his chest. He was beyond nervous—been that way for days. He'd nearly changed his mind at the last minute, but the American Airlines ticket was paid in advance. No refund was possible. Even though the trip was supposed to be a vacation, it was anything but.

Duty was calling.

"So you are Daniel's folks?" For two weeks, every unknown who walked through the same door, in the similar manner was a preacher or deacon. They were getting accustomed to it.

"Yes we are," Scotty said as they both rose from their seat, preparing for another cordial introduction from yet another preacher or deacon.

"Name is Horne."

"Scotty Harper...This is my wife, Susan."

"How's your son?"

"Nothing new to report," Scotty replied.

"There's been a lot of prayers go up for that boy."

"And we appreciate each and every one of them. Are you a minister?" Scotty asked glancing at the cross on his blazer.

"Yes I am."

"What church?" Susan asked, having seen at least a dozen, maybe more, from various churches and denominations.

"I'm a chaplain."

"You volunteer here?" Scotty asked.

"No, I'm not from here. I'm from out of town."

"I see. Where are you from?

"I'm a prison chaplain from Arizona."

"What brings you to Meridian?" Susan asked with puzzling suspicion.

Horne hesitated before answering then said, "Why don't we sit down and talk for a moment." Horne pulled a chair from the opposite wall. The legs of the chair squalled all the way as he eased it beside theirs, and sat in front of them.

"Mr. and Mrs. Harper, I've been following the story on the internet and the Lord has led me here to speak with you today."

"You came all the way from Arizona just to speak to us?" Scotty asked curiously.

"Listen, you may not want to hear what I'm about to share with you, but I ask you to withhold judgment until I've had time to explain myself."

Susan and Scotty both nodded in bewilderment.

"I have an inmate who's been praying for you. His name is Eugene Thompson."

"Dear God, not him!" Susan said, springing to her feet.

"Please Ms. Harper...Please sit down. I didn't come here to add to your burden. I came here to help you."

Scotty stood and took Susan by the arm. "Honey, let's hear him out." Susan slowly and reluctantly sat down, though Susan didn't dare make eye contact with the chaplain. Just the mention of *the killers* name made her blood boil. It was obvious she was upset and angry.

"Mrs. Harper, I know this isn't easy for you. You've been through so much..."

"Why are you here?" Susan emotionally spouted, quickly darted her angry blood-shot-blue-eyes into his unsettled ones.

"Please let me explain," Horne said softly, trying to calm her down.

"Maybe you ought to make it quick chaplain. I don't think my wife is prepared to dig up the past right now."

"I'll make it quick. Mrs. Harper…Eugene has come to know the Lord. He spends his time each day in prayer. I know for a fact that he's been praying for you nonstop...He's seeking your forgiveness."

"Forgiveness!" Susan yelled, "Who sent you here?"

"Please, let me finish and then I'm out of here...I promise. The Saturday of Daniel's accident, I went on my routine rounds at the prison. When I came to Eugene's cell, he was frantic, sweating and disturbed. He said he knew something was wrong in Mississippi. He sensed that you were in danger. I'd never seen him like that. He wanted me to check it out. So I did…on the internet. I found the articles. I read about Daniel and his accident. It couldn't have been a coincidence. I believe the Spirit of God clearly revealed this awful situation involving Daniel to Eugene."

"So!" Susan growled.

"So….If God revealed this to Eugene, there may be something important concerning your willingness to forgive. Praying for you has been Eugene's life for a long time. It's been his primary focus for two years."

"If you think I'm ever going to forgive the animal who murdered Dan you're wasting your time."

"Am I wasting my time in an attempt to be a blessing you? Eugene views it as spiritual warfare. His only desire is for God to be glorified."

"Eugene Thompson is the single biggest curse on planet earth Mr. Horne."

"Mrs. Harper, God has forgiven Eugene of his sins. He's my brother in Christ. I love him. He's been a tremendous blessing to me. I've witnessed this man go from a cold, harden person, to a strong compassionate Christian transformed by the power of Christ."

"That's great. God has forgiven him, that's fine by me. But I'll never forgive him," Susan bitterly responded.

"So you don't believe in forgiveness?" Horne boldly asked.

"I think we've heard enough," Scotty said.

"Jesus says that if you don't forgive, it will not be forgiven you." The chaplain knew he was taking it too far.

"I said that's enough Mr. Horne. Now would you please leave?" Scotty insisted firmly while glancing at a stranger seated in the corner of the room staring in disbelief at the commotion.

Horne didn't press the issue any further. He dropped his head and looked toward the floor. After a brief silence he said, "I've done what I felt was God's will. I'm sorry to have troubled you folks."

Horne got to his feet and slid the chair back against the wall on the opposite side of the room. He turned and started out the door, but stopped. He pulled out a card from his shirt pocket, walked to Susan and offered it. "Call my cell number on this card if you have a change of heart. I'll be in town for a couple of days. Before I go, could I ask you to do me a favor? Please keep this confidential. What I've done today could get me in hot water. This is something I've done on my own. Neither Eugene, nor anyone associated with the prison has the slightest idea that I'm here."

Susan didn't respond, make eye contact, or offer to take his card, so he laid it on an empty chair next to where she sat, and walked out.

Susan and Scotty sat quietly for fifteen minutes, not saying a word. At exactly 1:00 P.M., they went to check on Daniel.

Before leaving the ICU waiting room, Susan put the chaplain's card in her pocket. She was beginning to feel the guilt due to the manner in which she'd reacted to the chaplain. She was caught off guard and couldn't believe the way she'd handled herself. She felt that there must be more hidden bitterness and hatred in her heart than she was aware of.

Chapter 23

By the time Scotty's folks arrived at the hospital with Rachael and Rebecca, Susan was ready to get some fresh air for a change. Gazing out the second floor window of the ICU waiting area, she admired the bright afternoon sun. It was a perfect day to take a walk. She hadn't enjoyed the warmth of the sun on her face in two weeks. Maybe getting away from the hospital would calm her emotions and state of mind—possibly even change her perspective. Something wasn't right and she needed some time alone to contemplate.

She needed some time with God.

After a brief explanation to Scotty, the girls, and her in-laws, Susan left the hospital and started walking down Popular Springs Drive, south of the hospital. After walking ten blocks, she came to the corner of 8th street and 24th avenue. Susan could see her two shops from there and neither appeared to be very busy. For a split second, Susan thought she might drop in and check on things, surprising Ms. Ruby and Charlotte, but decided otherwise. In her opinion, she didn't look presentable wearing jeans and tennis shoes. Taking a left, Susan walked east, toward Bonita Lake Park. It was approximately two miles from downtown. The exercise was much needed, and the time to think and pray would be good.

By five o'clock, she was sitting on a bench a few feet from a man-made pond watching a flock of geese as they crept near to her feet. Some angry residence in the community had started complaining about the number of geese that were migrating to the park. Susan thought they were cute, lovable, and helped her mood. Obviously tamed and looking for a delicious handout, Susan wished for a loaf of bread to satisfy her hungry visitors. As the Geese came even closer, Susan's mind began to drift—

The conversation with the chaplain had stirred her. *What was she missing? Was God trying to communicate something?* She didn't feel much like a Christian. *A real believer wouldn't have spoken to a man of God like that. He had come so far from home.*

Susan began mentally drifting back to the convenient store, Dan's stiff body in the casket, the trial, Eugene's face and the verdict. She thought about Daniel; his baseball achievements, his dream, their random visit to Oak Grove, the sermon, the discussion with Big Jeff, the miracle of meeting Scotty and his connection to Dan, the accident, Daniel's coma. *What did it all mean? And what is the purpose behind Daniel's accident. Is everything somehow connected?* She recalled the testimony on behalf of Eugene at the trial, his wife's cancer diagnosis just prior to his entering the store, his certain drunkenness when the incident occurred, his lack of memory, the wrestling match, the gun shot—so deep in thought, Susan jumped when Eugene's gun fired, frightening the flock of geese. Being startled by the sound of a gun ten years earlier had occurred before in her night dreams, but never in broad daylight.

Then the face of the chaplain appeared in her thoughts, and Susan heard the chaplain again tell her of Eugene's conversion experience and his radically changed life filled with prayers for his victims.

Susan began to mumble to herself as she watched the geese gain confidence, hobbling closer to her feet. *"He's praying for his victims. He's praying for reconciliation with me. He knew about Daniel's accident the day it happened, though not the specifics. Nonetheless, God gave him a divine revelation that something wasn't right. Lord in Heaven, what are you saying through all this?"* Then she glanced to her right. There was a young black couple sitting on a blanket, enjoying a picnic lunch out on a grassy slope. They seemed so content and happy together. The flock of geese also noticed and began marching to make new friends. *Surely they have a handful of crumbs to spare.* The geese must be hoping.

For the first time Susan began to feel a slight sense of sympathy for her husband's killer. Eugene probably had similar picnics with his wife in years past. He lost his wife to cancer before the trial was over. For the first time, Susan felt a wave of compassion flood her soul for a man who would spend the rest of his life caged like an animal. He didn't even have the freedom of a pestering flock of geese.

But the sympathy passed as fast as it came. She still hated him.

She looked back at the water, then put her face in her hands and begins to cry. *"Lord, show me what you want me to do. Show me what all this means. I know you are doing something Lord. Show me Lord. I don't want to live with all this hate toward Eugene or anyone else. I don't want to live with a bad heart."*

Tears were streaming down her face. Lifting her head, she wiped the tears away with the back of her hand. As her blurry vision cleared, she noticed a different couple walking hand-in-hand on the other side of the pond. Their images were still rather blurry from tears, so she rubbed them again until the couple came into focus. *This can't be,* Susan said to herself. The man appeared to be Chaplain Horne. She rubbed her eyes again. It was either him or his twin. The woman she didn't know, but the man was indeed the chaplain. She was certain of it. Without even a brief hesitation, she reached into her pocket and grabbed the chaplain's card. With the other hand, she reached into the opposite pocket and retrieved her cell phone. She anxiously dialed Horne's cell number from the card.

Susan knew that if it was truly the chaplain, he would reach into his pocket for his cell, if he had it.

He did, and Susan almost snapped her phone shut, but instead said, "Mr. Horne, this is Susan Harper."

"I was praying you would call Mrs. Harper."

Susan could see every movement. Horne was motionless with the cell stuck to his ear. He was no longer holding the woman's hand.

"I've been doing some praying myself and God has given me an answer," Susan said.

"What is his answer Susan?"

"Why don't we meet and talk it over."

"I will be glad to meet you. Where do you have in mind?"

"There is a park on the Southeastern side of town. It's called Bonita Lake Park."

"That's a coincidence. I know exactly where Bonita is located, that's precisely where my wife and I are…right this minute."

"I think it is more than coincidental Mr. Horne, because that's where I am too…Look across the pond."

He does, and she waves from the bench.

"Susan, I see you. What are you doing out here?"

"I came for a walk to get some fresh air…away from the hospital. I ended up on this bench, praying and watching geese. Low and behold, there you stand on the other side."

"Do you mind if we ease around that way and have a talk?" Horne said with an obvious adrenaline rush.

"I wish you would."

After the phones were put back into their pockets, Susan watched as Horne and his wife strode around the bank of the lake/pond.

They sat together and talked until dusk.

During the approximately two hour conversation, Susan wanted to once again hear about Eugene's conversion to Christ—

with a better frame of mind. She told the chaplain about her life following the shooting death of her husband and the difficult years as a single mother. She opened up concerning her past rebellion to God and her recent marriage, life in general. Every supernatural event that had taken place over the years was verbally categorized. Susan wanted to know if the Chaplain thought the prayers of Eugene were a direct result of the blessings she and her family had been experiencing, to which the Chaplain said, *"That sounds like the God I serve."* She also wanted to know Horne's opinion on Daniel's accident and subsequent coma. Susan asked, *"Did God allow it to happen to bring my unwillingness to forgive Eugene under his submission?"* Horne once again said, *"That sounds like the God I serve."*

Before the conversation was finished, a plan was in order. Susan understood the seriousness of doing the will of God and following the leading of His Spirit.

It was her responsibility as a child of God.

She would fly back with the chaplain and his wife to Arizona at the break of day. From the bench in which they sat, Horne had called the airlines and booked an American Airlines flight.

Susan would come face to face with the killer of her husband in less than twenty-four hours. It was time to settle the matter once and for all. She was tired of the hate that had a grip on her life. She was willing to give Eugene a chance.

She was willing to give God a chance.

* * *

By mid-morning the following day, Susan spotted the runway from her window seat. She'd never traveled to Phoenix and she never would've believed her first visit would be to speak to someone who'd caused so much grief.

The day before, she made her intention known to her family. Except for immediate family, no one was aware she'd hopped on a flight bound for Arizona, not even Ms. Rudy and Charlotte. The shops had been on auto-pilot for two weeks and would remain in the capable hands of her trustworthy friends.

Once the aircraft had landed on the runway of Phoenix International, Susan began to have a churning feeling in her gut. Her heart was pounding and hands were cold, rapidly loosing circulation. *Am I making a mistake?* She kept asking herself.

Anxiety had officially landed in Phoenix.

Sensing her uneasiness, the chaplain looked passed his wife who sat between the two and replied, "Susan, try to relax. God will work this thing out. He's brought you this far, and will in no way leave you for a second."

Taking in a nervous gasp of air, Susan replied, "Chaplain, if there had been an ejection button on this seat, I would've parachuted over Texas.

"Trust me, you are right where God wants you," The chaplain reassuringly replied.

Both Susan and Mrs. Horne wore colorful dresses, yellow and dark blue, respectively. It was actually the first time in days she'd managed to put on make-up, fix her hair and look as if she cared. Mrs. Horne was a couple of inches taller than her husband. Susan had thought she favored *Little House on the Prairie's* Mrs. Olsen, but wouldn't dare tell her. Unlike the TV character, Mrs. Horne was charming and their conversation was constant during the entire flight. They chatted about everything from Daniel's untimely accident to cactus cake, a favorite dessert of the desert, though none of the ingredients came from the desert.

Within twenty minutes of walking off the plane, the trio were placing their bags in the back of Horne's small yellow station wagon. It was a hot mid-morning, nearing 100 degrees already.

Over the years, Susan had survived her share of warm Mississippi days, but in her memory nothing compared to the Arizona heat.

The chaplain knew the area well and without delay, sped out of the airport parking lot and onto the interstate. The prison was a two hour drive from the airport. Susan was surprised the air-conditioning worked in the old Toyota, though she was concerned about the rattling noise under the hood.

All necessary arrangements had been made with prison officials by Horne himself before departing from Meridian. In 1976, a program was instituted for victim families of violent crimes the opportunity for closure, thereby meeting with prisoners who were willing to seek forgiveness. Both sides had to agree to such a meeting. Horne hoped that Eugene was informed of the meeting, but wasn't sure if he knew that his prayers were potentially about to be answered.

They rode in silence.

Susan gazed out the window from the back seat, not at all enjoying the view of Arizona's barren landscape. Under normal circumstances, the scenery would've been beautiful. The chaplain behind the steering wheel visualized how everything would go down.

He hoped and prayed for *the miracle.*

* * *

The door quietly opened and Scotty walked in alone. The room was dim, the shades were closed. Daniel was motionless. Pulling up a chair next to his bed and slowly sitting down, Scotty put his hand on Daniel's clammy forehead. "You hang in there shortstop, you hear me. Hang in there my boy. You're going to come through this. Our God is awesome. He has a plan for your life. Scotty eyes darted to Daniel's fingers, his eye lashes, his feet, hoping for any sign of movement, any sign that would indicate he was coming out of it. Just a flicker, a twitch, something that might mean the coma was lifting. Daniel remained motionless, except for his chest cavity inhaling and exhaling. Scotty removed his hand from the forehead and placed it on Daniel's chest. Burying his face on the white sheets, Scotty began to pray for Daniel—and his wife.

* * *

Though still some distance, a mile or two ahead, Mulberry prison came into focus. As the prison facility grew larger with each passing moment, Susan's heart started to pound and the memory of Dan's death cut like a knife. The turmoil of the funeral and trial replayed visually, so visually that she closed her eyes to regroup. What would she have to say to the one she still hated with every fiber of her soul? She breathed a silent prayer for strength.

Horne was making verbal comments that seemed to be a thousand miles away. He was saying something about the mediation process. Susan was in another world. It was *the world* of a son whose life was in the balance and the killer who she despised. She wished to be at her son's side. She wished to be anywhere except on the road to Mulberry prison.

The prison was a perfect setting to house America's most violent—so remote, lifeless and isolated from society. Welcome to no-mans-land. Surrounded by desert, the prison was a world apart.

It was another dimension.

The walls and barbed wire surrounding the prison were mostly for show. If an inmate were to escape, there was nothing on the outside to hide behind, in, or crawl under. An escapee would die in the desert, or be caught within minutes to spend years in solitary confinement. A handful of attempts had been made, but none in the history of Mulberry were ever successful. There was nothing on the outside except sand, rocks, cactus and the blazing sun. Not to mention the snipe shooting guards stationed on the towers with itching trigger fingers.

This was the perfect place for murders.

The yellow wagon pulled up to the check point and the chaplain flashed his badge. A guard holding a rifle, probably illegal on streets, said, "Welcome back Chaplain." Their arrival was official and Susan was questioning her decision to come face-to-face with Dan's killer. The evening before she had a hint of sympathy for Eugene, but it was gone now, suppressed by years of anger and hate.

Chapter 24

Eugene realized the time had come. After four years of praying and trusting in all of God's promises, Eugene was about to get what he desired. A few hours had passed since the warden personally delivered the news. "*Eugene*," he had said while peering through the little hatch of the cell door, "*Sometime this afternoon, Chaplain Horne and a Mrs. Susan Harper will be meeting with you in the mediation room. They're flying in from Mississippi together. The chaplain has explained everything to me on the phone. Why Horne would spend his vacation time on your problem beats the heck out of me.*" Without waiting for a response, or asking any questions, the warden shuts the hole, keys it, and walked away.

Eugene had stood dumbfounded, his mind not initially digesting the information. After a moment of shock, his knees became weak and buckled. Falling to the side of his bed, Eugene praised God, and wept.

At 2:37 P.M., the hatch opened and the rifle carrying guard said, "Ready for your little chat?"

Eugene said nothing in response, only smiled, stuck his hands through the hole to be cuffed, the door opened and he walked out. He was at peace. There was no dread or apprehension. The Lord had well prepared Eugene to share from his heart and to confidently speak the truth. Eugene's sword of the Spirit was sharp and ready to do warfare against the powers of darkness. He believed from the moving of the Spirit which dwelt within him that victory was imminent.

Wearing orange prison garb, Eugene was escorted passed the dozens of cells and down a flight of narrow stairs until they came to a door. The control room personnel monitoring all movement within the prison replies to the guard, "all clear," which signaled the guard to punch the code on the wall's key pad. This was repeated three times as they made their way through the prison. Finally Eugene spotted a door at the end of a hall which read: *Mediation Room*. The guard opens the door and un-cuffed Eugene. "Your visitors will be with you shortly," the guard said. The room was empty except for a rectangular table with three chairs, one on each end and the other situated in the middle. "Sit in the far chair facing this door," the guard said, pointing his rifle. Eugene walked to his appointed place and sat. The guard promptly closed the door.

Alone in the room, Eugene prayed. "*God be glorified. Give me the right words to say. May your will be done. Be glorified Lord Jesus. Be glorified.*"

Chapter 25

The chaplain entered the mediation room first. Susan trailed behind and made no eye contact with Eugene. Horne greeted Eugene warmly, but purposely didn't want to overdo it. He was the mediator, impartial and composed. Horne had a ministry to accomplish and was to conduct himself in a way to be considerate to both. The chaplain slowly walked to the table and pulled the chair out which faced Eugene. "Susan, if you'll have a seat here." Susan shuffles to her place and sat as Horne very gentlemanly like, straightened her chair from behind. There was still no eye contact from Susan. She acknowledged Eugene in no way. Eugene's head was held high and watching every move of his visitors. After Chaplain Horne sat and adjusted his own seat, he briefly glanced to his right toward Susan. She appeared to be uncomfortable, nervous, unengaged and bewildered. Horne turned to his left and caught the bright eyes of Eugene, which suggested his confidence and controlled demeanor.

"Well…this has been a long journey for the both of you." The chaplain began, "I applaud you both for agreeing to this meeting. The success we will have today depends on a number of things. First, I ask you both to do your best to relax. I know this to be an emotional time. Secondly, it is essential to be honest, open and transparent about your true feelings. And thirdly, take your time. There is no time limit today. Eugene, I know you've waited a long time for this opportunity. Susan, you've come along way from home and have made an enormous sacrifice to be here today. You must not feel any pressure to hurry through the process. If either of you feel you need a break, let me know. There is juice, ice water and coffee on the table over in the corner. Help yourself if you like." Horne pointed his finger to a table with the cool refreshments. "Now do either of you have any questions?"

"No sir," Eugene said.

Susan shook her head slightly, *no.*

"Why don't we begin with you, Eugene, how would you like to begin?"

Eugene began by clearing his throat and then spoke, "I'd like to say how much I praise God for this opportunity. He has answered my prayer and I know that this wouldn't have been possible unless it was God's will. Thank you for coming all the way to Mulberry prison to give me a chance to meet with you. I know you didn't have to come, but you did. Thank you."

Susan looked angrily into Eugene's face and spoke with a trembling voice. "Do you really understand how hard this is on me? Eugene, I don't want to be here. My husband was killed by you ten years ago and my son is in a coma a thousand miles away. I don't really know why I'm here."

"Maybe we should view this meeting as God's plan. I heard about your son being in the hospital. The Lord knows all about it. I've been praying for his full recovery."

"Well, it would've been nice for Daniel to have had his father around. How do you feel about that?" Susan spouted back sharply.

"Mrs. Harper, I am so sorry about what happened. I make no excuses for my evil action."

"There were plenty of excuses at the trial. Being drunk is no excuse for shooting my husband. Killing my husband because your wife is sick is no excuse." Susan knew her comments were harsh. She had ten years of hatred that was erupting like a volcano.

"You are one-hundred-percent correct. There was no excuse. Not now, not then. If I could do something to change what happened I'd do it, but I can't. I can't change the past. I can only do what's right in the present, and in the future." After a pause, Eugene continued, "Mrs. Harper, I want you to know something. The Lord has changed me. I take full responsibility for what I did. The Lord has changed me on the inside. Thanks to Chaplain Horne and his prison ministry, I have come to view life differently. Jesus has totally changed my life. For many years now, God has been impressing on my spirit to seek forgiveness and confess to you this sin of taking your husband's life. I caused so much pain to your family. I took the life of your children's father. I committed a terrible sin and I have wanted to acknowledge my despicable action for some time now and to plead for your forgiveness. I want to tell you how very sorry I am."

Hearing his apology was expected, however, acknowledging it was something she wasn't prepared to do. "Dan was a wonderful person." Susan began to cry slightly as she continued, "I loved him so much. We had so much to look forward to. We had so much life to live. He loved me. He loved his children, now he's gone and it's your fault. You robbed me of my life with Dan. How could you do such a thing?" Supported by both arms, Susan's head fell to the table.

She wept loudly.

Chaplain Horne rose from his chair and placed a hand on Susan's back. "Susan, would you like a break? Can I get you something to drink?"

Susan slowly lifted her head, wiped her tears, took in a deep breath and replied weakly, "I'm Okay."

"Do you want to continue?"

"Yes."

Horne returned to his chair and Susan looked again into the eyes of Eugene. She noticed tears were streaming down both his cheeks as well. She stared at his tears for a moment. "Eugene, why was it so important to speak with me to the point that your Chaplain had to travel all the way to Mississippi to convince me to come here? Chaplain Horne could've picked a more pleasant vacation and I am fairly busy these days. I have my family to care for. My first born is in a coma. What are you expecting from me? Why can't you just leave me alone?"

Eugene wipes away his tears. "I don't want anything from you. I'm trying to help you. I'm trying to get you to understand that together, we have an opportunity to do a worthy thing. God has answered my prayers by giving me this opportunity. He's showed me how imperative it is for His children to forgive one another as He forgave us. This isn't for me. He brought you here because He loves you so much. He desires to bless you and your family. He wants you to have peace. I desire Jesus to be glorified in your life, as well as my own."

"Are you asking me to forgive you for killing my husband? Is that what you really expect of me Eugene? Do you think you really deserve forgiveness?"

"I deserve what I'm getting, and then some. I don't deserve forgiveness. I don't deserve anything. I'm a sinner saved by the grace of God. What you do is between you and the Lord. If you are all bent on hating me for the rest of your life, God will give you the freedom to live such a life. All I can do is what God wants of me and that's to seek your forgiveness. I'm truly so sorry, and I am asking for some measure of reconciliation. I'm speaking to you from the Spirit that He has placed within me. God has given me a love for you and your family. I'm asking forgiveness because that's what God wants me to do. This is His will for my life. What do you think is God's will in this matter?"

Susan didn't respond.

"Mrs. Harper, I'm saved and forgiven by God. I know that. I've asked Jesus to forgive me by the power of His shed blood on the cross. I'm not the same man that I was back then. God has given me a new life. He wants you to experience the same victory. Please Mrs. Harper...Please forgive me, I ask for your forgiveness."

Susan couldn't deny the sincerity of Eugene's words. He spoke words of truth and they began cutting like a knife into the depths of her soul. She knew about God's forgiveness. She had experienced His grace throughout her life. God had demonstrated his mercy by sending a wonderful man in her life. Through a host of unexpected circumstances, God had been moving in her life. Susan silently prayed, *God, what is your will?*

There was a peculiar stillness in the room. Something began to oddly invade her inner spirit. Looking into the moist eyes of the once hated, a sensation of compassion swept into her heart. She couldn't resist it. *Is this your will Lord? Do you want me to forgive this man?* Susan continued to pray within.

Susan glanced toward the edge of the table in front of Eugene and noticed tears had dripped from his chin and formed two small puddles. They were true tears of remorse. Those were the tears of a man who'd made a mistake in his life and wanted to make things right as best as he knew how. They were the tears of a fellow brother in Christ who'd spend the rest of his life in prison.

In an instant, Susan's heart softened. She began to feel empathy. God was doing something that was unexpected, unplanned. In a matter of seconds, Eugene wasn't the monster he'd been. He was a real human trying to make amends for his past. She knew without a doubt that Eugene was sincere. She had to admit that to herself. But was she able, did she have the strength to turn loose of her hate and embrace a new life of compassion? Did she have the power to go down a new path and accept his token of forgiveness? With

Eugene's tears, and her own, an unexplainable calm suddenly subdued her heart.

"Mrs. Harper, I'm so sorry, will you forgive me?" Eugene again sobbed, breaking the long silence.

Susan continued to focus on the puddle of tears, and then looked directly in the eyes of Eugene. Supernaturally, she felt nothing but unconditional love for Eugene. Taking a deep breath, Susan exhaled the words, "Yes, Eugene. I forgive you. I forgive you by the power and unconditional love of Jesus. I now know this is God's will for my life, and this is why He's brought us together today."

As those words flowed forth, an unmistakable heaviness was lifted from her body. The burden of hate vanished in the blink of an eye. It was though someone had lifted a heavy backpack from her shoulders.

"Thank you Mrs. Harper!" Thank you in the name of Jesus! The Lord Jesus is glorified!" Lifting both hands high into the air and looking toward the ceiling, Eugene continued to exclaim, "Your will has been accomplished on this day Lord God! Send your favor to this sister in Christ! Send your favor to her son Daniel! Be glorified Lord Jesus!"

In less than twenty minutes in the mediation room, there was an incredible breakthrough. Eugene had received what he'd long prayed for. Susan did what the Lord had pressed on her heart. As for Chaplain Horne, he just simply sat in awe at the mighty power of God.

* * *

Scotty didn't immediately notice that Daniel's eyes had gently opened. He'd been asleep for more than an hour, slouched uncomfortably in a chair next to Daniel's bed. Daniel's vision was blurred but was rapidly coming into focus. He could hear the air-conditioning hum and a beeping sound just to his left. He knew for sure that this wasn't the farmhouse. Looking around the room, he spotted Scotty asleep. Daniel's body was stiff and his head ached. He grimaced while attempting further movement. Slightly lifting his left arm, he spotted a tube protruding into his vein and taped to his forearm.

"Scotty," Daniel finally whispered.

Scotty was snoring.

"Scotty," He said somewhat louder.

Scotty didn't budge.

Daniel filled his lungs with air and with a strained puff, he said, "Wake up Scotty."

Daniel's voice jarred Scotty to attention as if a siren had suddenly sounded in the hospital. Upon seeing Daniel's eyes half-opened, but nevertheless open, Scotty sprang to his feet and proclaimed, "Daniel, you're awake!"

"Where am I?"

"Praise God, Daniel you're back! Praise the name of Jesus!"

"Where's mom?"

Scotty gently placed one hand on Daniel's chest and ran the other through his hair. "Your mother is fine. Everyone is fine and you're going to be just fine too," Scotty softly said, gathering his emotions. He didn't want to cause Daniel any additional trauma, so his composure was an essential.

"I'm thirsty."

"We'll get you something. I'll call a nurse."

"Am I in a hospital? What happened?"

"You fell from the loft of the barn," Scotty said in a similar relaxed tone.

"Could I have something to drink?"

"Let me get someone to help you."

Instead of pushing the emergency button for assistance, Scotty ran out in the hall and shouted toward the nurses station, "Daniel is awake! Praise God our Boy is back!" Scotty couldn't hold back his exuberance any longer. Everyone in the ICU unit simultaneously jumped at his abrupt expression of praise and excitement.

Chapter 26

Susan's cell had been turned *off* while in the prison facility. It wasn't until they'd pulled out of the prison gate that she realized an incoming call from Scotty had been missed. She checked the time of his call and it'd been just fifteen minutes prior. Sitting in the back seat of Horne's wagon, her heart raced out of control. She was almost accustomed to the sudden jolts to the heart. It'd been a very trying couple of weeks. *Daniel may have had a turn for the worse,* she thought. Susan immediately punched '*send*' on her cell and on the second ring Scotty answered. "Sorry I missed your call. How's everything going?"

Scotty asked excitably, "Susan, how are things going?"

"I'm fine. How's Daniel?"

"Hold on…there's someone here at the hospital who wants to give you the update."

The Horne's could hear the conversation, but pretended to be oblivious.

"It must be one of the Doctors," Susan said audibly.

"Mom?"

"Daniel, is that you?"

"It's me mom."

"Daniel your mom is on her way to see you." She replied, choking back the tears.

"That's good," Daniel said weakly.

"How's my boy…doing today?" Susan asked with tremendous joy, mixed with tears of emotion.

"Don't cry mom. I'm doing okay, I reckon."

"I'm just so very happy to hear your voice son."

"It's great to hear your voice too Mom. Sorry I fell out of the loft. I guess that messed everything up for everybody."

Susan understood that to mean his baseball plans. "Daniel, get some rest and don't worry about anything."

"They say I've been resting for sometime now."

Susan laughed slightly through her tears. "Daniel, it's going to take me a few hours to get to the hospital, but your mama is coming. I'm coming son."

"Great…I love you mom. Guess I better let you go now. Here's Scotty."

"I love you too son." Susan said, knowing that the cell phone had already been handed to Scotty.

Horne pulled over to the side of the desert road. Both he and his wife were straining their necks to share in the good news. They were smiling ear to ear as Susan continued to speak on the cell.

"Can you believe it Susan?" Scotty asked.

"The Lord has done this Scotty. When did the coma break?"

"About twenty minutes ago."

She knew without a doubt what had happened. That was precisely the time when she had forgiven Eugene.

"Scotty, God has done this and I praise Him for it. Listen to me. I'm just leaving the prison and it was about twenty minutes ago that I forgave Eugene Thompson.

"Unbelievable! This is absolutely incredible!"

"Scotty, this is a God-thing."

"No question mark in my mind."

"What are the doctors saying?" Susan asked.

"Well, the on-call physician was pleased to say the least. He said everything looks great."

"Scotty, we have about a two hour drive back to Phoenix International. It'll be well after dark before I arrive."

"You guys be very careful. Daniel's not going anywhere."

"Hallelujah, thank you Jesus! I'm coming Scotty! Tell Daniel his mama is coming!"

"There's power in forgiveness, is there not darling?"

"You got that right. Love ya'll. Tell Daniel I love him."

"We all love you too sweetheart."

"Yes, thank you Jesus!" Susan shouted again, snapping her cell shut. "Well, let's get a move on it. I've got a boy to go see."

"On-ward we go," Horne responded with satisfied expression. Mrs. Horne reached into the back seat and slapped Susan's knee and said, "You got your miracle honey."

Horne's antique Toyota Station Wagon spun off the side of the sandy road and back onto the single lane. He was surprised the vehicle wasn't even rattling anymore, and the red *check oil* light wasn't seen.

With Mulberry prison at the rear, Susan turned and looked out the back windshield and whispered, "Thanks for the prayers Eugene…and I truly do forgive you."

As the wagon sped down the road, Susan had an enormous sense of gratitude for her new friends. *The chaplain may have saved Daniel's life by taking his risky trip to Mississippi.* She also speculated on the likelihood that Daniel would have never awakened had it not been for her trip to Mulberry, and willingness to be obedient to God's spirit—to forgive Eugene. Even though Oak Grove Church sang contemporary praise music which she thoroughly enjoyed, a song came out of thin air and entered into her soul. The song radiated throughout her being. God had given it for the occasion. *"There is power…power…wonder working power, in the blood…of the*

Lamb. There is power...power...wonder working power, in the precious blood of the Lamb." Initially Susan was humming the tune, but by the fourth run-through, she was singing the spiritual to the top of her lungs.

The Horne's joined in, and they sang old-time gospel hymns most of the way to International, rejoicing in the miracle that had just been performed by the Lord.

Susan would surely miss her new friends—the Chaplain Horne and his wife.

Chapter 27

Daniel was lying flat in the bed with his left leg propped up with a couple of pillows. Some three hours earlier, the sun had lowered over the western horizon and he was expecting his mother any moment. They'd spoken three additional times as she made her way through both airports. Susan's last call came as she loaded the carry-on bag into her parked vehicle at the airport in Meridian. She held her breath with each call hoping Daniel hadn't somehow fallen back into his coma. To her great pleasure, Daniel was more articulate and lively with each conversation.

By the time Susan entered his room, Daniel was well aware of all the circumstances of his injured leg and the two weeks that followed. He knew where his mom had been and what had happened with Eugene Thompson. Throughout the long day, Daniel had frequently stated to Scotty, the doctors and nurses, his twin sisters, his step-grandparents and to his mom by phone, how appreciative he was for the prayers and concerns. He was just glad to be alive and felt God had brought him through.

Daniel was aching from the top of his head to the bottom of his feet. He'd lost nearly twenty pounds and was stunned by the loss of his muscular frame. Daniel wondered if he'd ever walk normal, much-less play baseball. He was extremely stiff, weak and felt a sense of shame. One minute he was in the loft preparing for a long hard day on the farm, and now life had drastically changed.

His future was in the balance.

"Well, well, what do we have here? You sure are a sight for sore eyes." Susan pleasantly said as she walked to the side of the bed.

Daniel sheepishly smiled, "You are really something mom."

"Well give your mama a hug," Susan ever-so-gently squeezed her son.

After the embrace, Susan walked over to Scotty and likewise gives him a hug and kiss. Susan again returns to the side of the bed and replies, "Have you had a good meal yet?"

"I had some ice cream and jell-o. I've been thirsty all day. I think I've tanked three gallons of water."

"Well that's understandable. You need all the hydration you can get."

"This is a real bummer isn't it mom." Daniel's countenance had a rapid change.

"You're going to do wonderful. I just know it. It's going to take time to get going, but you'll get there."

"Baseball is shot out of the water."

"Did God say that or is that coming from you?"

"Mom, it's obvious. Look at my banged up leg. Look at me, I'm all skin and bones," Daniel frustratingly replied while looking down at the metal contraption secured just below his knee. There were four silver metal rods protruding through his skin, to the bone."

"Baseball's not everything. You're sitting up speaking to your mama right now. That's more important than a game."

Scotty walked over and put his arm around Susan and interjects,

"They're planning to move Daniel out of ICU and into a regular room tomorrow. The doctor even suggested that at the current rate of improvement, they'll release him all together by the end of the week."

"Wonderful," Susan emphasized with both thumbs in the air.

"I can't even move my leg. I hope I don't disappoint the Doctors."

"You just have to trust God and do the best you can do. That's all you have to do, and we'll be there cheering you on all the way."

"Mom, don't you need some rest? You look so tired. Go home with Scotty and get some sleep. I'll see you guys tomorrow."

"Daniel's right Susan, it's late and you look exhausted."

"I would feel terrible to leave. I just got here. Daniel, are you sure you don't want me to stay the night with you?"

"I'll be fine. You need to go home and see about the girls."

"They were here earlier with mom and dad. We had a semi-party here in the room a couple of hours ago," Scotty said.

Susan hadn't noticed the colorful balloons floating in the corner. "I suspect everyone was excited to see Daniel?"

"Everyone was thrilled, and by the way, the news hit the media this afternoon. I suppose most everyone in Meridian knows by now. Big Jeff gave me a call and said Daniel was the headline this evening on TV33. The media rush will probably begin first thing in the morning, if it hasn't already begun in the lobby and out in the parking lot. The staff here at Piedmont have been wonderful at keeping them at bay."

"Mom, I'm in good hands here, go get some rest."

"Okay Daniel, I'll take you up on the offer. We'll be back at the hospital bright and early."

"When you come back tomorrow, bring my Bible."

"We'll surely do that," Susan said.

"Goodnight son." Susan kissed Daniel on the forehead and Scotty gave him a fist pump.

Just before they closed the door, Daniel said, "Mom,"

Susan stuck her head back in the room. "What is it son?"

"I love you."

"I love you too…Sweet dreams. And don't worry so much."

Susan shuts the door, and Daniel grimaced in pain.

* * *

It had been near daybreak before Daniel finally dozed-off. After no more than two hours of sleep, a young girl entered the room and nudged him slightly on the shoulder. After opening his eyes, it didn't take him but a second to become fully alert. She was definitely on the cute side with her shoulder length straight brown hair, perfect complexion, awesome figure and a smile that would lighten the darkest of rooms. *One of the benefits of being crippled and hospitalized,* so he thought.

It was breakfast time and the rising of the sun brought an attractive girl into the room holding a tray of eggs, grits, toast and orange juice.

"Hope your appetite is good this morning," the girl replied.

"Thanks," he managed to say while transfixed on the pretty girl.

She didn't appear old enough to be an official nurse. She was much too young, and cute. The dress she wore was noticeable different than the other nurses. He'd seen too many of those. The more serious looking nurses had entered into Daniel's space every fifteen minutes since popping back into reality.

This girl was close to Daniel's age—seventeen, eighteen at best.

Throughout high school, Daniel had a few casual dates with a couple of church girls, but nothing came remotely close to materializing.

"How long you been nursing?"

"Some call us Candy Stripers."

"I see…why?" Daniel asked while gazing at her red stripes on her otherwise white uniform.

"I'm a volunteer. I think the term *Candy Stripe* is a little silly," she said while placing the tray on a table and rolling it in front of Daniel.

"Hope the food is suitable to your liking this morning." The girl was pulling the aluminum cover off the small orange juice container.

"Yummy…this should be fine." Daniel rubbed both hands on his stomach. "Do you want to be a nurse one day?"

"One day, I hope. I'm entering the nursing program at MJC in the fall."

"Well, I reckon that perfectly qualifies you to be a Candy Stripe girl," Daniel replied humorously.

"Guess so," the girl said with a bright smile.

"Well, is there anything else I can get for you?" She asked.

"Nothing I can think of just yet, but if I do, I'll push the emergency button."

"You do that and you'll most likely get a real nurse to assist you. I work each Thursday, Friday and Saturday from eight to one."

"Can you tell me what day this is?"

"It's Thursday."

"Sorry for the ignorance. They tell me I've been out of it for a few days."

"I know all about your story. Who hasn't?"

"May I ask your name, or shall I call you Candy Stripe?"

"Brook."

"Does Brook have a last name?"

"Brook Millard." She said, completely aware there was some flirting going on in ICU.

"It's good to officially meet you…Brook Millard."

"See you at lunch, now be a good boy and eat your breakfast."

Brook turned to leave, but just before the door clicked shut, Daniel throws another line her way, "Looking forward to lunch... Brook Millard."

Now alone, Daniel quoted her name in his mind—*Brook Millard…Where have I heard that name before?*

* * *

Susan and Scotty arrived just as Daniel was scrapping his plate of the remaining egg crumbs. After a rather typical morning conversation, Daniel finally asked, "Hey mom, does the name Brook Millard ring a bell?"

"Sure, I remember that name. Why do you ask?" Susan was perplexed that Daniel had asked such a thing.

"I've been working that name around in my head and I'm drawing a blank."

"Daniel you've heard that name before, though not recently. Why do you ask?" Susan was acting rather curious as she pulled the breakfast table away from the bed and rolls it to the side.

"A Brook Millard served me the breakfast I just ate."

"It couldn't be the same person then. She wouldn't be old enough to work here."

"She's around my age. She works as a volunteer. Come clean mom, what Brook Millard do you know?"

I'm sure it's just a coincidence, but you know the little girl who your father rescued the night he was killed? Her name was Brook… Brook Millard."

"That's it. I remember now!" Daniel exclaimed.

"I'm sure it's not the same girl. The last time I saw her was at Dan's funeral. She was a precious little thing. I suppose the Millards still live in Philadelphia," Susan said.

"Wouldn't it be something if she's the same girl?" Scotty said, breaking his silence.

"Yea, wouldn't that be something," Daniel echoed with an obvious smile of anticipation.

Chapter 28

Daniel successfully convinced Susan and Scotty to eat their lunch in the hospital cafeteria while he eagerly waited for his. But it wasn't food Daniel craved. It was information.

Brook was on time. She entered the room with the exact same wonderful smile. "Ready for your lunch Daniel?"

"Ready and eagerly waiting," In the history of Piedmont's ICU, Daniel was the most excited patient ever—the grin suggested.

"She began the usual routine of organizing the food tray for consumption and Daniel wasted no time in pursing the issue.

"Where are you from Brook?"

"Philadelphia, it's about a thirty minute drive, but I don't mind."

"You don't say," Daniel said with raised eyebrows.

"Why do you ask?"

"My family is familiar with a family from Philadelphia by the name Millard."

"Oh really?"

"Really," Daniel was completely uninterested in lunch. "Can I ask you something?"

"Sure."

"Has your father ever worked at a convenience store?"

"When I was a little girl, why do you ask?"

"This is crazy Brook…when you were a little girl was that store robbed, and you held at gunpoint?"

"How did you know about that?"

"It's you, this is amazing!"

"What is amazing Daniel? How'd you know? I haven't spoken about that in years. We don't even mention at home. It's sort of something we have put in our past, a horrible nightmare."

"You better sit down for what I'm about to tell you."

"Okay then." Brook pulled up a seat from the corner and curiously waited for Daniel's explanation.

"My dad was the one who was shot and killed. You remember don't you, the police officer?"

"Officer Patton, he was your dad?"

"That's correct."

"Your dad is the one who saved my life?"

"Correct again."

Brook places both her hands over her face, and then removes them. "I probably wouldn't be here today if it weren't for your dad."

"You are probably correct there too, though we can't be sure." Daniel pushes himself up as straight as possible, and growled, after a stabbing pain. "Now I know why all of this has happened." Daniel said with a painful voice.

"I wish you would share it with me. I'm stunned right now."

"It's because of someone in Mulberry. I've been told that there's been some prayer's going out of that place."

* * *

"When do you think is the right time to tell Daniel about the Atlanta Braves Scout?" Susan asked while stirring the cream in her coffee in the crowded hospital cafeteria.

Scotty picked up a chicken leg and takes a bite, "We haven't yet told him the full story about his leg. How are we going to tell him about the scout, if he doesn't know about his leg Susan? Nobody has even mentioned the portion of bone that had to be removed to repair the leg."

"I know Scotty…the news will send him into a depression. I know it will."

"He deserves to know the details. It is better he knows now, rather than later. He's the kind of person who'd want to know," Scotty firmly said.

"According to the specialist we've spoken with, Daniel will probably never play sports competitively again. His left leg will be slightly shorter than the other one. He'll have a permanent limp," Susan somberly said.

"I still think it is best we go ahead and tell Daniel before he finds out from someone else. It's best he knows the whole truth now rather than later," Scotty reiterated."

"Daniel's a smart young man with a level head on his shoulders. He is going to be fine. Everything is going to be fine. God is in control of everything. Haven't we seen Him working? Okay then, after lunch it'll be. We'll tell him about the leg and the Braves Scout after lunch," Susan said.

"I agree. After lunch it will be."

Twenty minutes later, Scotty and Susan stepped out of the elevator onto the ICU floor. As they made their way to Daniel's room, a young girl was leaning on the counter of the nurses station obviously looking in their direction, as if she had been in-waiting. "Excuse me, are you Susan Patton?" The girl in a candy stripe uniform asked.

"Yes I am," Susan responded, stopping in her tracks.

"Hi, my name is Brook Millard."

"Oh, hello there, I've heard Daniel mention your name. Did you two get a chance to clear things up on the mistaken identity thing?"

"Yes, I believe everything is clear as a bell, only thing being, it's not a mistaken identity thing. I'm the little girl Officer Patton gave his life for…I'm thrilled to finally get to meet you."

Susan looked at Scotty. Her mouth flew open, but nothing came out. She just stood there, dazed and confused.

"I just wanted to tell you that Officer Patton was a brave and very great man. He's obviously a hero to me and my dad."

"Yes, I agree…a great man," Susan squeezed out of her lungs.

"Well, I won't trouble you any longer. Maybe we'll have another opportunity to talk another time."

"Yes Brook…I think that would be nice."

"See you soon. I'm actually off-duty right now. My shift ended at one."

"I hope we'll be able to get to know each other in the next couple of days. We're hoping to take Daniel home by Monday."

"I'll look for you tomorrow, I promise. I'll be on the ICU floor and I know about the plans to place Daniel in a regular room. I will not be on your new floor, but I'll be sure to find you."

"That would make me very happy Brook, and might I say that you sure have blossomed into a beautiful young woman. The last time I saw you…you were just a little girl. Thank you for waiting to speak with me."

"It was my pleasure."

"I'll see you tomorrow then."

"You can count on it. I already promised Daniel to pay him a visit. We've got each other's phone numbers. We plan to stay in touch."

"Brook this is incredible, you and Daniel…friends."

"Daniel said it was all God's plan."

Suddenly Susan remembered Eugene. "I believe that with all of my heart Brook."

"See you tomorrow."

"We will be here. Look forward to it."

As Brook walked to the elevator, Susan elbowed Scotty in the side. "What is going to happen next? I mean, what if Daniel and Brook got—"

"Serious," Scotty said, completing Susan's sentence, "Didn't you notice the glow in Daniel's eyes this morning when he was talking about Brook? Now we've seen the same glow in Brook's eyes—Two-plus-two-*equals*-love-at-first-sight. I know about that because I remember the first time I laid eyes on you."

Susan elbowed Scotty in the side for a second time as they continued their walk toward Daniel's room. "That's silly. They just met...She is a charming girl though."

* * *

By late afternoon Daniel had moved out of ICU, and within three days was released altogether. During those final days in the hospital, Daniel had a constant flow of visitors. Even with the disturbing revelation concerning the leg, his spirits were surprisingly high. Brook's daily visits were essential to Daniel's sound disposition. Along with Brook, there were dozens of other visiting well-wishers from students, teammates and members of Meridian High's coaching staff. Big Jeff enthusiastically dropped by on three occasions and without fail laid a firm hand on Daniel's damaged leg in earnest prayer for rapid recovery. Susan pledged not to return to her shops until Daniel was released and resting comfortably on the farm. Scotty hadn't been as regular as Susan. The chores had piled up and the farm work couldn't be postponed any longer. Each day the twins had skipped into the hospital along with the grandparents, smuggling in hidden treats for Daniel's sweet tooth.

All the attention was nice, but one of the happiest days of Daniel's life was when he was wheeled into the farmhouse. Home at last, albeit with one leg slightly shorter than the other and stiff as a board, but nevertheless he was home.

In the days that followed, Daniel would've most certainly battled extreme discouragement, had it not been for Brook. Her friendship put pep in his personality that might otherwise not be on display. Her faithful visits out to the farm gave Daniel the most pleasure. Her company was what he looked forward to the most.

Additionally, they spoke by cell phone regularly, especially at night. Brook was a never-ending source of encouragement. Hours were spent getting to know one another better. They'd mutually concluded that it was the providence of God which had brought them together, though Daniel understood its meaning more than Brook. Daniel couldn't deny himself one particular truth, and that being, the first time he'd laid eyes on Brook, something unusual happened. He wasn't sure what, but something definitely happened—inside his heart. *Was it love at first sight? Or was it only infatuation?* He'd concluded it was definitely *love.* However, he wouldn't dare reveal the truth of his inner feelings to Brook.

It was completely too early in their friendship to unload the *'L'* word. It was way too earlier for that.

Chapter 29

Beginning therapeutic rehab was one of the most challenging feats Daniel had ever attempted, much more challenging than hitting a ninety-mile-an-hour fastball. It was grueling. Rehab began the day doctors removed the metal rods which protruded into his leg and the cumbersome support contraption. The specialist at Piedmont had stated that the bones had grafted together satisfactory, and instructed Daniel to begin a seven-day-per-week program to restore movement and flexibility. Twice a week, he would return to their rehab facility at Piedmont, but the remaining days would require self-motivation.

Brook volunteered to be Daniel's personal *candy stripe* girl. Susan and Scotty were thrilled to see how Brook had taken this kind of initiative to help Daniel. Just the thought of it made Susan rather emotional. The same girl who was rescued by her late husband ten years earlier was now instrumental in helping her son. This was one of those phenomenal gifts from God that no one could explain. It was yet another astonishing God-thing.

By September Daniel could walk without crutches, though a cane was necessary. Every evening Daniel and Brook went for strolls on the farm. It'd been three months since the accident and Daniel was up and about with *soul mate* by his side, he secretly determined.

It was Sunday afternoon shortly following morning worship at Oak Grove in which Daniel and Brook arose from the table to take one of their usual afternoon walks. It'd been a good day already. This was the first occasion that Brook had accompanied Daniel and his family to church. Big Jeff had preached a sermon entitled *'The Sovereign Hand of God.'* It centered on how God operated in the lives of others in miraculous ways to bring about His purposes. The preacher didn't refer to Daniel directly, but everyone who followed the recent happenings out on the Harper Farm understood its applications. The Sovereign Hand of God had been moving in peculiar fashion.

Following the message, Susan prepared a huge meal. Brook seemed to enjoy every last bite of fried chicken, butter beans, and cornbread. She particularly enjoyed the sweet taste of apple pie, topped with vanilla ice cream. The new girl in the house was beginning to feel just like family.

"Thank you for lunch Mrs. Harper, everything was very tasty." Brook responded with her usual smile.

"You are quite welcome. I'm glad you enjoyed it."

"Can I help with the dishes or anything?"

"No…you and Daniel go ahead and get your exercise in for the day. We'll handle everything in the kitchen."

"Can we go with ya'll?" Rebecca pleaded on behalf of her sister. Occasionally, the twins would accompany the two. Brook had bonded with Daniel's sisters. She thought they were hilarious. Daniel thought they were becoming a nuisance. They were interfering with his time alone with Brook. Scotty and Susan were beginning to sense the nuisance part, and came to the rescue. "No, you girls stay back this time and help your mother clear the table." Scotty replied as he began stacking plates. The girls pouted.

"Are you ready Brook?" Daniel said grabbing his walking cane which had been leaning on his stiff leg during lunch.

Daniel limped out the back door and Brook courteously holds it wide. When they were a safe distance from the house, far from peering eyes, Daniel reaches out his free hand and Brook gently interlocks his fingers with hers. This wasn't the first time they'd privately held hands while out and about on the farm, but it was the first time Brook had snuggled this close to his side. Daniel was determined to give Brook a first kiss when the time was right, but that special time hadn't come, yet. Maybe that electrifying first kiss would be today.

He sure hoped it would be today.

"Daniel…how come you've never taken me into the barn to show me where you fell from?" Brook asked, wondering if it was an appropriate question.

"It's just an old barn. It means nothing more or nothing less to me…just an old barn."

"Doesn't it trouble you to think about what happen, you know, the fall and all?" Brook probingly asked.

"Well, if it hadn't been for that old barn, I probably wouldn't have met you. I have no residual anxiety toward it. In a way, the barn's been a blessing."

"What about baseball? That must not make you feel so great, you know, the timing of your accident and all."

"Guess you could say the accident is bitter sweet. I know I'll never go to sleep in a barn again. I spent my whole life to get to the point I was at, and now look what happened…just like that." Daniel said snapping his finger.

"So you're not upset at the barn, but you are upset about what happened. All this time getting to know you and I haven't heard you complain much. You haven't seemed bitter. You must have been a great ballplayer. All those things I've read about you and heard what others have said. I can understand how a person with that kind of future ahead of him would be frustrated out of his mind."

"It hurts like crazy, but I can't do anything about it. All I can do is take one day at a time and live as normal a life as possible. I had planned to play baseball for God's glory most of my life. Baseball was my life, my passion. I just don't understand it Brook. All these years of witnessing God do things. You know…miracles. The way my mom met my coach who is now my stepdad. The way my real dad, who by the way saved your life, is the same real dad who was instrumental in winning my stepdad to Jesus long before we knew him. The way I came out of the coma the minute my mom forgave the man who killed my father, who by the way is the same man who once held you at gunpoint. And the way I met you at the hospital the day after coming out of a two week coma. I could go on and on. It all has to be connected to the purpose of God. I haven't even told you about the vision I had when I was just twelve which started this whole unbelievable cycle of miracles. Boom, boom, boom, it's been one miracle right after another. I don't understand why I'm limping around out here re-learning how to walk again. Maybe God never wanted my life to be in baseball, maybe he wanted my life to be with you." They continued walking slowly, holding hands and enjoying their time together. It was a beautiful Mississippi day.

"Have you considered that baseball may still be in your future? You can have both you know," Brook emphasized.

Daniel liked the ring of the word, *both.*

"Everything will be revealed in time. God hasn't brought us this far to leave us now," Daniel replied, using the word *us* to counter her word, *both.*

"Sometimes life doesn't make sense. Daniel, I've been doing some thinking lately. I'm open to the possibility that Eugene's prayers may possibly be a factor in all those things happening, but that suggestion troubles me. Is it possible that God would honor the prayers of someone so ruthless and despicable? He is the one who walked into a convenience store and scarred me for life. Daniel, he is the one who viciously took your father's life. I can't think of anything he's done that would remotely suggest a blessing. Sometimes I get confused by the whole idea."

Changing the subject, Daniel points his cane forward and replies with a scary tone in an attempt to impress with humor. "Come my dear, I will now take you to the infamous barn and further explain a few things to you."

"Yes master," she said with equal wit.

* * *

Once inside the barn, Daniel and Brook sat on a single bale of hay. There were only three bales in the whole barn. It always puzzled Daniel why Scotty seemed to always have a few bales of hay on-hand. They didn't have any livestock. Maybe they were for show. More likely, they were for sitting. Most every barn in the south had at least some hay, and this barn was no different.

With the swinging door half open, cracks throughout the boarded walls, and small holes in the aluminum ceiling, the bright afternoon sun made for sufficient lighting. The beams of light which penetrated into the cracks of the wall and tiny holes from above set off a laser-like spectacle. Daniel pointed his cane upward to the loft. "Right there's where I fell asleep and there's where I landed among all those tractor parts," Daniel said, while slowly moving his cane down to the spot of impact. "They tell me that blood was everywhere. Guess mom made sure all that was cleaned up good."

"That's a high fall, I didn't realize it was that high," Brook replied taking in the scene.

"I sure don't remember it. The last thing I recall is climbing up there, laying down and looking at the ceiling. I'd stayed up most of the night before, thinking and praying about stuff."

"One thing we can't do is change what's happened," Brook said.

"Like I said, it must've been God's plan to bring you into my life."

"You really mean that don't you."

"I totally mean it Brook." Daniel was now gazing directly into Brook's gorgeous brown eyes. He leaned closer and gently kissed her on the lips. Relishing in the first kiss with the girl in which he'd fallen in love. He pulled back and gave a shy smile. The ice was finally broken.

"That was nice," she said

"Very nice," he agreed.

"What took you so long?"

"I like to pace myself."

"Could I have one more?"

"At your service…master."

After their second tender kiss, Daniel shifts his head, admiring the display of lights shooting through the barn and romantically said, "This reminds me of what has happened."

"What do you mean?" Asked Brook with love in her eyes.

"Look at all these beams of light going in all directions."

"Beautiful…isn't it?" She responded, rivaling his romantic tone.

"This is how God operates. His light shines in the dark places of life. His love will find a way to penetrate even the hardest of hearts."

"Even the heart of someone like Eugene Thompson?"

"Of course Brook, even his heart. The love of God can change anyone. That's why Jesus died on the cross for our sins. Everybody is a sinner and needs his love and forgiveness. According to Romans 3:23: "*All have sinned and come short of the glory of God.*"

"I don't know if I want Eugene to be forgiven. I know that sounds mean, but that's just my true feelings."

"It's important for you not to hold a grudge against that man. He is a Christian now. His sins have been wiped clean. My family has forgiven him. Why don't you consider doing the same?"

"I'll try, but it's not going to be easy. He didn't kill my father, but I still feel his grip. I still to this day smell the alcohol on his breath. I still recall the evil in his eyes. I can't go into a store without the fear that a madman might jump me and shoot me in the head."

"God can, and will take away your fear, if you will trust Him."

"I'm willing to trust God but I don't know how. There is something missing in my life. I don't have this peace and assurance that you have. I don't have this same confidence in God to protect me. This is an evil world we live in."

"Brook, I want to ask you an important question that's been on my mind."

"You can ask me anything."

"Has there ever being a time in your life that you asked Jesus to come into your life and forgive you of your sins?"

"Honestly, I can't say there has."

"The most important thing you'll ever do is give Christ your life, asking Him to change you and give you a new outlook. He loves you and died on the cross for you, personally. Jesus desires to be in your life. His love will penetrate your heart like these beams of light has penetrated this barn."

"I've been thinking about it ever since church this morning. I didn't say anything because I wasn't sure I was ready."

"When are you going to be ready Brook?"

"I'm ready now Daniel."

"That's wonderful."

"Well…what do I have to do?"

"I'll tell you what I did when I was little. I just prayed to Him with faith. I told God that I believed that Jesus, His only Son died for my sins on the cross and that he rose from the dead. I asked God to forgive me of my sins because I wanted to go to Heaven when I died."

"That's it?"

"That's it—would you like to pray to receive Jesus as your Lord and Savior Brook?"

"Yes Daniel. I'd like that very much."

Daniel reaches over and gently secures her hand. He prays a simple prayer as Brook repeats each sentence. On the 20th day of September, Brook Millard, with a beam of light strategically shining on her heart from a single hole in the roof, became born again into the family of God.

Chapter 30

"I feel free Daniel," Brook said with a crisp expression as they walked through a gate and onto the farm's baseball field. The grass hadn't been cut in weeks suggesting baseball wasn't a recent priority.

"That's the Spirit of God inside of you," Daniel informed.

"All those negative feelings I had toward Eugene are gone too. I have this peace about me. It's as though I could fly right over this field." Brook throws open her arms as if she was flying.

"That's what having your sins forgiven will do. Burdens you didn't even know were there, have been lifted. Christ did the same thing for me when I was little. I know what you're feeling on the inside."

"Daniel, why don't you try to play baseball again? The Lord will help you. Why don't you get back out here and play. If Jesus can do this for me, I know anything is possible with God. Anyway, it'll give us something to look forward to. I'll help you."

"I can't even walk without a limp. It hurts every step. I wish—"

"I wish I could play, but I can't," Brook said cutting him off. "My dad always tells me, *can't never could.* Daniel, I can't think of any better rehab than to get you back out here doing some drills.

You know...light stuff. What is it? You don't think a little candy stripe girl can coach you?"

"Mom would go crazy if she saw me heating up the pitching machine."

"I'm not talking about heating up anything."

"Baseball is all about hitting, running, fielding...it's rougher than you might think."

"I've enjoyed our walks, but aren't you getting bored with it? Aren't you ready for something a tad-bit more challenging?"

"My motivation right now is to walk without this cane in my hand, not fielding ground balls and hitting line-drives."

"You don't have to start there."

"Where do you figure I should start?"

Brook picked up a bat leaning next to the fence. It'd been left at the field months ago as scrap lumber after one of Daniel's former power swings put a crack in its handle.

"Put down that cane," Brook insisted, sounding more like a drill sergeant than a girlfriend.

Daniel rolled his eyes in apathy, hesitated and finally did as he was told. He couldn't believe that someone who'd prayed the sinner's prayer just twenty minutes prior had become so tremendously bold—but still altogether beautiful.

"Here, hold this." Brook hands the fractured bat to Daniel as he attempts to balance himself on the strong leg."

"Don't just stand there...give me a swing."

"Brook this is useless," Daniel said as he pressed the knob of the bat on the ground for balance.

"Daniel Patton, put that bat in the air and give me a swing or I'll never give you another kiss again," She threatened.

"I knew you'd use that kiss against me," Daniel replied with a half smile. Daniel gingerly lifted the bat, balanced his body and swung. Immediately loosing his balance, he fell to the earth like a bag of potatoes. With the sun shining directly into his face, Daniel squinted while looking up toward Brook and replied, "Satisfied now?"

"No, get back up and do it again." In a flash, Brook's facial expression changed from bossy, to sympathetic, "You didn't hurt yourself did you?"

"No. . . I'm fine, a little humiliated, but I didn't break anything, I don't think."

"Good, get up and try it again." Her tough demeanor returned as quickly as it had departed.

Daniel wedges his bat onto the ground and forced his way to his feet. This time he takes an easier, more controlled swing without loosing his balance."

"Much better...See there's nothing to it."

"Easy for you to say," Daniel replied with a touch of sarcasm.

"Now give me ten more swings."

Daniel swings the bat and with each effort, picks up the pace until he heard a familiar *whiffing* sound. It was nothing compared to the old days of just three months ago, but there was definitely a *whiff* heard. He was surprised that he could generate that much bat speed with most of his weight balanced on the right leg.

"Well. . . did I pass the test?"

"We're probably not ready to heat up the pitching machine, but it'll do for now."

Daniel was impressed with her baseball lingo.

"Now bring the bat and follow me to home plate."

"What now?"

"Come on, don't wimp out on me and don't dare pick up that cane."

Daniel limped weakly to home plate leaving his walking cane in the grass. Brook leads the way, never once looking over her shoulder as he struggled to keep pace. After reaching their destination Brook insisted, "Now get in the batter's box and get in your hitting stance."

This side of Brook's personality was something new and Daniel was pretending not to be enjoying it. He instead rolled his eyes in dread even though things were beginning to get interesting. It was the most exciting day since his final ground out to end his high school career—a kiss, winning someone to the Lord, and now being forced into submission by a beautiful girl. Life was sweet at the moment. Daniel figured it must be the Lord who'd given this gal some new self-confidence. She was exploding with energy, zeal and personality.

After getting into the best stance possible, Brook continued, "Now peer out at the pitcher and give him a snarl."

"There is no pitcher out there."

"Do I have to go out there and be the pitcher Daniel? *PRETEND*...like there's a pitcher and give him a snarl."

"As you wish, Ms. Candy Stripe," Daniel replied already exhibiting a snarly expression.

Daniel balanced and increased the expression making it the most intimidating snarl known to mankind.

"Good, now take a swing at that fast ball and take-off."

"Take-off where?"

"To Mars...Daniel, where do you usually run when you hit the ball? You do know where first base is, don't you?"

Daniel laughs slightly at her relentless drive to motive and proceeds to swing with enough force to hear the *whiff* of the bat again. He couldn't deny that he still enjoyed the feel of his swing.

"Are you going to just stand there?...Run Daniel, you just got a base hit!"

"You have got to be kidding."

"I'm not kidding Daniel. Run the best you can. The game's on the line here. Don't let me and your team down."

Daniel drops the bat and does as Brook demanded.

It takes a couple of minutes to reach first.

After his long and very awkward limp, Daniel turned to face Brook who stood ninety feet away, and gives her one of those looks as if to suggest, *you satisfied now*. Then he asked, "What do you think? Was I safe or out?" Daniel was gasping for air.

"I think if you raced an expectant mother you'd come in third. Now come back here and do it again."

"Come on Brook, my leg is hurting."

"That's not all that's going to hurt if you don't come back to home plate and do it again. This time you're going to do it quicker."

"Guess I don't have a choice in the matter, do I?"

"Nope," Brook stated while folding her arms together.

Daniel slowly returned to the batters box, repeats the swing and hobbles to first. Only after three additional times was Brook satisfied, and calls it a day.

Ten minutes later, they sat in the overgrown grass, leaning against the backstop fence a few yards from home plate. Daniel continually wiped the sweat from his brow. Brook sits close to his side and displayed the pleased facial expression of; *mission accomplished*.

"I didn't know you were so tough," Daniel said wiping more sweat and trying his best to straighten his stiff leg flat on the ground.

"I didn't know I was that tough either," Brook calmly agreed, with her former personality suddenly resurfacing.

"You're right, this is more exciting than walking around the farm counting cotton."

"I thought it might be good for you. And by the way…thanks for leading me to Christ," Brook said leaning over quickly to kiss Daniel on the side of his wet face."

"Keep that up and we might make this a habit."

"Just doing what any good little candy stripe would do."

"Candy Stripe my foot—more like Rambo."

"You should've seen your face," Brook said laughing loudly.

"I know it's funny to you, but I probably won't be able to walk for days. The way you punished me today, I'm going to be sore as all-get-out."

"Don't worry about the soreness. I'll work it all out of you. Just give me time."

"If it means spending my day with you, I'll count it as joy."

"We will call it a date then. Tomorrow say, nine or so in the morning."

"I don't know if I'll be able to move, but okay, it's a date. A definite painful one, but nevertheless a date it is."

"I'll bring my softball glove. I played a little softball in the recreation summer league program a couple of years ago. I haven't used it in a while, but I still might surprise you at how good I can catch and throw."

"And I might surprise you at how bad I catch and throw."

"There's only one way to find out," Brook insisted.

Spending another hour talking, Daniel thought about the month-on-end which Brook had traveled to the farm almost every day.

She even helped him to study for a couple of test the school system required so he could receive his diploma, but those were easy. The school system gave him a major break on ninety-five percent of the work. But it was time she could've spent doing other things. It meant more to him than he could express. She was an angel out of heaven. She was more than he could've ever dreamed. He liked the *before Christ* Brook, but he adored the *after Christ* Brook. Jesus had come into her life and she was certainly making the most of it. She radiated with joy. In an instant, she had been changed for the better. Daniel didn't know if he would be able to keep up with her new enthusiasm.

But he would certainly give it a shot.

Chapter 31

Eugene felt a sudden jolt as the razor sharp blade plunged deep into the center of his back. His leg muscles gave and forced him to his knees. Instinctively, he reached toward his back in panic without screaming, or as much as a whimper. He made no vocal noise whatsoever. The only sound being the weight of Eugene's lanky body collapsing to the cement, severely smashing his face on the hard surface. Instantly aware of being stabbed, he knew this to be his chosen hour.

He successfully spotted the shoes of the blood thirsty perpetrator hurry away. The *Hell's Chosen* prison gang was in the process of claiming yet another victim for bragging rights. It was the feet of the dreaded *Hell's chosen* Eugene saw as the appointed one hurried from the scene to hide among his friends with pride. Their mission had been accomplished and carried forth to perfection. The guards in the towers hadn't seen a thing.

Every Christian prisoner at Mulberry was aware that any day could be the last in the *blood yard.* Eugene wasn't only aware, he'd anticipated it. Within seconds, his eyes closed and his body trembled in a puddle of blood, then he became motionless. This would be the day Eugene would leave Mulberry prison and go live with his Lord.

In the Prison Medical Emergency Room lying prostrate on a cold metal table, Eugene heard a voice from above. He knew this wasn't heaven. There was still too much pain. The voice vaguely heard produced a momentary smile even in midst of imminent death. There were other voices in the room. Those voices came from the prison medical staff doing the job they'd done many times before. The stabbing was another routine day for the crew as their rambling instructions were only background noise. Eugene's ears were channeled to the voice of comfort. It was the familiar voice of his trusted mentor and friend, Chaplain Horne.

Eugene couldn't see the blood, but felt its warmth running down each side, and beneath. As the blood was frequently being toweled, the chaplain hovered over his dying friend, repeating his name, "Eugene, Eugene, can you hear me Eugene?"

Gasping for breath, Eugene mumbles, "I…hear-ya…Chap."

The *blood yard* would soon have another victim added to its troubling statistic, but Eugene was grateful for the opportunity to make one more request, before his soul departed.

"The Lord is with you my friend," The chaplain said in tears.

"I…know…He…is," Eugene said, in a gruff and pain-stricken voice.

"Hold my hand tight. Everything is going to be alright. You just hang in there."

The prison medical staff had seen Chaplain Horne on many similar occasions, but had never witnessed him so emotional.

"We…did…good…didn't…we?" Eugene replied, straining to gather in air.

"We did our best for the Lord. No regrets," Horne affirmed.

"No…regrets," Eugene said.

"Is there anything I can do for you?" Horne was squeezing his hand. He knew there wasn't much time left.

"Just…one," He whispered.

"What is it my brother?"

"Tell Daniel…" Eugene coughs up blood in his attempt to speak. The chaplain grabbed a towel at the foot of the table and wiped the blood from Eugene's mouth. He heard the name Daniel and didn't have to speculate who he was referring to.

"What do you want me to tell Daniel?" The chaplain asked.

With every bit of strength, and a final push of air, Eugene clearly said, "Tell Daniel…God…Is…His…Enabler."

With those final words, Eugene slowly discharged his last breath from his lung, his body relaxed—and died.

Eugene Thompson was finally at peace. He was finally free from his earthly confinement. He'd fought the good fight and the victory was his. The spiritual warfare was over, the battle had been won.

Chaplain Horne continued to squeeze the relaxed hand of Eugene and pressed his forehead on the blood stained back of his deceased brother in Christ.

The Chaplain grieved for his friend.

Chapter 32

Daniel was exhausted from the impromptu Sunday afternoon workout and was sound asleep on the couch when Susan's cell began to chime. Brook had left and gone back to Philadelphia. The rest of the family was lounging comfortably watching a re-run of the *Andy Griffith Show.* Neither the high volume of the television, nor the sound of the cell could breakthrough the sleep world of Daniel. A freight train or fog horn couldn't wake him. He'd always been a sound sleeper, but this was ridiculous. If the house caught on fire they'd have to drag him out and he still would be snoring. *The recent coma must've relaxed the portion of the brain that controls sleep,* the family rationalized.

Susan retrieved the cell from the front pocket of her jeans, snapped it open and read the name of the incoming. It was the chaplain. She'd programmed him in with the hopes of staying in touch. "It's Chaplain Horne, turn the TV down."

Susan answered her cell after Rebecca quickly picked up the remote from the coffee table and tones the volume down. "This must be the long lost chaplain?" Susan said with an upbeat zeal.

"How's everything in Mississippi Susan?" Horne replied in a more low-keyed manner.

"Everything's kicking right along and how's everything out West?"

"Something happened earlier today and I thought you'd want to know," Horne said somberly.

"What happened?" Susan asked curiously.

"Well it's concerning Eugene—he was killed...fatally stabbed here at the prison a couple of hours ago."

"What?"

"I was with him when he died." Horne's voice was cracking. He was still shaken from the tragic episode.

Susan tried to think of something to say but words didn't come. Her eyes were wide and expression blank. Scotty and the girls were staring at her. They knew something serious had happened. Daniel never budged a muscle, but continued to snore the evening away, while hogging the family couch.

"I'm sorry to hear that," Susan sympathetically said.

"He's in a much better place. He's much better off."

"I believe that with all my heart Chaplain."

"Listen, I'm going to be in Philadelphia for the funeral. I thought maybe we could all get together. I'd like to meet the rest of your family, especially Daniel."

"That'd be fine. So you're saying that Eugene's funeral will be in Philadelphia." The rest of the family was starting to catch on, except for Daniel.

"That's right. His children have requested that I conduct a graveside service. I guess Eugene has mentioned me in the past. I just spoke with the eldest son right before I called you."

"When's the funeral?"

"Tuesday afternoon."

"We'd love to have you come here to the house. Are you flying into Meridian?"

"Yes, I'm going to arrange my flight after I speak with you."

"Do you need a ride to the funeral?"

"I intend to rent a vehicle at the airport."

"No need to rent anything, we'll pick you up and take you."

"I wouldn't want to trouble you folks."

"It's no trouble. We'll all plan to go with you, if you think it will be appropriate?"

"Susan, do you really mean that?"

"With what God has done through the faithful prayers of Eugene how couldn't I? I'm completely saddened by what's happened. I want to meet his family. They may need healing as much as I needed it. Do you think it'd be risky showing up unannounced?"

"I'll call them and ask. If there's a problem, I'll let you know. But I seriously doubt there will be. I'm sure they knew Eugene's heart. I'll call you tomorrow with the flight time."

"If there's anything I can do for you while you're here, don't hesitate to let me know."

"I appreciate that Susan. And by the way, there is one thing I wanted to tell Daniel if you don't mind."

"Daniel is sound asleep. Can I relay the message?"

"It has to do with something Eugene told me. It was his last words before dying. You just have to understand Eugene to know that everything he said carried spiritual significance. He'd walked his final years filled with God like I've never seen in any other Christian."

"Eugene spoke to you before he died and told you to tell Daniel something?"

"That's correct. I have his last words to relay to Daniel."

"I've learned never to underestimate the words of a praying man. I'm just surprised his last words were for my son."

"I was surprised too."

"What did he say?"

"Well, that's just it Susan. He told me to tell Daniel. I feel compelled and obligated to reveal it to him first."

"I understand Chaplain. I truly understand where you're coming from."

"Hold on and I'll try to wake him."

"That's not necessary," Horne quickly said. "I'll tell him on Tuesday. Do you think he'll be able to attend the funeral?"

"If I know my son, he wouldn't have it any other way."

"Great, we'll settle everything then. Listen, I better run. It's been one of those days and it's still not over yet."

"I'm so sorry to hear about Eugene."

"Like I said, he's in a much better place, and you made his life very meaningful."

"I was simply doing God's will. It was His plan all along."

"God bless you…and your family."

"See you soon, have a safe trip."

After ending the startling conversation, everyone in the room stared at each other without speaking. They'd heard Susan's side of the discussion and filled in the blanks. Scotty finally broke the silence and asked, "How'd it happen?"

Susan told her family as tears of unconditional love welled in her eyes.

Chapter 33

Ninety minutes later, Daniel woke to an empty room and stared calmly at the ceiling fan, being refreshed by its breeze as it gently blew across his body. He didn't move a muscle while considering what he'd just experienced.

Daniel had another dream, much like the one from his childhood. It'd been so vivid and real that everything about the experience suggested more than a regular dream. It was like another vision. He could still smell the flowers and feel the wonderful sensation of the grass as its blades touched the bottom of his bare feet.

Daniel had returned to Heaven.

Daniel felt it had to be Heaven. He'd spoken to his father once again, with Jesus to his side. There had been an extra person. While the dream lasted, the color of the third person's skin wasn't even the slightest of an issue. Now fully awake in the flesh, he knew the man to be black.

The black man standing alongside Jesus and his dad was Eugene Thompson.

Daniel had asked Eugene *what he was doing in Heaven*. Eugene said that *it was his time to come and live with the Lord Jesus*. Jesus had both arms around his dad and Eugene. Both men were at total peace. They both had love for Jesus and one another. He didn't have to ask. He could feel it—sense it. Love flowed out of their Heavenly bodies as the river flowed. Their perfect love penetrated into Daniel's heart as he stood in awe.

The three stood on the opposite side of the river, which seemed to be the same river of his previous dream. In every direction, the same flowers sang as if all the choirs in the universe were harmonizing their praises to Jesus. He couldn't remember the words to the song, but knew the tune glorified the Lord.

Daniel was told by Jesus that a message was forthcoming and to handle it with all care. He'd asked Jesus *what would be the message?* Jesus simply smiled lovingly and reassuringly, but didn't verbally answer the question. There was no audible response. The Lord's eyes penetrated into his being pure love until he knew the message without it being spoken.

Daniel tossed his stiff leg off the couch and onto the floor, grabbed the cane and made his way to his feet. He glanced at the clock on the wall. It read 8:25. He limped to the window of the TV room and pecked through the white shades. Daniel spotted them sitting in lawn chairs under one of the numerous oak trees. It was the traditional family gathering for that time of the evening. Oak Grove didn't have an evening service, making the most of the one service they did have each Sunday. Big Jeff was a huge promoter of quality family time before the work week began, and the Harper family, for one, made the most of their Sunday evenings.

Daniel eased his way out the back door and approached the group. They held clear plastic cups with ice cold reddish kool-aid.

"Feel better after your nap?" Susan asked after Daniel limped to within ear shot.

"Sure do."

"Do you want me go get you some kool-aid?"

"I'm fine," Daniel said, taking a seat in the last remaining chair.

"Daniel…I received a call while you were sleeping."

"Who called?"

"It was from the chaplain in Arizona. He had some bad news to pass along to us."

Daniel wasn't surprised, but he went along for the time being. "What's the bad news?"

"There's been a stabbing at the prison...Eugene's been killed."

"I already knew he'd died and gone to heaven. I just spoke to him."

"You just what!" Susan exclaimed.

"Mom, I had another dream, like the one when I was twelve. Eugene's with dad now. They're the best of friends and Jesus is right there with them. You wouldn't believe how happy they are."

"Go on son tell us everything about your dream," Susan said highly interested, but not totally alarmed.

"I got my message mom. I know what I'm supposed to do."

"I can't wait to hear what you are supposed to do."

"The Lord wants me to go for it. Jesus revealed to me that He'll enable me to play baseball again."

"That's wonderful son." Susan didn't know anything else to say. After all, it was just another typical, supernatural day. Scotty sipped his kool-aid and stayed silent. This was definitely more exciting than the bachelor days. The twins were already changing the subject to something more interesting. It's hard to impress young teen girls.

Chapter 34

Tuesday afternoon was a windy, overcast Mississippi day as Chaplain Horne preached a message of love, hope and atonement. Pressing his notes on the wooden podium to keep them from blowing off, Horne suddenly thought of an appropriate illustration that wasn't previously written in the two pages of handwritten material. In fact, He hadn't thought of it until he began to speak.

The chaplain wore his best suit, the only one he owned which was reserved for such an occasion. The refreshing breeze made the graveside service one that could be endured. Without it, the heat index would have made it unpleasant, especially for a chaplain with suit and tie.

There were only eleven people reverently assembled around the fresh heap of red dirt. It wasn't unusual for a State owned coffin to be placed in the ground and covered up before a funeral began. The delivery was on the dime of the taxpayers, so efficiency was necessary. Eugene's body was in the ground thirty minutes after arriving to the cemetery the day before.

Three of the eleven people present were the children of Eugene. They'd introduced themselves by name: Alfred, Terry and Donna. Scotty, Susan, Daniel, Rachael and Rebecca along with Brook and her father, Keith Millard, stood by the grave with the wind sending their hair and clothing into a frenzy.

Mr. Millard had been captivated by intrigue. Normally, he wasn't a man of strong personal faith. But the testimony of his daughter and the evidence of what he knew to be fact brought him to his knees in submission to Christ earlier that same morning. He too had forgiven Eugene for the episode at the convenient store and desired to join his daughter for the funeral. He had the opportunity to meet and thank the family of the man who saved his daughter. He regretted he hadn't already called.

Eugene was laid to rest next to his wife. Engraved on her small headstone was the name: *Eloise Thompson*. Under her name was inscribed: A *Precious Wife and Mother*. At the grave of Eugene, there was no headstone or any other official marker. Only a single, beautifully arranged assortment of flowers stood, having been placed there by his three children.

"Eugene was a very dear friend of mine who had a giant faith in the Lord Jesus," Chaplain Horne proceeded to proclaim. "He ministered to me more than I ministered to him. He demonstrated his faith in God in so many ways. He was a praying man, a caring man. He loved his family and his friends. He went to be with the Lord having given all he knew to give in this life. He had no regrets at death. He had no guilt that I am aware of. He made peace with those from the past. The families present today are a witness to that truth. What he has accomplished through prayer alone should remind us all of its power. Eugene broke down walls of hate, bitterness and despair from his lonely prison cell. He had inspirational faith which was second to none. Eugene absolutely believed that the confinement of his tiny prison cell could not hold back the power of God in the lives of others." Horne paused dramatically, folded his prepared script and slipped it into his coat pocket. He continued with the illustration God had revealed to him. "What we are witnessing today on this windy September afternoon is nothing short of a miracle of God. In my humble opinion, the miracle we're witnessing is equal to the parting of the sea and the feeding of the five thousand. God has revealed a truth to me by this wind that we have with us today…for it is the Wind of God's Holy Spirit that has been touching lives. The Wind of God's favor has been blowing into each of our hearts as a direct result of the prayers from Mulberry penitentiary…."

The chaplain continued for another few minutes with his eloquent message on the Wind of God's Spirit moving in supernatural ways, and those present couldn't doubt the truth of every word spoken.

Following the closing prayer, Susan was first to move forward and respectfully place a single rose on the top of Eugene's grave. She then turned to Eugene's children and one by one warmly embraces them. Tears began to flow. They weren't tears of sorrow, but of joy and love. This set in motion a chain reaction as everyone freely embraced one another. Heaven opened, the September wind was blowing, and showers of blessings fell on all eleven at the funeral of Eugene Thompson.

Daniel had driven his own truck to Brook's house, parked it there, and arrived with Brook at the funeral in her late model VW Bug. The chaplain's opportunity to speak with Daniel prior to the funeral was lost. It wasn't until requesting a word with him following the service that Horne had the opportunity to reveal Eugene's dying words. Daniel was humbled, but not taken-aback. Horne's delivery of Eugene's message was, however, a confirmation to what Daniel already believed. Horne seemed relieved to get that bit of spiritual business off his chest.

Ten minutes later, everyone was invited to the house of Alfred Thompson, the eldest son of Eugene. He'd become a well-respected doctor in Philadelphia. Dr. Alfred Thompson pursued the field of medicine shortly after his father was convicted and sentenced. The sudden loss of his mother to cancer, and father's incarceration, subsequently drove him toward a career in medicine. With no parental guidance or financial support, Alfred had courageously gone back to school and finished his final two years of college, and graduated from medical school four years later. Then he endured three years of Internship at Emory University Medical Center in Atlanta. During his education years, Alfred worked third shift at various factories and studied by day. He borrowed all he could, and earned the rest from his low-paying factory jobs.

Dr. Thompson was motivated to help people who were down on their luck, much like himself. His private practice in Philadelphia accepted families with no insurance. In fact, he didn't file insurance papers at all at his practice. The charges were within budget, a mere $35.00 per-person, per-visit—mostly walk-ins. On average, he would treat more than fifty individuals each day, five days a week. He was known as; *Alfred, the Good Doctor,* by his patients in and around Philadelphia.

Dr. Thompson's residence was the only house big enough of Eugene's children to comfortably accommodate the group. The chaplain planned to fly out first thing in the morning, so the suggested after-funeral-get-together suited him perfectly. Everyone appreciated the unexpected invitation of the Doctor, and for nearly two hours swapped stories. The most interesting conversation began after *The Good Doctor* asked Daniel about the surgery on his leg. They were all sitting in the modest living room and enjoying a variety of non-alcoholic chilled beverages. "They took a chunk of bone out and mended me back together. My left leg is a little shorter than the right," Daniel informed the Doctor.

"Will you allow me to take a look at your leg Daniel? I haven't seen a patient all day and I'm getting antsy." Doctor Alfred suggested.

"Sure, I don't mind." Daniel slid up his left pants to just over his knee. The scar from the surgery extended approximately eight inches and wrapped around his leg just below the knee.

"It appears the incision has healed nicely. Are you experiencing pain?"

"I feel pain when I walk."

"How's the feeling in the lower part of your leg? In other words, is there a tingling sensation in your toes?"

"Most all the time in the toes, but the feeling in my calf, ankle and foot seems close to normal now. After the surgery, everything from the knee down was almost completely numb."

"That's a good sign. The nerve damage is being restored with your rehab and exercise. Keep that up."

"Has your Doctor given you a support brace to pull over the knee area?"

"They have, but I don't wear it much. My knee is really not my problem. The pain extends down my leg when I walk and I'm having serious trouble with balance."

"I see."

"Do you have any suggestions on what I can do to regain my balance? I want to get back to playing baseball."

"So I've heard…We'll, I think I do have a recommendation. I don't know if it will help with balance, but it will possibly strengthen the leg and help with circulation."

"I'm all ears Doc."

"Do you have access to a swimming pool in Meridian?"

"Before my accident, sometimes I'd go swimming in the pond on the farm."

"Are there snakes in your pond? It would be awful if you got attacked by a snake?" Doctor Thompson said with a smile and quick shiver.

"I've only seen a couple, but they're more scared of me than I am of them."

"So they say...well, I don't know if I want to recommend a pond with snakes, but you use your own judgment."

"I've been going to Piedmont Hospital to rehab in their whirlpool twice a week."

"That's not nearly enough to stretch the leg muscles. Daniel you need mobility. Your muscles have contracted and the tissues must be stretched. They need to be expanded. The blood flow is being restricted. Swimming is the best thing I know to rehab this sort of injury and it's going to take more than a few minutes twice a week."

"What are you suggesting?"

"How about one hour of swimming…every day. If you're really considering playing baseball again, go to a pool somewhere in Meridian every day and swim your heart out."

"What about the pond?"

"Don't tell anyone I said this, but if you must, the pond will be fine. Just don't drown, or get snake bit. If you do, just remember I've given you fair warning." The Doctor and everyone listening laughed, including Daniel.

"I'll start tomorrow," Daniel said, before continuing, "Doc, can I ask one final question?"

"This is free advice. I'm not billing you by the hour."

"Do you think I'll be able to run one day?"

"Sure, but time will tell how fast."

"What about the limp?"

"You may have to live with a slight limp. Your body however is a highly complex thing. The signals from your muscles to your brain and from your brain back to various muscles effects your overall balance. You may be surprised how your body can adjust to the limp. It's even possible that you'll run faster, if that's your focus and drive. I believe that swimming regularly will help in every area—balance, strength, pain, everything."

"Thanks Doctor Thompson, you gave me something to think about."

"You are more than welcome. If I can do anything for you, come and see me. Walk-ins welcome, of course I expect you to be running-in."

"You can count on it," Daniel said looking toward Brook.

**

By four o'clock in the afternoon, everyone had departed from Dr. Thompson's place, including his younger brother and sister. Like his other two siblings, Alfred had never married. They teased each other on who would be the first to take the plunge.

Now all alone with his thoughts, Alfred pulled out his wallet from his back pocket and unfolded it. He gazed at a small picture of his dad through the plastic. The picture was the only one he owned except for a much larger family portrait which hung in his bedroom. But the portrait was much older, making his father and mother younger in the picture, and he a small child. The one he carried in his wallet was the most recent picture, taken about two years before his dad was sent to prison.

As Alfred stared at his dad's face, the emotion of gratitude came flooding into his soul. "*Thank you for being my father. Thank you for the prayers. I'm going to keep living my life to help people overcome their obstacles, just as you did. I am so proud of you Dad.*" Alfred said with a tear.

He gently eases the picture out of the plastic and presses it upon his heart. Alfred was proud that he was this man's son.

Chapter 35

The lamp beside Daniel's bed was shining sufficiently upon the words of the Bible as he read passages from the Old and New Testaments. He was lying under a blue bedspread with his head propped on two pillows. The top pillow was folded long-ways enabling the best angle for his neck. His feet which stuck out from the bedspread displayed a rather large hole in one of his white tube socks. A big toe was sticking out. He wiggled the toe when a fly landed for the third time. *What is it about my big toe that this fly likes so much?* Daniel pondered. Occasionally he scratched his head with the pencil in deep thought. A few verses had been jotted on a notepad which was resting on his chest. Other verses were hidden in his heart from years of nightly study. These inspirational nuggets from God's Word would be his motivation to do the hard work ahead.

After more than an hour of reading and scribbling notes, he shut the Bible, eased himself from underneath the covers and delicately got down on both knees. Praying before going to sleep was the normal routine but this night was anything but normal, or routine.

It was the lull before the storm.

It'd been an extremely long and draining day. After Eugene's funeral, Daniel went back to Brook's place in order to fetch his own truck, but decided to stay to get to know Mr. Millard better. The three were so involved in conversation that it was dusk before Daniel left Philadelphia. Although he hadn't driven his truck in months, he was satisfied with having carefully navigated it back to the farm, making sure the bad leg didn't interfere with his ability to drive safety. With the eventful day behind him, Daniel prayed silently to the One who'd promised to enable him in his pursuit to play baseball again. He was to be a testimony to the power of God to prevail in the midst of great odds. He was ready for the challenge.

After his prayer, Daniel sat on the edge of his bed and glanced around his room. The lamp produced enough light to see the dozens of baseball trophies and action photos from various newspaper articles framed to size. Shelf-after-shelf held significant home run balls with the game and date written on each. The wall was memory lane. The awards from past accomplishment were no longer on display to impress himself or anyone else. They'd taken on new meaning. If there was any pride within his sinful nature before the accident, it was now totally gone, being diminished to the last degree. As he sat contemplating *the comeback*, there was a tap on his door. "Daniel, you still awake?" It was Scotty.

"Yes sir, come on in."

Scotty eased his way in and stood in the room. "You've been rather quiet the last couple of days and I just wanted to check on you."

"Yea, I guess I've had a lot on my mind."

"You barely said a word when you came home tonight. Is there anything you want to talk about?" Scotty asked as he proceeded to sit next to Daniel on the bed.

"Tomorrow it all starts."

"You're really going to go for it, aren't you?"

"I'm going to give it my best."

"What's the plan?"

"That's what I've been thinking. I've written out a workout schedule to follow." Daniel opened the top drawer to his night stand, pulls the schedule out and hands it over.

"Look's incredibly challenging." Scotty said after a brief time to digest Daniel's plan of attack.

"I've been working on it in my spare time for a couple of days."

"This is a six day a week program, for six months. Are you sure you can manage this by yourself?"

"I'm going to do the best I can with what I have. Brook volunteered to help as much as possible."

"I want to run something by you that I feel the Lord has placed on my heart. Can I share it with you?"

"Sure."

"How would you feel if I helped you? I've finished the busy season on the farm and I'm available. I have some time on my hands."

"Scotty, I think that'd be great."

"Do you think Brook would get offended? I don't want to get in the way of, you know, your plans with her."

"Don't worry about that. When I showed her this same workout schedule this afternoon, I think it scared her a little. I don't really think she was all that excited about what I'm going to have to do. When Brook is around, I'm sure she will be happy observing. She understands now how serious this is. I'll call her before I go to bed and give her the heads-up."

"That settles it then…I'll be your personal trainer and coach."

"Just like old times."

"You got it. Just like old times."

"I think we better hit the sack. According to your schedule, we're out of here at daybreak." Scotty said.

"I'll meet you downstairs at six."

"I'll be there. You can count on it…Coach."

Chapter 36

At first light Daniel and Scotty stood in the outfield of their make shift ball field. Daniel had grown an inch taller than Scotty over the years, but he'd lost his athletic frame in just three months. Still rather frail from inactivity, the weight scales in the family bathroom showed he'd gained back half the weight that was lost.

They each wore blue sweats and their footwear were black rubber-cleats. Daniel's shirt was white with red lettering on its front which read: *IT'S POSSIBLE*. The phrase being shortened from one of his favorite verses in the Bible: *All things are possible through Christ Jesus our Lord.* After departing from Philadelphia the evening before, Daniel stopped by a small shirt-shop on the outskirts of Meridian. He requested the iron on lettering and purchased three at a discount.

"We'll follow your schedule. I'm just here to help with what you've planned. If I have any suggestions, I'll let you know," Scotty emphasized with the schedule in his hand.

"Sound's good," Daniel said, without his usually companion in hand—The Cane.

For the next hour, Daniel was aided by Scotty in stretching every known muscle in his body, especially in the legs. A towel was placed on the dew covered ground, but this didn't prevent his backside from getting soaked. After getting himself thoroughly flexed, he began doing one-hundred standing knee lifts, grunting with pain and discomfort. He rotated his legs equally. Whatever he did with the good leg, he did with the bad one. The injury had been below the knee, so he could swing it up in amazing fashion. Every morning until the end of October, Daniel had committed himself to the exact same workout. After October, a more advanced workout was planned.

Following the leg lifts, he proceeded to endure one hundred pushups and one hundred situps. He strained to do as many as possible per set until collapsing in pain. Five laps around the field followed, which took ninety minutes to accomplish. He ran about the same pace which he had sprinted for Brook—very slowly, and limping every step. The water was still warm enough for swimming. He had figured that Doctor Thompson's recommendation was sound and swam the length of the pond several times with Scotty rowing in a small fishing boat to his side. Scotty constantly barked words of encouragement as Daniel gasp for air, struggling to keep his body afloat. Wildly swinging his arms and kicking his feet, he splashed the muddy waters to kingdom come. Continuously throughout the grueling, torturous long day, Scotty constantly shouted out words of encouragement; "You can do it!" or "Keep it up Daniel!" or "We're almost there! Just a few more!" or "Give me all you got son!" Scotty's voice could be heard all over the countryside. However, with Susan at work and the twins at school, the only ears who heard were Scotty's parents, who sat on their porch and prayed. Scotty's enthusiasm reminded Daniel of little league, except more intense. It was a grind—blood, sweat and tears.

Brook had promised to stay her distance even though the invitation was open. *"Don't worry about me, I'll be thinking and praying for you. I'll come see you every other evening, so we'll have time for just the two of us,"* he remembered her saying. Daniel only hoped that he had the time, or the strength left for anything after what he intended to put himself through.

Scotty was engaged with Daniel's every move; every lap around the field, every pushup or situp and every stroke in the pond. He carefully monitored it all, and Daniel was thankful for his stepfather/coach/friend. Had it not been for Scotty, his quest would be awful lonesome.

Susan arrived home from her business responsibilities and prepared a quick, but nutritious meal. She was slightly concerned about Daniel's maiden workout, but knew this was his decision. After barking a few motherly suggestions—off she'd go to *sell, sell, sell, and sell* to Meridian's main street shoppers. That business sparkle had returned to her personality. She was back on track.

Soon after digesting the good grub, the soft-toss drill began. Daniel had several wood bats he'd purchased and stored in his closet just in case there was a need down the road. The time to use them was now. He'd made up his mind that pro ball was the target, not college. At the professional level, aluminum bats weren't allowed. The adjustment from aluminum to wood had to be made by every high school or college player who was fortunate enough to get a shot.

From a squatting position, Scotty tossed Daniel balls from the distance of approximately five yards, and he would hit them into a green tarp draped over the fence along the right field foul line. He could still hit, nothing like before, but he could still make fairly good contact. His balance was off and timing mediocre, but the bat was striking the ball consistently. On a few occasions, he stumbled and fell to the ground, but he always got back to his feet, dusting himself off, and continuing the drill. To the duos benefit, they had more than seventy well-used brownish baseballs for the drill. After each ball was hit into the tarp, time would be taken to gather them into a large white bucket. A total of four buckets of balls were hit into the trap before the drill was complete. His hands quickly blistered and soon blood was visible. The bat's handle eventually became stained with his blood, but Daniel wouldn't dare quit, often spitting into them before his next swing. Toughening the hands was all part of the process. Calluses had to be formed, therefore batting gloves were off-limits.

The only kind of glove Daniel planned to use was the Wilson used for fielding. With glove in hand and at a modest distance apart, Daniel got the cobwebs out of his throwing arm, softly throwing a ball with Scotty for thirty minutes. Daniel hadn't thrown a baseball in three months, so he was extremely cautious. He didn't want a damaged arm to go along with his already damaged leg. His body ached and his leg was killing him, but through it all, a smile appeared on his face at being able to throw and catch a baseball again. The ball sounded good popping the leather.

They both realized the obvious truth. Daniel couldn't presently make a single baseball team on the globe, high school or otherwise. Yet they weren't about to give up after only one day. Nothing was going to diminish their drive for progress. Nothing could sidetrack the vision, not one day, one week, or one month. They were committed to stay the course for as long as it took.

* * *

Every day according to schedule, Daniel and Scotty repeated the same exercises and drills. Day after grueling day, week after week, clear skies or inclement weather, the workouts continued until Daniel eventually showed signs of significant improvement.

Brook purposely stayed out of the way. She often sat in a lawn chair near the action and watched the workouts. Occasionally, Daniel would give her a wink or smile, but not as often as she would have liked. It was all about baseball. It was nearly dark before she got her few minutes with Daniel. Brook now missed their one-on-one walks on the farm, but the romantic walks would have to wait.

As the movement and agility of Daniel's leg improved, so did everything else. Eventually, he began hitting from the portable pitching machine. By December, Daniel was hitting the ball with power. With regularity his swings sent balls well over the fence in left field. He still had his limp, but was getting used to it. There were times each day when he thought about his unorthodox style of play. The new mannerism would probably be unusual to others when compared to before. He didn't worry about what others thought. All he knew to do was keep on running, hitting, catching, throwing, stretching, exercising, swimming, and in the end, he was confident God had a plan for his life. Adjustments were being made and they were pleased with the progress so far.

Chapter 37

The beams of light weren't shooting through the barn on this particular occasion. It was late in the evening on Christmas Eve, and with winter temperatures slowly dropping, the evenings were cool, but not yet cold. Sometimes Mississippi didn't have much of a winter.

Earlier, Daniel had worked up a good lather despite the chill in the air. It was his most vigorous workout to date, and he would purposely shut-down the baseball drills tomorrow. While most everyone were sitting around open fires spending time with family and friends, watching holiday movies, or just taking a day to rest the Eve before Christmas day, Daniel worked on his game to near sundown. Traditionally, his family would spend Christmas Day together—eating, opening gifts and listening to Christmas music. So in honor of Christ's birth, Daniel would spend the twenty-fifth enjoying family time and of course, the company of his sweetheart.

An hour prior, Daniel had showered and put on a brand new pair of jeans and a not-so-new blue sweater. He'd anxiously waited for Brook's arrival. The small box had been wrapped and he was nervous. Daniel had never given a girl a promise ring before. He hoped she wouldn't get the wrong impression and think it was a wedding proposal. There was a chance a proposal might be somewhere in the future, but marriage wasn't on the immediate agenda. He'd had the ring for two weeks and couldn't wait to get it out of his possession.

The setting was perfect in the old barn as they sat on their favorite bale of hay. The sun had disappeared, but the light of the evening was sufficient. "It's beautiful Daniel." The ring Brook held in her hand had a small stone imbedded and it sparkled as Brook held it up for viewing. It reminded Daniel of the stone the night of his vision on the field, though not as big. It wasn't a real diamond Brook was looking at, but it looked like one.

"It's a promise ring," Daniel quickly informed.

Brook slid the ring down her finger and gave Daniel a tender kiss of appreciation. "I guess this means we're steady," Brook implied.

"Steady as a truck-load of cotton," Daniel responded, not knowing if he'd heard that line before or if it was an original. "Brook you've been so patient with all that's going on right now."

"I understand what's going on right now. You're doing something that's important to you."

"Yea but…I haven't been showing you the attention you deserve."

"I admire what you're doing. I've never seen anything like it."

"My goal is to attend spring training with the Braves, but no one knows about that yet. I don't even know if the Braves will invite me to spring training with all that I've been through."

"What's on the shirts you wear every day? I believe anything is possible too. I believe in you Daniel, and I think you're doing the right thing. I've seen your passion out there. You've come a long way in the last three or four months, and I'm just proud to be a small part of it."

"You're a huge part of it!" Daniel emphasized. "Your sacrifice on my behalf is incredible. I know you have dreams of your own to be a nurse. That's important work. I'm as proud of you as you are of me, and I just wanted to give you the ring as a token of my love for you."

"I love you too Daniel, thanks."

This wasn't the first time they'd exchanged the spine tingling four letter word, but it was the most meaningful. They both admired the ring and after a couple of smooches, went into the house to eat dinner with the family.

Daniel had heard the story of Brook's family life. She was an only child. Her mother ran-off with another man when she was a baby. She never talked about her mother because Brook never really got to know her. This was the first Christmas she'd spent with a large family. She cherished every second with Daniel's family. Brook's father was tickled pink that his only daughter was courting a nice young man like Daniel, especially the son of the man who saved his Daughter life. Brook promised her father that he'd get equal time for the holidays. Mr. Millard had no problem with the arrangement. He just wanted his daughter to be happy and safe.

* * *

January and February were the coldest months. Swimming was out of the question. Surprisingly, Daniel managed a handful of swim drills leading up to Christmas, so a few adjustments had to be made. However, Daniel did continue his workout through a snow blizzard by Mississippi standards. It snowed almost one inch on February 17th, the first blanket of white stuff the cotton farm had worn in five years. The snow day found Scotty and Daniel completing every single drill without missing a beat. A half-hour snowball fight did breakout however—a little fun to go with the business of baseball.

By noon the following day, the snow had completely melted. Daniel adjusted his chair to prepare to eat lunch with the entire family, including the grandparents from the other side of the trees.

"I think I'm ready," Daniel said shortly after the giving of thanks.

"Ready for what?" Susan asked as she took her first bite of greens.

"I'm ready to give it a go." Daniel wasn't chewing on anything just yet, unlike the rest of the clan.

"Give what a go?"

"I'm ready to give that Braves scout a call. I'm going to ask for a tryout. I want to attend spring training in March," Daniel said assuredly, turning his head to give Scotty a long confident stare.

Everyone seated around the table lowered their forks, except for the teen twins who continued downing their heaps of mash potatoes and gravy piled high on their individual plates.

"Well, that's…that's exciting news I suppose. Do you really believe you're ready?" Susan questioned.

"He's ready," Scotty proudly said in support of Daniel's decision.

"Mom, I was going to be drafted, probably in the top five of the Braves draft just nine months ago. I know they haven't forgotten about me already. At least I hope they haven't.

Susan knew the Braves hadn't forgotten about Daniel. She'd spoken with Robert Walker on two occasions. The scout had called three days after Daniel snapped out of the coma, and the other being a distant four months earlier. Walker knew the extent of the surgery and the rehab in progress. He didn't have an '*I can't wait until Daniel can come to spring training*' tone to his voice. It was more of an '*I hope Daniel can live a fairly productive life*' type of conversation. He'd been respectfully thoughtful and concluded with, "*I wish you folks nothing but the best.*"

Susan had kept the calls to herself.

"Probably number one in the Braves draft," Scotty replied while slicing the fat from a pork chop.

"His name is Robert Walker. I've got his cell number," Susan informed.

"What do I have to lose? I'm strong. My limp is barely noticeable…to me anyway. We've clocked my quickness to first, and I can hardly believe it myself…but I'm just a few fractions slower than my best times in high school. My hitting has come around. My fielding and throwing is back. I feel strong as ever."

"The boy is ready. Now everyone eat. Daniel's got a scout to call after lunch." Scotty rolled his eyes toward Daniel and winked while continuing to divide his pork chop into small bites for proper digestion.

* * *

Everything Daniel wanted to say was written on a piece of notebook paper, but he was still sick to his stomach. What if after months of hard work, the Braves were no longer interested? What if the scout didn't believe him? He began to have doubts as he sat alone in the back yard under a bright blue sky.

After closing his eyes and saying a prayer, he punched the cell phone while reading the ten digit number from the top of the paper.

"Robert Walker." The scout's voice indicated professionalism.

"Mr. Walker, this is Daniel Patton from Meridian Mississippi."

"It is nice to hear your voice Daniel. How are things going?"

"Thing are going great. How's everything with you?"

"On the road as usual…how's your family?"

"The family is great."

"I spoke with your mom sometimes back and she said you were doing better. That accident was something else, but I'm glad everything is looking up for you now."

"Thanks…me too."

"Glad you gave me a call...what's on your mind?"

"Baseball is on my mind," Daniel said while preparing to read the five pre-written sentences.

"I thought it might be," The scout said in a not-so-surprised manner.

"Mr. Walker, I have been working out since last September. All I ask from the Braves is to give me a good look this spring. I'm not begging you for anything. I'm simply offering my availability to attend spring training. All I want is a chance to show the organization that I can still play." Daniel rapidly said without stopping to catch his breath."

"That sounds impressive Daniel. What about the leg? Are you a hundred-percent?"

"I'm one hundred and ten percent."

"I'm surprised to hear this Daniel." The scout paused dramatically. "I'll tell you what. Give me until this same time tomorrow. I'll make a few phone calls and see what can be worked out. I wish I could personally come to Meridian and see a workout myself, but the Braves front office has me on a tight schedule this time of year. The rosters are already set...not a whole lot of wiggle room with availability. In fact, most of the pitchers and catchers reported to spring training two weeks ago. But hold tight until tomorrow and maybe something positive can come out of this."

"I'll talk to you tomorrow then," Daniel said.

"Thanks for the call Daniel."

After the conversation, Daniel folded the piece of paper and said another prayer. He thought the conversation had gone well. A hint of excitement was in the scout's voice.

Chapter 38

The butterflies in Daniel's stomach prevented him from eating lunch with his family the following day. Daniel sat in the same chair, in the same location as the previous day. Scotty and Susan were giving Daniel his space. They were in the house with not much of an appetite either. As for the girls, they ate like they didn't have a care in the world.

Daniel held his mom's cell tightly in his hand. Shortly after one o'clock in the afternoon the phone began to chime. Daniel saw the number. *It was Mr. Walker*. Decision time was at hand.

"Mr. Walker?" Daniel's stomach was in knots.

"Are you ready for some good news Daniel?"

"I'm going to spring training?" Daniel exhorted.

"You're going to spring training son," The scout exclaimed.

"Thank you sir…I won't let you down," Daniel promised.

"You are to report to our rookie camp down in Orlando on March 3rd. I'll pass along the pertinent information in a day or two."

"I'll be there," Daniel said with firmness in his voice.

"Listen Daniel, I can't make any promises but the organization is excited to be able to take a close look at what you can do. Just go down there and do the best you can."

"I intend to Mr. Walker. Thanks for everything you've done for me."

"It's my pleasure Daniel. Let me know if I can help you."

"I'll do just that."

"And do me a small favor…don't go near that God-forsaken barn," the scout said with all seriousness.

"I'll try not to," Daniel said, knowing that the barn had been a tremendous blessing—not at all God-forsaken.

"See you son."

Both Daniel and Mr. Walker snapped their individual phones. The call was over and Daniel Patton was on the Braves list of walk-on participates in Orlando.

* * *

This was Bob's best day in months. To be a conduit in potentially helping make a dream come true for a deserving player was special.

Bob sat at the Chick-fil-A in Valdosta Georgia shuffling through the contract he once intended to offer Daniel. He'd been prepared to beg and plead Daniel at that point. The million-dollar-kid was a past bad memory. He hoped for a good ending even though the former contract was now void. Taking a bite of a grilled chicken sandwich, the Scout only hoped Daniel still had what it took to be competitive in the world of professional baseball. He recalled what Daniel had deep within that most players never discover. Daniel Patton had desire in his heart. That's what the Scout remembered most about his once number one draft pick in the entire country. Even though his name never appeared in the Atlanta Braves draft of last June, Daniel Patton would always be one of the most deserving players he'd ever scouted.

Every eye was glued on Daniel as he opened the door and stepped into the house. The family was seated in their respective places at the large table. By Daniel's even expression, nobody could tell if he was excited or disappointed. Susan had glanced out the window ten minutes earlier and saw him talking into the cell. They knew the matter was now settled and done with. They attempted to read the verdict on Daniel's face as though they were courtroom observers studying the faces of a jury strolling into the courtroom after a long deliberation.

Daniel slowly walked to the table and stood between Scotty and Susan. "I'm headed to the Atlanta Braves Spring Training Camp in Orlando," Daniel said humbly.

The pandemonium of exuberance was instant. Everyone immediately pushed their chairs back and jumped to their feet. It was though each family member exhaled in unison. One by one, they give Daniel an embrace. "I'm so happy for you son," Susan tearfully said while hugging Daniel. "You deserve it. You've worked awfully hard. Now show those Braves what you can do. I'm proud of you son."

Scotty rivaled Susan's embrace with a bear hug of his own. "This is great news Daniel. You're going to Orlando."

The twins simultaneously wrap their arms around Daniel. With one clinging on his left hip and the other on his right, Daniel said, "With God all things are possible."

Chapter 39

Daniel couldn't remember ever having to say goodbye to his family. Now nineteen-years-of-age, he'd never lived without his family close by. Part of the sacrifice of chasing a dream would be departing from the family he loved, the farm he adored, the hometown he'd been raised up in, and the entire State of Mississippi where he'd spent his entire life. But it was a sacrifice he was prepared to make.

Daniel's truck was packed with all the necessities. He had a blue tarp covering the back portion to prevent his valuables from getting wet in case of rain. Orlando, Florida seemed like a world away from the farm.

He'd received all the instructions from the Braves organization on where to report, how to get there, what to expect and what to bring. He wasn't left in the dark about anything. The Braves had a top-notch, well-managed system. Daniel even received phone calls from a couple of coaches associated with rookie camp. The coaches didn't promise Daniel he'd be offered a contract, big or small, but all were positive he'd get his chance to prove himself. It was even noted that a professional staff of trainers and physical therapist would be on site to work with any residual ailments with his leg. Daniel was confident that he'd get every opportunity to show he could contribute to the organization. Most any other prospects wouldn't get the same consideration by simply calling a scout, but Daniel had been highly regarded within the organization before his accident.

"Well, I guess this is it," Daniel said, not paying much attention to the Meridian Star newspaper photographer standing from a distance snapping pictures.

"Call us the minute you get there," Susan ordered as she placed both hands on Daniel's broad athletic shoulders. The thousands of pushups had paid dividends and his stature was more impressive than ever.

"Ya'll just be praying for me. I'm going to give it all I got and then some," Daniel said after giving his mother one last embrace before taking his seat behind the steering wheel.

Daniel salutes the twins with a humorous smirk etched on his face. "Now you have the house to yourself for a change. Aren't you lucky to not have a big brother to tell you what to do all the time?" This was Daniel's attempt to ease the emotions of the moment.

"We'll miss you and I can't wait to see you on TV," Rachael added. Daniel blushes slightly at the premature comment.

Scotty, who'd been standing by his parents, walked to the opened door and shakes Daniel's hand firmly.

"I wish you were going too," Daniel softly said.

"A part of me wishes the same, but this is something you have to do on your own. I'll be right here on this farm praying for you every step of the way. You've put in the work, now go get after it." Scotty was still gripping his hand and staring intently into Daniel's blue eyes.

"I intend to. I definitely intend to do just that. Thanks for everything you've done for me Scotty."

"It's been my great pleasure. Call when you can and Keep us informed."

Daniel nodded affirmatively, shuts the door, turns the key and pulls away. Daniel adjusted his rearview mirror to see those who he was leaving behind. He blew his horn continuously as the truck kicked dust into the morning air. Down the winding farm road he drove admiring their waves until the trees blocked his view. Now alone, he wondered if the tarp in the back was tied down sufficiently due to its violent flapping. Under the unsettled tarp was one suitcase of clothes, a few bathroom supplies and his baseball equipment.

His Bible was upfront, on the dash.

For the next hour, all he could think was how enormously grateful he was that the people he left behind were his family.

Chapter 40

The baseball hopefuls had been arriving throughout the evening. The twelve hour drive was indeed draining, but the instant Daniel's eyes fixated upon the vase Atlanta Braves facility, he had an adrenaline rush. The anticipation of competition overshadowed any residual driving fatigue.

After being cleared at the entrance gate, registering in the front office and picking up his spring training uniforms. Daniel parked his truck in the designed area for all players. He then un-tied the tarp and began lugging his things to a building which resembled a two-story motel. He proceeded up a flight of steps, located room number-48, keyed the door, went in and placed his things on the floor. He'd been told by the young lady at the front office to report to the conference room located just off the lobby for orientation, which would begin promptly at 9:00 P.M. He had a little more than an hour to unwind before it all began.

That was plenty of time to do as he'd promised.

Daniel reached in his pocket to retrieve his cell, and called home. After the brief phone call, Daniel completely organized his clothes into a dresser and hung his three Braves uniforms in a tiny closet by the bathroom. He gazed at them admirably and hoped they would all fit.

Within thirty minutes of entering the room, he heard the door being keyed and a black fellow eased his way into the room. Daniel had just slid his hand into his glove and was in the process of beating a baseball into its leather as his *expected* roommate arrived. "You must be Daniel from Mississippi?" He asked. The athletic looking fellow promptly placed his bags on the floor and walked over to shake hands. Daniel throws the ball into his glove, rises from the side of the bed and shakes his hand.

"Nice to meet you—"

"Dexter Lewis…out of the great State of Texas," he informed.

"Long drive from Texas," Daniel inserted.

"Tell me about it. I've been driving since yesterday."

"Good grief," Daniel sympathetically said.

"Say Daniel, are you the shortstop I've heard so much about?"

"I don't know. What have you heard?"

"Are you the one who was going to be drafted last year, probably number one, but you had some kind of a fall on a farm that put you in a coma for weeks and shattered your leg something terrible?"

Without verbally answering his question, Daniel smiles, sits back down on the bed and rolls up his faded jeans just enough to show Dexter the enormous scar just below his knee."

"I guess that's definitely a *yes*. Proud to know you Daniel Patton from Mississippi…you are quite the story. I saw it on ESPN last night in a Motel 6 somewhere in South Alabama."

"You mean they were talking about me on ESPN?" Daniel asked surprised. "I didn't know that."

"Now you do."

"What do you know about that…I wonder how ESPN knew I was coming to spring training?"

"Word travels fast in the world of baseball. Folks love that kind of stuff…*Mississippi boy attempts to defeat the odds by chasing his dream.*"

"Did they say that last night?"

"Don't get too excited comeback kid. They covered every team in baseball in a two hour special on spring training, but you did consume around three minutes of air time. They even showed some footage of your high school days. Think you can still play like what I saw on the tube."

"I sure hope so. I guess we'll soon find out. Where'd you play?"

"Got drafted in the 24th round of the winter draft out of UT."

"The University of Texas?"

"That's what UT stands for. I'm a proud LongHorn, starting centerfielder for three years."

"Awesome." Daniel's amplified his being impressed.

"Well I better get some of this stuff unpacked. We got a meeting to go to in a few."

Now having formally met his thirty day long spring training roommate, Daniel wasn't in the State of Florida without a friend. The difference between the two wasn't mentioned. Dexter had already signed a contract. Daniel was hoping and praying that one would be offered by the end of March. If not, it'd be back to farm life, working the cotton fields with Scotty. At least that's what he kept telling himself for additional motivation.

Fifteen minutes later, the two roomies made their way into the crowded conference room, took a seat in the back and listened intently as several minor league coaches expound upon their decades of baseball wisdom. There were a total of fifty-six rookie ballplayers hoping to be playing on one of the Braves farm teams in April. The management plainly said at least sixteen would be cut before the end of March.

Daniel felt confident that he'd be in the top forty.

Occasionally during the two hour session, Daniel's mind drifted to the information Dexter had revealed. *Why hadn't his mom mentioned something about it on the phone? They must've heard about it even if they weren't watching ESPN at the time. News traveled fast in Meridian too. His high school friends would've been calling. His coaches would've called. His church family would've started one of their usual prayer chains.*

During the last several months, Daniel and his family had made the commitment to keep his workouts private. He and Scotty didn't want any media out at the farm distracting from the goal. It wasn't until Daniel's departure earlier that morning in which Scotty invited an Oak Grove Church family friend who was employed with the local newspaper as a photographer. The man promised that the article of Daniel's spring training invite wouldn't be published for at least three days. *Surely, the phone was ringing off the hook at the farmhouse prior to his call. Maybe they didn't want to distract. Maybe they didn't want to put more pressure on me…Maybe they just forgot about ESPN.*

Daniel's first spring training pep rally/meeting was in the books by 10:30. Daniel and Dexter stood casually conversing with several other players. No matter their hometown, whether from nearby Jacksonville Florida, or as distant as Bozeman Montana, Venezuela or Cuba, most of the players made an effort to meet Daniel—the ones who'd heard about his fall, anyway.

Matthew Townsend, better known as *Matt the Cat,* the Braves Farm Director who'd been one of key-note speakers, strode to Daniel with a warm greeting. It seemed everyone wanted to pat Daniel on his back and wish him good luck. Whenever Daniel heard the words *good luck*, he'd think, *I pray for it everyday*. Daniel didn't believe in luck or chance when it came to baseball, or life. He'd personally witnessed the providential hand of Almighty God for years. Too much had happened in the past to hope for luck. Surely the same Wind that had blown in Mississippi was more than capable of blowing its blessings of favor in Florida. What Daniel desired was GOD—not l-u-c-k.

Daniel and Dexter beat the imposed 11:00 curfew by just two minutes. They'd quickly walked around the rookie baseball field, which was positioned just behind their living quarters. In all, there were five well-manicured fields. However, only one would be used by the fifty-six hopefuls. The other four much more elaborate fields were for the big boys of the Braves organization.

Within twenty minutes of entering room number-48, both Dexter and Daniel were sound asleep. The 7:00 a.m. breakfast was but a few winks away. By eight o'clock, every player would be on the field beginning their warm-ups. Daniel couldn't wait until daybreak, for it was time to shine under the bright Florida Sun.

It was time for the Wind to blow.

* * *

Daniel's normal routine of rising before the break of day to prepare for his daily workouts were already programmed into his system. Dexter had set his small alarm clock to sound at 6:30. An hour before, Daniel stood in front of the bathroom mirror checking the fit of the Braves spring training practice uniform. Since little league, he'd always been issued number-8, his favorite. The Braves had assigned him number-2. The jersey was blue with a red tomahawk on his chest. The white pants had double-red stripes running down the side. The blue cap displayed a white *A* on the front. After a brief pose, he was shaken to reality. If he didn't earn the right to continue wearing the uniform of the Braves, it'd be a short-lived memory.

The professional uniform wouldn't get to his head, not now, not ever.

As players and coaches were making their way for breakfast, they noticed a lone figure out on the rookie field. Some wiped sleepy from their eyes to gaze through the foggy morning to catch a glimpse of the number-2 jersey. Daniel would mimic his swing at home plate and sprint to first.

"That's my roommate," Dexter said as he walked among his fellow spring trainers.

"Is that Daniel Patton?" asked one of the coaches after appearing out of nowhere.

"Yes sir…that's him," Dexter informed the coach.

"He'll get plenty of that after breakfast. Run out there and tell him to come get some grub, he'll need it."

Within five minutes, Daniel quickly walked into the room and along with Dexter, grabbed a plate and proceeded to get breakfast from the buffet-style-format. Daniel placed an orange, a banana and a couple of sausages onto his plate, and reached into a refrigerated cooler for a pint of milk. Daniel hurriedly sits with Dexter at a center table with four others players. "Patton, you've already worked up a good sweat this morning," an unidentified player said.

"It's a habit of mine that's hard to break."

"Your movement looked pretty good out there," Dexter responded positively.

"Thanks, I'm working on it," Daniel replied with a smile.

After eating the fruit, inhaling the sausage and absorbing the pint of milk, Daniel politely left the group while they continued to devour their individual helpings of eggs, grits, bacon and toast. In less than five minutes of being in the congested cafeteria, Daniel was darting back to the field. There'd be no leisure time until he had a contract in hand.

A table of coaches observed Daniel's eagerness and one replied, "I think the kid came to Orlando to play some baseball."

"We'll have to see how he holds up," another coach replied after sipping black coffee. "If he knew what lies ahead, he might be pacing himself right about now."

"You can say this much for him. He's out to prove he means business," a different coach responded.

"It's refreshing to see a player so eager this early in the morning. Hope his leg is strong enough for the challenge," Farm Director Matthew Townsend said, while biting into a piece of toast layered with grape jelly with the intensity of a *cat.*

After the breakfast for champions, every player was huddled and resting on one knee as the coaching staff spoke with authority as to what was expected each day—*hustle at all times, no walking on or off the field of play, wear your caps at all times and wear them correctly, keep your shirts tucked in properly, stay hydrated, listen to the staff, on and on*. For fifteen minutes coaches tag-teamed in preaching the essentials to the wide-eyed fifty-six. There was already activity on the other fields. The more advanced players in the organization were stretching their athletic muscles for the long spring training day ahead. Daniel recalled the words of Farm Director Townsend. He specifically recommended the importance of focusing on the job at hand. *"Don't get carried away in admiring the guys on the other fields. If you want to advance to their level, you better pay attention to what's going on between your own white lines!"*

They were the words of the wise, though Daniel hoped to meet some of the well-known big leaguers after practice—if possible.

Chapter 41

After an hour of stretching and throwing, infield practice began. A well organized system of rotating each player was utilized. Daniel had always been a shortstop—nothing more, nothing less. But with Daniel's mobility in question, the Braves made the decision to position him at third base. His scouting report stated that Daniel had *soft-hands and an above average throwing arm*, both were essential at the hot corner. His range was of most concern and the third-base-position required less lateral movement than shortstop. The position was new, but Daniel felt that if he could play short, he could play anywhere on the infield.

A coach by the name of Beasley began hitting grounders to each infielder. The outfielders were in two separate groups shagging pop-ups. There were two players other than Daniel at third base, and each proceeded to rotate in and out after each grounder. Daniel fielded each ball cleanly and his throwing arm felt strong. He was tested on a couple grounders in which he made driving catches before jumping to his feet and gunning the ball to first. It wasn't much different than high school ball, except for the caliber of athletes. Daniel was locked-in and holding his own among his fellow third-basemen. He noticed the agility of those at shortstop and figured he could've competed at his now former position too. However, Daniel was content to get his opportunity regardless of the position.

After every player was thoroughly tested defensively, batting practice followed. Daniel had been hitting for the past six months off the pitching machine on the farm, so he reminded himself of the obvious. *See the ball, hit the ball.* Each player would get twenty swings at live pitching from a coach stationed behind a screen half the distance to the pitcher's mound. This sped-up everyone's bat, and required less effort from the coach. Of the twenty swings, Daniel hit mostly line-drives in the gap to left-center, and a couple to right-center. Four balls left the ball park altogether, three soaring high and deep over the left-field-fence. The one drive which traveled over the center-field-fence even caused the big boys on distant fields to pause in an attempt to get a glimpse of the one responsible. The ball bounced into the parking lot—a good fifty-feet beyond the 405 marked fence, though the player who owned the Mercedes wouldn't be too impressed when he discovered the ball put a small dent in the door of his *pride* and *joy.*

The players were allowed a forty-five minute lunch break, but Daniel needed only ten to grab a few bites. He once again left the others in the air-conditioned cafeteria for extra batting practice. During the remaining lunch break, Daniel punished two buckets of balls off a tee. The pounding sound of the balls striking onto the tarp echoed, and faintly was heard by those still enjoying lunch.

Nothing went unnoticed at spring training. The management of every professional sports organization was aware that you can teach fundamentals, but you can't teach passion. After Daniel's half-day of spring training, there was no question concerning Patton's passion for the game, and his aggression to prove he could still play. Daniel was determined to stick-out like a sore thumb when compared to the other players. It was as if his life depended on success. He was going to give it his all. In reality, the Lord Jesus was who he was pursuing.

After lunch, situational fielding practice ensued. Using only nine positioned players on the field, a coach would hit a grounder, a fly, one in the gap to left-center, right-center, down one of the lines, through the infield, a blooper, or a bunt out in front of home plate. "Give me runners on first and second with one out," a coach would bark. A couple of available runners would instantly sprint to the bases and the coach would proceed to rip a grounder to an infielder, who'd normally complete the twin-killing-double-play. When Daniel wasn't at the third-base-position, he was available to run the bases. Every player was utilized either on the base paths, or at their respective position.

During the two-hour session of live fundamental defensive practice, Daniel not only demonstrated his ability to perform defensively with fluidity of movement, but also showed he could still run the bases effectively. A couple of occasions he ran first to third on base hits to the outfield. If Daniel had a handicap, it wasn't something that was holding him back. His all out base running style was more like a race-horse sprinting around the final bend of the track. He'd re-invented his running, and every gear was clicking just fine.

During the defensive and base-running drills, countless double-plays were turned on the infield, hundreds of cut-off men were hit with throws from the outfield, a ton of pop-up slides into bases were performed—including two hard slides by Daniel who effectively bounced up like he had a spring on his hindquarter.

As the day progressed into the evening, there was more batting practice and Daniel was getting into his groove, blasting six towering balls over the fence. But this was hitting off a fifty-something-year-old coach who tossed them conveniently into his sweet spot.

The real test would begin tomorrow when the rookies were divided into two teams for a late afternoon nine inning scrimmage game. The first day of spring training was an opportunity for the players to get their feet wet. The scrimmage would be blue-team against red-team.

No doubt the coaches were pleased with what they saw in Daniel. But could he be as effective in the daily afternoon scrimmages? Daniel was out to prove to the Braves decision-makers, he was up for any challenge, including the scrimmages.

* * *

After each daily scrimmage the *Most Valuable Player* of the game was acknowledged at dinner. Daniel topped every rookie in spring training by receiving the honor four times in the first seven games played. He was eleven for twenty-four at the plate with three home runs. His blue-team named him their team captain and was feared by the red team every time he came to the plate. His defense was highlighted with several head long driving stops, springing to his feet and throwing lasers to first. He was fearless in his demeanor and welcomed every challenge with the courage of Biblical David facing Goliath. Like David who'd previously killed a lion and bear with his bare hands before his confrontation with Goliath. Daniel had faced his giant long before the start of spring training, and God had brought him through the fire.

It was March 18th, the fifteen day of spring training. Daniel sat in the spring training office of Farm Director Townsend along with two other coaches. He knew this was the day to find out if his dream of being a legitimate professional baseball player would be realized. He'd already made up his mind he'd try other teams if the Braves rejected him. This particular evening disrupted his after-dinner workout session. The meeting was at the request of the Farm Director.

It was make-it or break-it time, Daniel naturally figured as he sat in the surprisingly tiny office. *What other reason would Townsend and two coaches gather to meet with me?*

He sat in the only available chair across from Townsend's desk, Daniel calmly waited for him to speak. The other coaches were seated on both sides of Townsend, like they were there as witnesses. "Daniel, you've been incredibly impressive this spring," *the cat* began to say. "This is one of the easiest decisions the organization has had to make in sometime. We want to make an offer to you… first, may I ask if you have an agent to represent you?"

"Not in an earthly sense," Daniel said, wondering if he should've mentioned it.

"What do you mean by that?" the Farm Director asked.

"I mean the Lord is my only agent, except he doesn't represent me, I represent Him," Daniel said, knowing they probably didn't understand.

"Well that's fine then," he said with a perplexed expression. He tried to continue, "Daniel we want to make you an offer. The front office of the Braves has given me the go-ahead to make this offer. If you're not satisfied, we'll go back to the drawing board to see what can be done. In other words, the Braves are prepared to do what's necessary, within reason, to make your contract satisfactory."

"You're telling me I made the cut?" Daniel softly asked before allowing himself to get overly excited.

"We're telling you…if there ever was a more deserving player to sign with the Braves organization, I haven't met him... congratulations son."

"That's great," Daniel exclaimed as cool as possible. Part of the character he'd developed was one which kept his emotions in-check. He didn't get too high when things were going his way. He didn't get too low when they weren't. Every step would be one of trusting God, knowing that in the end all things would work together for the good. He was at spring training to do his best and leave the rest to God.

"It's great for you, the Braves, and especially the fans. We think you have a bright future. And if you keep it up and your leg holds true to form, we think you'll rapidly move upward through the Braves system. Who knows, you might get a shot in Atlanta before it's all over," Townsend said with a satisfied smile.

"I plan on it," Daniel maturely and confidently said.

Farm Director Townsend picked up several papers from his desk and stacks them evenly, as one would a deck of cards. "The contract we want to offer you includes a $100,000 signing bonus which will be drafted into your account on the opening-day-date of April 3rd. You will be paid $3,000 per month which is substantially higher than the average pay of our rookies. There are also several bonuses for performance as stated in the contract. One, if you advance to our Double-A team in Jackson Mississippi within two years of April 3rd you will receive another $100,000 bonus. On top of that, your salary will be doubled to $6000 per month. Two, if you make the minor league all-star team in either Double-A, or Triple-A within three years, another $25,000 bonus will be awarded. And three, if you make the Majors by the time of your 23rd birthday you'll receive another $250,000 bonus, plus a major increase in your monthly pay, being contingent on the minimum Major League salary at the time. Do you have any questions about anything?"

"I don't think so," Daniel said sheepishly. He'd never really considered money being part of his goal. He'd never had a checking account. Once every few days, a letter from his mom would come with three or four twenty dollar bills to buy the essentials, but that's it. Things were about to change financially for Daniel. Townsend and every executive in Braves world knew that less than a year ago, Daniel would have become a teenage millionaire had it not been for the accident. They also were conscious of the fact that if everything went Daniel's way, he'd still get there, eventually.

"Would you like some time to think about it? The contract in my hand is ready for your signature. What do you think?" Townsend said while turning the contract in Daniel's direction and sliding it toward him across the desk.

"Do you have a pen in this office?" Daniel asked without hesitation.

After a pen was handed over, Daniel signs the contract and became an *official baseball player in the Atlanta Braves organization.* Daniel wished his family could've been present for the occasion. He knew the Meridian Star would've loved to snap a picture of the signing. His thoughts shifted to Brook. He couldn't wait to call her. Lately, the phone calls had been brief, much to Brook's dismay.

First things first. Daniel made sure the contract was signed on the right line, which would be followed by a call to his family, and then Brook.

He longed for them to be at his side. They'd be thrilled at the scene.

Chapter 42

"Mom, I've got some great news?" Daniel proclaimed into his cell the instant his mother answered. Daniel was still blown-away by everything that happened fifteen minutes earlier. He left Townsend's office and was now standing beside the left-field-fence of the darkened field attempting to stay composed.

"You made the team?" Susan shouted.

"I made one of the teams. I'm starting out in Single-A—Myrtle Beach, South Carolina in a couple weeks."

"Hallelujah!" Susan yelled loudly through the house. "Daniel made the Braves! Go get Scotty quick!" She screamed to Rachael and Rebecca as they sat on the couch watching a rented DVD.

Scotty was in the barn tidying up things after a long day in the fields. The spring planting season had rolled around again and it was all Scotty and his father could do to stay ahead of demands.

"Daniel, Rachael has gone to get Scotty."

"He must be working hard this time of the year."

"He has son…They've been planting corn this spring. I'm so proud of you. When'd you find out?"

"A few minutes ago, I already signed the contract."

"Even though I'm excited, I'm certainly not surprised. From your calls, I could tell you were proving yourself in a big way." Susan said with happy tears.

"I hope it didn't sound like I was bragging?"

"No, no, I just took every detail I could pull out of you and multiplied it by five. You're my son. I knew something good was going to come out of this thing just by the sound of your voice. Plus, there were Braves spring training reports on-line. How come you never told us about those MVP games?"

"I guess I forgot."

"Right, I'm sure you did," Susan said just as Scotty quickly opened the door and rushed into the house. He had an excited expression plastered across his dirty face. Scotty already knew there was good news from Orlando by the way Rachael summoned him to the house. *Daniel is on the phone and are you going to be forever happy!* She had said, not to totally spoil it for Daniel.

"Hold on Daniel, Scotty is here," Susan said about to burst.

"What's happening sport?" Scotty had zeal in his voice as he spoke into the tiny cell.

"Not much other than signing a contract to play pro ball with the Braves."

"You don't say. That's wonderful! How does it feel to be a professional baseball player at nineteen-years-of-age?" Scotty slapped his dusty thigh with his cap and chuckled in delight.

"Feel's like it's happening according to God's timing."

"Amen to that. Listen, our local TV station and paper have been reporting what we already knew from the internet. I think everyone in the area and especially the church won't be that shocked by the news."

"Yes sir, mom already told me, but she didn't tell me about the reporting. That means by tomorrow everyone should know about the contract."

"Can't keep this from the attention of the media, nor should we want to. This is a big deal Daniel. Have you called Brook yet?"

"I wanted you guys to be the first to know. I'll call her when I get back to my room."

"Well, I reckon you'll be getting paid now," Scotty couldn't help from mentioning.

"Yea, can you believe it, paid to play a kid's game." Daniel didn't volunteer any financial information, yet.

"Do you mind telling us how much you'll be making?" Scotty asked out of curiosity.

"$100,000 bonus and $3000 per month, to start."

"Good…gracious…a-life, what are you going to do with all that money?" Scotty exclaimed while jerking off his John Deere cap again. It was as if Daniel had just struck gold. Susan, with eyes wide open silently mouthed, *how much?*

"I don't know yet. I'll have to pray about it." Daniel was telling the honest-to-goodness-truth.

"You're no longer a poor country boy."

"I never was a poor country boy."

The conversation ended with another shout-out to his mother and he was ordered to repeat the money totals. Baseball was paying dividends, but what made them the happiest was Daniel having overcome long-odds. He'd dreamed of the day since little league. Scotty clearly recalled the ambition of the young boy in the blue Mustang uniform.

After all, he was the coach.

Without mentioning it, Daniel and his family thought of Eugene Thompson. Had it not been for the prayers from Mulberry, they were totally positive that things would be much different. Scotty wouldn't be in the picture, he may have died, and Brook wouldn't be waiting in the wings to share in the excitement.

Three minutes after speaking with his family, Daniel entered room-48 looking forward to his upcoming one-on-one with his love bird. But one of the happiest, most anticipated days of his life had a turn for the worse. Dexter's things were all packed and sitting neatly in the center of the floor. Daniel didn't have to ask, he knew right-off what'd happened. "I wanted to wait until you got back before I left," Dexter said while sitting in the only chair in the corner of the room.

"They cut you?" Daniel asked in frustration. "I thought you already had a contract?"

"Those contracts are just a piece of paper. When they get ready to dump you, they just tell you, contract or not," Dexter replied, trying to make mental sense of the business side of baseball.

"They can't just release you just like that," Daniel said angrily.

"They just did…and it wasn't just me, it was eight others."

"Dexter, I saw you play the game. I saw your talent. You were doing a great job out there."

"Thanks, but it wasn't good enough in their view. It doesn't matter what *we* think, it's what *they* think," Dexter said as he slowly got out of the chair and began picking up his things.

"So, where…will you go?"

"Back home, get a job. I have a degree in Business Administration you know, from UT…go LongHorns.

"Can't you hook up with another team?"

"That's not likely. I heard that once you get released, it's almost impossible to sign with another organization. This appears to be the end of baseball and the beginning of a new chapter in my life. I wish it could've lasted longer…much longer."

"I'm sorry Dexter."

"Yeah, me too," Dexter replied while turning the door knob with his free hand. Before walking into the night, he turned toward Daniel, and with a *brave* smile said, "I'll see you at the show."

"What show?"

"You know…I'll be watching you in the Majors before long. You're an unbelievably talented baseball player. It's been an honor to room with you. Just don't forget me when you get rich-and-famous."

"I won't forget you whether I make it or not. Let's stay in touch," Daniel said as he grabbed the heaviest bag from Dexter's shoulders. "I'll help you carry your things"

"A future big leaguer is helping to carry my luggage." Dexter's remark was an obvious attempt to lighten the situation.

"It's an honor to carry the luggage of a terrific ball player and might I add a perfect roommate."

They walked slowly along the second floor wing and before reaching the stairs, Dexter mentioned, "I know my smelly feet and snoring had to bug you."

"Overlooking the feet and snoring, you were perfect," Daniel replied, sharing a final laugh together.

After reaching a rather odd looking and faded, baby-blue sports vehicle of some sort, they place the luggage in the trunk, exchanged a farewell handshake, and Dexter got behind the wheel.

Dexter drove from the Braves parking facility to begin his dreaded drive back to Texas. Daniel stood in the parking lot and watched the red tail-lights dash into the night.

He didn't have the heart to share his exciting news with Dexter. The time wasn't right.

As the tail-lights flickered in the distance, and finally disappeared altogether, Daniel's mind raced back to an article he'd read at the age of fifteen from a baseball magazine: *What It Takes to be a Major League Prospect*. The article mentioned: *for every one thousand players who signs a professional contract only one would eventually see action in the Major Leagues.* Dexter fell among the nine hundred and ninety-nine who'd be released before realizing his dream. Daniel understood more than ever that it was a long road to the *show* and an even longer road if he made it. He encouraged himself with the words of his undershirt: *It's possible.* Daniel truly believed he'd be that one-in-a-thousand. But when the time came to hang up his spikes, be it tomorrow, or twenty years, Daniel hoped he'd do it as courageously as Dexter had.

Chapter 43

The media hounds were out in full-force, but Daniel purposely limited himself to one interview per day for the remainder of spring training. The buzz of his comeback was picked up on the national news. CNN and Fox networks told viewers the remarkable story of the kid from Mississippi who was defying the odds to get his chance. The Braves front office loved the national attention. Daniel, on the other hand, was determined not to let the hype get to his head. "*I haven't proven anything yet,*" Daniel repeated often.

One young FOX Sports Reporter had asked, "*How does it feel to be in the Braves organization when your Doctors gave you little hope of playing competitively again?*"

Daniel replied with a slight grin, "*I didn't hear the Doctors say that...I was in a coma.*"

A few days prior, Daniel didn't know if he'd be playing professional ball or picking cotton. However, the recent personal clarity didn't prevent him from his extra daily drills, nor did it diminish his zeal during the closing days of spring training. Various members of the coaching staff brought it to Daniel's attention that he'd already made the cut. *He could relax a bit—save a little for opening day.* But Daniel continued to play the game as if he were out to prove himself all over again. In fact, he played at an even higher level in the waning days of spring training. He anticipated opening day in Myrtle Beach, but not so much that he overlooked the baseball of the moment.

He was notified on the final day of spring training that he'd be assigned as the starting third baseman for the Single-A-affiliate of the Atlanta Braves. He was informed that the Myrtle Beach *Pelicans* were the only minor league team in the Braves organization who'd been branded with a different name than that of their parent club. According to sources familiar with Myrtle Beach, the wind blew hard making it difficult for power hitters to hit the long ball. Traditionally, young Pelican players had lousy batting stats, which in turn caused emotions to run high. Myrtle Beach was notoriously nicknamed, *knock down alley*. The wind would minimize an otherwise well-hit-ball to nothing more than a routine out. But Daniel wanted to get off to a good start, gale force winds or not.

* * *

Following spring training, Daniel had only two full days to make the drive to Myrtle Beach, rent an apartment, and find his way to the field. He spent one of those days checking ads with a couple incoming Pelican teammates. At $900 per month, Daniel, Jeff Billings and Bruce Wilson unpacked their sparse belongings into a furnished three bedroom apartment located one-half-mile from Pelican Park.

Jeff was a catcher from Rocky Mount, North Carolina, and built like a freight train. He sported a crew cut that'd make the U.S. Marines envy. Daniel had noticed his physical superiority in the *Braves Minor League Profile Book*. Jeff was five-foot-ten and weighed two-twenty—nothing but pure steel. He bragged that he could bench three-twenty. Jeff's barrel-lunged voice easily was heard from every corner of the field. A voice of authority was a bonus for the catching position.

Bruce on the other hand was a soft-spoken, cowboy ballplayer type, and the only baseball standout to have ever signed a professional contract from his hometown of Bozeman, Montana. When Bruce wasn't wearing a baseball uniform, a pair of pointed-toed cowboy boots stuck out from his tight fitting jeans. But it wasn't the boots alone that made the Myrtle Beach locals turn their heads for a second look. A solid black cowboy hat with a leather band rested perfectly on his round head, and tilted low to the eyebrows. His speech was slow and deliberate. He reminded Daniel of a quick-drawing Marshal out of a Western flick. Daniel felt, in a humorous way, that with even the slightest irritation Bruce would whip his six-shooter out, but this cowboy didn't pack, thankfully. On the field of play, however, Bruce transformed himself into a quick-handed second baseman. He could turn a double-play at the speed of light. Daniel had never before seen anyone bounce around the infield with rabbit-like reactions like Cowboy Bruce.

Cotton Farmer Daniel from Mississippi, Marine Jeff from North Carolina, and Cowboy Bruce from Montana became good-enough friends in spring training to now agree to be roommates.

They hurried to get their stuff into their new apartment. It was almost time to go and checkout their new playing conditions.

Chapter 44

The flag in center was stiffly blowing. Daniel could feel, and to his disbelief, even taste the salty wind. It was his first official at-bat as a Pelican. Head Coach Skip Roland shouted encouragement from the box next to third. Coach Roland had the reputation of getting the most out of his players despite the deplorable wind conditions. "*You bonehead's who have the habit of swinging for the fence, forget it. Think line drives. If you want to advance beyond Class-A Myrtle Beach, you got to hit the ball low and hard, through the infield.*" He'd told his eager team in the dressing room prior to game-time.

Daniel recalled the quote as he glanced toward his new manager, and then stepped to the plate for his first at-bat as a professional. After fouling-off two curves into the opening day crowd of more than eight thousand, Daniel connected on a fastball, stroking a low and hard line-drive which skimmed off the top of the left-field-fence, taking a small splintered chunk of wood from the top of the wall.

It was a two-run-homer, and it vandalized the wall in left.

The cheering fans leaped to their feet in unison as the laser blast knuckled its way over. It was a rarity for the locals to witness home runs, so they made the most of it as Daniel rounded the bases quickly. In the sixth inning, Daniel drove in an additional run with a double to the right-center-gap, going two-for-four in his first game as a Pelican.

After the 6-4 Pelican win, Coach Roland came by Daniel's locker on his way to his office. "Nice game tonight kid." The leathery Coach offers Daniel an obligatory fist pump. "Think liners, low and hard."

"Thanks, I will."

"If I can get it through your thick heads to level off on the ball, it will cut through the wind like a knife. Anything hit high in the air is useless." Roland walked away either in disgust or joy. Daniel didn't know which one. But he did know that as long as he played in Myrtle Beach, he'd take to heart every recommendation from his first professional manager. He'd seen hundreds of players come and go in his seven-years at the helm. The manager knew a thing or two about what it took to be successful.

After the game, Daniel, Jeff and Bruce chose to eat at Denny's, which was just across the street from their apartment. Bruce bit into a burger and wiped mustard from the corner of his mouth and said, "I've got to get used to these wood bats. I've been swinging aluminum all my life." For the time being, the black cowboy hat was off his head and sitting in the booth by his side.

"Daniel, what size wood are you swinging? You turned nicely on a couple tonight?" Jeff's hair was sticking up like a porcupine. He was the only one of the three who didn't have to blow dry before leaving the clubhouse.

"I'm going with a 35-inch, 31-ounce for the time being." Daniel sat straight to inhale after folding too many fries into his mouth. "But I'm thinking about switching to a 32-ounce. I got around a little too quick on a couple of curves. I'm not used to seeing so much off-speed stuff. The pitcher…I forgot his name, but anyway, that dude had a wicked arsenal of curves."

"You're the current team leader in homers, with one. Every ball I hit tonight got sucked-in by mother wind." Jeff's thick arms were propped elbow-first on the table as he chewed on his burger. "I can't wait to go on the road so we can play under normal conditions."

Daniel takes a sip of coke from his straw. "The wind is a test. You can make it your friend, or your enemy. If you resist the wind, you'll get frustrated like all the other players who didn't make it up the ladder." Daniel was privately thinking of the spiritual implication of what he'd just said—need he explain it to his new roomies? "Welcome the wind as being among a friend. Don't fight against it. That's the challenge of Myrtle Beach."

Jeff continued to chomp away at the last of his burger and was in search of the waitress to order another. One burger wouldn't be enough for someone who could bench over three hundred pounds. "At least I did manage a bleeder to right," Jeff mentioned, while smacking his chops and wiping the mustard from the corner of his mouth with the back of his bare-hand.

Bruce picked-up his tall greenish glass with a straw sticking out the top and held it stationary over the center of the table. "I propose an opening day toast to one rocket shot that broke the left-field fence, one bleeder to right, and my one walk with three-strike-outs."

"All three laugh uncontrollably and click their drinks together over the table."

"Maybe you didn't get a hit in the opener, but we couldn't have won without your glove and two very *sweet* double plays." Daniel had always believed that a good offense begins with sound defense.

"What can I say? My big sister taught me everything I know." Bruce confessed jokingly.

"Serious?" Daniel gullibly asked.

"Daniel… I don't have a sister...My mom taught me."

"Really?"

Bruce and Jeff glanced at each other, and laughed at Daniel's expense.

Within fifteen minutes, they were crossing the busy street and heading toward their apartment complex. Luckily, they didn't have to deal with climbing any stairs. Having previously walked the half mile to the park, and back again, the only thing on their minds was sleep. After briefly checking out the availability of stations on the furnished TV, each took to their rooms. It was 11:15 on a Friday night. Tomorrow morning, they had to be fully dressed and on the field by 10:30 to prepare for an afternoon affair with the visiting Class-A Pirates out of Nashville. It would be the second game of a three game series. In fact, they wouldn't get a single day of R and R for two weeks. The beach was just a couple of blocks from their apartment, but it would have to wait. It'd be pretty much nothing but baseball as long as they were playing in the Braves organization.

And that was fine with Daniel, at least.

* * *

In his darkened bedroom and lying under a single sheet, Daniel correctly felt it was too late to call home, but decided to anyway. With the hour change, it'd only be 10:30 Mississippi time. "Hey Mom," Daniel timidly said.

"How's my pro ball player doing?"

"I'm great. I miss everybody, but Myrtle Beach is interesting… I guess. I have a good place to get my feet wet."

"Did you already go to the beach?"

"I'm not talking about getting my feet wet in the ocean. I'm talking baseball-wise. The fans are awesome. I hit a homer tonight in my first at-bat."

"That's wonderful!"

Daniel knew his mom was still half asleep.

"Scotty...wake up, honey, Daniel hit a home run tonight."

"How are the girls?"

"Just fine...Rachael has been asking to move into your room. What do you think?"

"Okay by me."

"Hold on Daniel, Scotty wants to talk with you. Congratulations on the home run son. Here's Scotty—"

"Daniel, what's happening slugger?"

"Sorry for calling so late. I'm just now getting back to the room."

"We'd be disappointed if you didn't. How was the opener?"

"We won 6-4. Pelican Park is going to be interesting. It's a lot bigger than I'd expected—410 straight away, 385 in the alleys, 345 down the lines. The locals really come out in droves. The grass is perfectly manicured. The lights are much brighter than Meridian High. Most players complain about the wind gust from the coastline, but all-in-all these are by far the best playing conditions I've ever played in."

"Keep up the good work. I know it's going to be difficult being away from home for so long. Maybe we can take a few days off in May and come be with you. Son, your mom just elbowed me to tell you that Brook called about an hour ago wondering if we'd heard from you. She also wanted to know how things went with the opener."

"I'm going to give her a call just as soon as I get off with you."

"That's good. We don't want to keep you on the phone long then. Congratulations on number one tonight...we're praying for you."

"Tell mom I'll call her after the game tomorrow afternoon."

"Afternoon game...yea, of course, we pulled up your schedule on the internet, printed it out and taped it to the frig.—1:05 starting time. Wish we could be in the stands, but just know we are thinking and praying for you daily."

"I need all the prayers I can get. I'll be sure to pray for all of you too."

"I believe God definitely has a special plan for you. I know you believe it and I know your mom believes it." Scotty knew the conversation could get longer than expected.

"I know He does. I can feel it. But I honestly don't know the details yet. Maybe soon things will be clearer."

"When the time comes, you'll know what the Lord has for you to do. God's plan isn't like a blueprint to be viewed all at once. His plan and purpose for our lives is more like a scroll which unrolls little-by-little, one day at a time. Look for those little opportunities to glorify Christ as things *roll along*."

"Good advice Scotty...Well, guess I better give Brook a call. Talk to ya'll tomorrow."

"Sleep good slugger."

"You do the same and tell mom I love her."

Two seconds after clicking his cell shut, Daniel punched the rapid dial for Brook and she answered on the first ring, "Thought you'd forgotten about me."

"Now how could I've forgotten about my Mississippi girl?—"

Their conversation lasted until 12:35. At one point Daniel had to get out of bed, cut on the light, scramble through his unpacked suitcase to find the small cord to charge the cell.

The last thing mentioned during their late-night/early-morning, boyfriend/girlfriend, rambling with repetition, on and on romantic conversation, was the possibility of Brook accompanying his family when they came to Myrtle Beach—possibly sometimes in May.

Chapter 45

Eleven-year-old Drew Robinson was still excited a day later, and nothing had changed as he was being tucked into his bed. Despite the diagnosis of brain cancer three days earlier, he wasn't going to be denied the opportunity to attend the Pelican's opening day game.

A couple of weeks prior, young Drew had begun feeling light headed and complained of headaches. It wasn't until his parents took Drew for a routine check-up with their family doctor that they began to worry. Drew's parents figured their son had been experiencing normal childhood growing pains, until their Doctor ordered an immediate scan of the head, and the *mass was discovered.*

The young boy was going to be in a battle for life, and treatment would include an assortment of tablets for pain relief before beginning radiation at Myrtle Beach Cancer Institute.

It was clear to the sick child's parents, Andy and Nancy Robinson, that the game may have been just what Drew needed before beginning his two weeks of radiation. Both Andy and Nancy sat on each side of Drew's bed, and put on their best face, but inside, their hearts were shattered. It'd been a nightmare for the last few days. *How could a loving God let this happen to a precious child? How could it happen to this gift that they'd cherished for eleven years?*

They worried about the cost of treatment. Drew was in construction, Nancy had recently started taking classes at the Community College, and neither had reached the age of thirty-five yet. The young couple had $275 in a savings account and less than that in checking, with no medical insurance.

"Did you see Daniel Patton hit that ball against the wind? Nothing was going to keep it in the park." Drew was still glowing from the game he'd witnessed the night before. It had been twenty-four hours since the opener, and he was still talking about Myrtle Beach's newest slugger.

"You better believe I saw him hit that ball son. I think we got us a solid third-baseman this year. I hope he stays with the Pelicans the entire year." Andy was glad he'd made the decision to take his sick boy to the opener. He deserved to have every joy in life, every opportunity to cheer and clap his hands like any other child, but sadly he may not have another happy occasion for some time.

"Do you think he might go all the way to Atlanta some day?" Drew whispered in a sleepy manner.

"We may see him in a Braves uniform one of these days. He's a top-notch prospect according to what I read the other night," Andy recalled.

There was something in Daniel Patton that had inspired the boy. Something about the way he played the game. His dad had purchased a *player profile* at the opener and read the brief article to Drew. It described the details of Daniel beating the odds to be playing Minor League Baseball. After Daniel's homer, Drew had watched Daniel's every move. He purposed in his little heart that *if Daniel could survive that fall from a barn, he could also survive his condition*. What Drew saw in Daniel was hope.

Andy and Nancy had been upfront with their child. They'd explained the tumor as best they knew how. Drew had to be told of the series of radiation treatments to come and all they would entail. He was heartbroken to learn that the treatments would require him to miss the rest of the school year.

"Sure hope he goes to the Majors after all he's been through," Drew said in a slurry manner. He was having trouble keeping his eyes open, and after a couple of slow blinks, closed them entirely for the night.

Nancy bends down, lifts his hair, and kisses his forehead lightly. "I love you so much son."

Andy and Nancy tiptoed their way out of Drew's small bedroom holding hands. Before closing the door, they turned for another loving and worried gaze at their precious sleeping child.

Drew was at peace in his dreams.

Chapter 46

The Pelicans' coaching staff was amazed at Daniel's tremendous start to the season. During the first ten games of the season, Daniel had hit a whopping seven homers, drove in nineteen, and owned a batting average of .395. Defensively, Daniel was as smooth as a cucumber making only one error in fifty-eight chances. The team was off to their best start in their history with eight wins and two losses. Privately, manager Roland credited Daniel for the team's early success. Daniel had become the spark-plug and inspirational team leader. Additionally, attendance was up fifty percent from last year when the Pelicans finished a distant fifth in the Carolina League.

Roland didn't want recent good fortune to cause his outstanding sluggers to develop an ego. He had informed Daniel after his seventh homer, "*Make sure you stay back as long as possible before you commit to swinging. I've seen more guys in the Carolina League fall into a heck of a slump when they think they've arrived, then the super-stud mentality sets in, and they are ruined for life.*" The manager had a way of keeping promising young players humble.

It was his job.

Publically, he treated everyone the same regardless of how their stats-on-paper looked, but intuitively the coach knew that Daniel wouldn't be in Myrtle Beach very long. The Double-A Mississippi Braves would soon be beckoning for his star third baseman.

* * *

In early May, Daniel got the surprise of his life. While warming his arm before a Tuesday night game, he heard a familiar voice from the stands. "You look good in that uniform sport." Instinctively Daniel glances quickly in the direction of the loud voice.

Their surprise worked perfectly.

Scotty, Susan, his sisters and Brook were standing right behind home dugout, smiling. Daniel focused upon their familiar faces, and then nearly sat down on the outfield grass because of light-headedness. He didn't have a clue his family would be at the game. He was thrilled they were in the park, although his stomach immediately knotted. After a final toss of the ball back to Bruce his roommate, he thought it was best to jog over to greet his family—and Brook. They all worked their way to the railing beside the dugout and waited for Daniel to reach them.

"Who on earth do we have in the stands tonight?" Daniel asked as he approached.

"Thought you might be surprised, now give your mama a hug."

"How did ya'll get here?" Daniel proceeded to hug his mom in shock.

"We drove. We left Meridian early this morning."

"You drove, how come I didn't know about it?"

"It wouldn't have been a surprise if you knew beforehand." Susan finally released Daniel so he could hug the rest, with Brook being the next in line.

"It's great to see you Daniel." He grabbed her tight and squeezed. He lifted Brook to the point of nearly pulling her over the short railing and onto the field.

"I'm so glad to see you Brook." He released his hold slightly and lowered her back to the ground, promptly giving her an appropriate kiss. He couldn't restrain himself from placing a power blast right square on her lips, and his family didn't seem to mind the moment of tenderness. There first public kiss was out of the way, now he could move to the others.

Scotty worked his way to the railing and stuck his hand out, but Daniel wouldn't have any of that. Scotty got a bear hug as well. "Looking forward to watching you play tonight." Scotty was like a kid in a candy store.

"I don't know if I can play now. I'm in shock!"

He then embraces both sisters at once. "How in the world are you girls doing?"

"We came to see you hit one out tonight." Rebecca points to the fence in the outfield.

"Yea, hit a long one for us Daniel. We drove all day." Rachael replied.

"So you're putting pressure on me, are you?" Daniel squeezes their respective shoulder blades.

"Daniel, you go focus on what you have to do. We'll catch you after the game. Let's go out to eat…my treat," Scotty was becoming concerned their surprise was a distraction.

"Alright then, I'll meet you after the game. Ya'll say a prayer for me. I'm going to need it." Daniel smiles and jogs back toward the outfield. He then stops in his tracks, turns, and shouts, "Meet me in the parking lot. You should see my truck…and the food is on me." Daniel had never picked up a tab in his entire life. He could afford it now, and they knew it.

A big deal hadn't been made of Daniel's substantial available funds, although, his family had been informed of the $100,000 he'd deposited into a savings account in Meridian. To them, he was just regular Daniel, preparing his best to play another game.

Fans were piling into the stands by the thousands as Daniel's surprise visitors returned to their seats. In three minutes, the twins were at the concession stand purchasing five hotdogs and five cokes. The game was a new experience for the Mississippians. They had never attended a minor league baseball contest before.

"Scotty, this place is bigger than I thought. The pictures we've seen on the internet doesn't do it justice." Susan glanced around at the arriving crowd. She thought the ten foot mascot was adorable and humorous in its colorful Pelican costume. The vendors were already out in full force selling peanuts, cotton candy and cold beer. She hoped a fan wouldn't request the cold beer in the vicinity of her family. She and Scotty despised the stuff.

Twenty-five minutes later the first pitch of the game was thrown. The stands were at near capacity. The five hotdogs had long been consumed, and the peanuts were being cracked. As the sun lowered, the shadows on the field thickened. It would be the fifth inning before the lights would be turned on.

Daniel was an expert at devoting his full attention to the game at hand. His senior year helped him mature beyond his age in that regard. In high school, he had scouts by the dozens watching his every move. He didn't feel any undue pressure because his family was live and in the flesh. He'd give it his all for the Glory of the Lord, as always.

And as usual, the wind was blowing in from the coast.

Daniel went two-for-four, which included one triple off the wall in right-center, and one single back up the middle. To the distinct pleasure of his partial family, Daniel seemed to be one of the fastest players on the field. "*He runs like a jack rabbit! Look at him fly around those base!*" Scotty had declared in the seventh inning as Daniel slid head-first into third completing his triple in dramatic fashion. They were seated on the third-base-side, so they were able to watch Daniel field several balls and fire over to first. In their opinion, he was obviously one of the more gifted ballplayers on the field, but of course they were family. They also noticed the announced crowd of nine-thousand-four-hundred-and-twenty-three seemed more electrified when Daniel stepped to the plate. It was clear to them that Daniel had become a fan favorite. At every plate appearance the packed crowd began chanting his name, seemingly to impress his family—they knew that couldn't be the case. The fans liked Daniel's game. At Meridian High, there were the old milk jugs with rocks inside. The noise those things produced seemed to rattle and distract every visiting team. Two hundred people could sound more like a thousand, but nothing in their memory compared to their first Class-A minor league game to watch Daniel play baseball. Rally milk jugs were not used during the game, but *the excitement was still brain-rattling*—Scotty had said.

Chapter 47

The Mississippians' stood by Daniel's truck and waited patiently. The congested parking lot had nearly emptied as attendants with flashlights directed the hundreds of vehicles on their way. The Pelicans won the game 7-5. Daniel didn't hit a home run, but one shot did ping high off the wall in right-center, so the twins were almost satisfied.

Daniel finally walked out of a door from underneath the stands and headed in their direction. Susan noticed he hardly had even the trace of a limp.

"You played a wonderful game son," Susan said, hugging him the second he reached her. In fact, everyone received another post-game hug, but Daniel purposely saved the last one for Brook. His arm remained wrapped around her shoulders.

"How long are ya'll going to stay in Myrtle Beach?"

"We figured we'd stay for a couple of more games." Scotty wanted to stay the entire season, but that wasn't realistic.

"That's great." Daniel was smiling wide. His hair had been bleached to the blonde of his youth, as a result of the constant coastal sun. Even the dampness from the clubhouse shower didn't darken it. Brook had both arms wrapped around his waist and he squeezed her in close. "Where are ya'll staying?"

"We managed to check-in at the *Cove.* We have an ocean view, but we were only there for about fifteen minutes before we came to the park. Everyone was so anxious to see you," Susan said.

"You'll enjoy the beach while you're here," Daniel said, glancing in the direction of his sisters.

"We haven't been to the beach since we were babies." The twins didn't remember the occasion, but they'd seen pictures.

"I remember that." Daniel thought of his vision from God following his final game of high school ball.

From the shadows of the parking lot a stranger approaches, breaking up their conversation. "Daniel Patton." The man was now standing next to Daniel. "Hope I'm not interrupting you."

Everyone figured he must be someone who attended the game. Daniel had signed many autographs for fans, and another one was forthcoming. "No sir, you're not interrupting us. Can I help you with anything?" Daniel stated.

"Can I have a word with you in private?" The man appeared troubled and serious. He looked to be around thirty, maybe forty-years-old, dark hair and casually dressed.

"Sure…no problem." He released Brook, smiled to reassure his family, and walked a few yards away with the man at his side.

"My name is Andy Robinson. Listen, thanks for taking the time to speak with me." The man and Daniel shake hands.

"It's nice to meet you Mr. Robinson."

"I know I'm going out on a limb. I realize you don't know me from Adam's apple. But I've got something for you to consider." The man's voice trembled, and Daniel was intently listening. "It's my son Drew. He's eleven-years-old. He has a brain tumor. We listened to the game tonight by radio from the Myrtle Beach Cancer Institute where he's undergoing treatment. My son talks about you all the time. He wanted to come to the opener several weeks ago even though he knew he was sick, so I granted him that wish. He loves Pelicans baseball and really enjoyed your home run that night. You see, your story has inspired him, and to make it short, I was wondering if you might stop by the hospital and pay him a brief visit? He's had a real hard month, but he insists on listening to every Pelicans game—cheers for you in particular. It'd be a complete surprise, and it'd mean so much to him."

"It would be great to visit with Drew, how about tomorrow morning?" Daniel was touched by the request. "My family and girlfriend are visiting from Mississippi for a few days. Do you mind if I bring Brook." He points in her direction, and she wonders about the details of the conversation.

"Sure, that'd be fine. Do you know how to get there?"

"No sir, I'm still learning my way around."

"The Institute is located on Blue-Gill Road about three miles from where we are standing. It's right across the street from Sprint Telecommunications. You can't miss Sprint. It's the tallest building in the area. His room is 213, and his name is Drew Robinson." Andy reminds Daniel of his sons name with emphasis while continuing to point in the direction of the hospital.

"We'll be there sometimes mid-morning." Daniel reached out his hand for a confirmation handshake. "Mr. Robinson, me and my family believe in the power of prayer. Would you join my family for some prayer time?"

"Thanks…that'd be great." Andy's reaction suggested that he was totally overwhelmed at the gesture.

Daniel and Andy eased slowly to join the conveniently huddled group. Daniel explained the situation concerning Drew, and each laid a hand on Andy's back to intercede on behalf of his child.

Scotty placed his left hand on Andy's shoulder and raised his right toward Heaven. The prayer began penetrating the Mercy seat of God.

Chapter 48

The tap on the door came at 9:45 in the morning. Andy and Nancy thought it must be their little surprise. "Come on in," Andy said as he and his wife stood to their feet. They'd spent the night on two cots, which had already been folded and rolled out by a nurse. Daniel and Brook eased their way into the room. Andy and Nancy remained standing, absorbing the moment. Drew was sitting up in his bed watching a cartoon on a television hanging high off the wall. Drew didn't immediately say a word, but his eyes widened as Daniel slowly walked to the side of his bed. Most of Drew's hair had fallen out except for a couple of patches above both ears—the results of intense radiation treatment.

Daniel briefly acknowledged Andy and Nancy, but intentionally gave Drew all his attention. "How's it going Drew? My name is Daniel Patton. I play for the Pelicans." He reaches out his hand to offer a shake.

Drew stuck out his small hand and placed it into Daniels'. The boy was in awe. He glanced at his parents who were still positioned by the window, and with his mouth still wide-open exclaimed in disbelief, "Dad…It's Daniel Patton of the Pelicans!"

"I know who it is son. What do you think about that?" Andy catapulted on his tiptoes and back down again. He was ready to blast out of the room in euphoria.

"I think it's awesome!" Drew said with his mouth still open.

"Drew...I want you to meet my friend Brook." She smiled and exchanged a friendly handshake.

"I hear you are big into baseball." Daniel had become somewhat accustomed to wide-eyed children, especially youngsters who came in packs to every game. Some of the players called them *clubhouse rats* because of their persistence in accumulating autographs from anything and everything in a baseball uniform. But Daniel had a way with the children and took the time to show respect when signing his signature at each child's eager request. However, this was Daniel's first hospital visit to encourage a precious boy who was very sick. It wasn't long ago that he was in a hospital—he could empathize.

"I love baseball. You're my favorite Pelican of all-time."

"Well thanks Drew...that makes me feel important." Daniel even blushed slightly at Drew's sincere compliment.

"Me and my dad listen to every game on the radio." Drew turns his head to the small radio which sat in the window. "I wish I could be there every night to watch you play."

"Maybe it won't be too long before you can. You know God is able to help you get back to the park before you know it."

"Yea, and if you did it, I can do it too."

"That's the spirit Drew. We never underestimate what the Lord can do." Daniel was touched by Drew's attitude and determination to fight. He also began to realize the impact his story may be having on others. That thought had never penetrated his heart until that moment.

"You were sick in the hospital not long ago and now look at you." The child still remembered the facts of Daniel's coma and leg injury from the player profile in the free program. The program is provided to every person who comes through the gates, and Daniel noticed the copy lying next to the phone.

"That's right, and I owe it all to the Good Lord. He's my Helper." The words came out like the Lord was speaking through him.

"The Lord sure did a good job of helping you. You're the best player the Pelicans have ever had."

"Thanks, but I'm sure there have been some great players to come through Myrtle Beach in the past, much better than me."

"Not as good as you. The wind can't even stop you from hitting home runs. It has everybody else's."

Daniel shares a grin with Andy and Nancy, but Drew is straight-faced and completely serious. Daniel glances at Brook and says, "Well Drew, we just wanted to stop by and say hello. It's been a real pleasure to meet you, but before leaving, I've got a neat idea. Why don't we be friends from now on? You know, keep in touch, and all that good stuff. I tell you what...the next home run I hit, know that I'm rounding those bases thinking of you."

"You really mean it?"

"I absolutely mean it...under one condition."

"What's the condition?"

"You be praying for me to hit a home run and I'll be praying for you to get better."

"That's a deal." Daniel and Drew shake on it.

Nancy steps to the side of her son's bed, while Andy follows Daniel and Brook out the door. Once in the hallway, Andy expresses his appreciation to both. "Thanks a-bunch for coming. You'll never know how much this means."

"I meant it when I told Drew we'd be friends. I also want to be friends with you and your wife. If there's anything I can do, let me know. I'll get back with you in a day or two and we will exchange cell numbers."

"Sorry...Nancy and I presently don't have cell phones."

"That's okay, how about your home phone number?"

"We don't have a phone at home either."

"I see....Well I guess I'll call the hospital." Daniel noticed Andy was acting rather uneasy. "Mr. Robinson, did I say something wrong? Is it alright if we stay in touch?"

"If I'd have known—" Andy couldn't finish the sentence, and after a few seconds continued, "It's unreal to not have insurance in times like this. I'll probably lose everything I own...but the important thing is to get the best treatment I can for the best child in the world." Andy was obviously distraught. He was beginning to feel the pressure of mounting hospital expenses. He knew the medical cost involved in battling the life-threatening tumor would be astronomical. "If I lose everything including the kitchen sink, so what, it's just stuff. My son is going to get the care he deserves, no matter the cost." Andy clenches his fist in determination.

Daniel's mind was at work. He couldn't abandon the child. He'd already committed to being a friend. After a slight pause in the conversation, Daniel looks intently into Brook's eyes and speaks frankly to Andy. "Maybe there's something I can help you with."

Andy was listening in bewilderment.

"Maybe I can talk to the team's General Manager and have a fundraiser. You know...a game to raise money for Drew's medical expenses."

"Daniel, are you serious?"

"I've never been more serious about anything in my life. Why else would the Lord have me come here today? I've seen God work in mysterious ways all my life. He wants me to go into action and demonstrate his love." Daniel had chills run down his neck and back when he mentioned the fundraiser. He felt the anointing power of the Holy Spirit.

"I hope you don't think I brought you here to ask for financial help of any kind. I probably sounded like a beggar."

"No, no, Mr. Robinson. This is God's plan. He wants me to help you. I've needed a lot of help myself at times. I sense it in my heart or I would've never mentioned it."

"Thanks for the thought...You do have a great idea."

"Again Mr. Robinson, this isn't my thought. It's the Lord's."

* * *

A few minutes later, Daniel and Brook were climbing into his truck. They had a lunch date with the family at a popular seafood place near Daniel's apartment.

His roommates had agreed to join them.

Chapter 49

Manager Roland stuck his head out of his office and shouted toward Daniel who was seated in a chair lacing up his spikes in front of his locker, "Patton, come see me before you leave for the field."

Daniel was completely dressed in his uniform and game ready, but all he'd been able to think about for the better part of the day was how to approach General Manager Steven Willington concerning the fundraiser for Drew. He didn't have any idea what his field manager might want. In his experience, the couple of times Roland had called a player into his office, it was always bad news. Three struggling teammates had been released from the club in the first month alone, being instantly replaced on the roster by newcomers.

Daniel walked into the office with trepidation. Roland sat at his desk with a pre-game cigar tucked tightly into the corner of his mouth. The cigar was new to Daniel. He didn't know his coach smoked.

"Sit down Daniel. I've got something to tell you."

Daniel pulled up a metal chair and sat without saying a word.

"How do you like the cigar?" Roland pulled it from his clenched teeth and points the thing at Daniel. The aroma of its smoke filled the room, and Daniel was on the verge of gagging.

"You know kid…I never smoke one of these disgusting things unless it's a celebratory moment."

Daniel was aware that the team's seven-game-winning-streak was probably the longest in Roland's tenure as Pelicans Manager. *Possible it was the winning streak he was referring, Daniel thought.* "Let's make it eight in a row tonight," Daniel replied.

"If we do, you won't be around to help us with number nine." Roland said while leaning over to thump a pile of ashes in a trash can next to his desk.

"What do you mean by that?" Daniel's heart had jumped into his throat.

"I was informed a couple of hours ago that you've been called-up to the AA-Mississippi Braves. Congratulations kid, you're headed to Jackson."

"You mean—"

"I mean this is your last game in that Pelicans uniform. You got talent son. You're on the fast-track. You're scheduled to start at third in Jackson tomorrow night." Roland rises to his feet. "Now go out with a bang tonight kid and don't swing for the fence. That wind will knock it down every time." He smiled at his own comment and tucks the cigar slowly in his mouth with satisfaction.

Daniel rose from his chair, walked to the door, and turned for one more look at Roland just before leaving the room completely. His self-absorbed Manager was relishing the moment by inhaling on the moist end of his very long cigar.

Daniel wasn't smiling. He'd developed a good relationship with his teammates, the coaching staff, and the faithful Myrtle Beach fans. He knew this changed everything. In a way, he felt he was abandoning everyone, including a very sick young friend named Drew. At the same time, he knew he was on a mission to make the Major League level, and this was a significant step in the right direction.

"Thanks for all you've done for me. You're a great manager."

"You're welcome...Now get out of here. You got a game to play." Roland tilted back in his chair, and smiled again, while moving the cigar slowly toward his mouth—puff, puff.

Daniel walked out without any hint of excitement.

As Roland began writing the official starting line-up, he continued to tug away on the nasty cigar, even if it made him sick.

Chapter 50

Drew Robinson sat propped up with pillows in the hospital bed with his parents in chairs on each side. The Pelicans game was perfectly dialed to clearly hear every sound of the play-by-play action. It was the bottom of the ninth with the game tied 1-1, two outs, and his friend Daniel was at the dish. Daniel was 0 for 3 in the game so far. It'd be the perfect time for Drew to say a silent prayer for his friend. *Dear God, help Daniel hit a home run to win the game, just this one time God.*

Andy and Nancy noticed that Drew had tightly closed his eyes and locked his fingers together, placing them underneath his chin. They remembered the mutual pledge between their son and Daniel to pray for one another. Drew was being true to his word.

Before Drew had time to open his eyes, the announcer said, "And here is the 0-2 pitch, Patton swings, there's a line drive to left! This ball is going deep…back, back, back!! This ball is out of here!!! And the Pelicans have won the game!!!! Daniel Patton has just delivered a game-winning home run to give the Pelicans a 2-1 win!! That kid is amazing!! Listen to this crowd!!"

Drew came off the mattress in excitement. All three yelled so loud a nurse came running into the room. Drew was pumping both fists into the air. The announcer on the radio declared, "And the Pelicans have extended their winning streak to eight off the mighty bat of Daniel Patton! And this crowd is on their feet as nineteen-year-old Daniel Patton has just delivered a walk-off home run—against the wind!!"

Helping the Pelicans' announcer, Andy added, "Daniel Patton has just slammed a walk-off home run for Drew Robinson!"

"Thanks Daniel," Drew softly said, "And thank you Lord for helping my friend." His face was beaming, and for this brief time, Drew forgot all about his illness. The excitement of the home run enabled Drew to totally forget about his frail, weakened body.

No pain at all, even if it was for a few fleeting moments.

Chapter 51

It was their last game to be with Daniel for no telling how long—so the Mississippi delegation thought. They wanted to enjoy a memorable late-night meal at the popular *Ocean View Seafood Diner*. The Atlantic was dark, but they knew its waves were crashing into the shoreline just beyond the window.

Daniel's promotion to the Mississippi Braves was an unknown fact to Brook and his family. He was saving the news to perfection. Even the media wouldn't know until the morning papers were distributed. The fans would surely be disappointed, but the promotion was intuitively expected by the local baseball community. All of the best-of-the-best eventually got the call, and Myrtle Beach would indeed have a new third baseman by tomorrow night.

"The flounder platter looks like a winner to me," Scotty suggested with his reading glasses tilted on his nose in order to read the fine print of the menu.

"That sounds good by me too," Susan said.

The twins didn't care what was ordered. They were just ready for some food, any food. Brook and Daniel studied a single menu together. Brook didn't have much of an appetite. It'd be their last hour together for a long time—so she thought.

Daniel felt it was the right time to make his announcement. He patted Brook on the knee and placed the large menu on the table. "I've got something to tell everyone." Daniel cleared his throat and everyone noticed. He paused dramatically to make certain he had everyone's full attention.

"What is it Daniel?" Susan was pondering Daniel's expression. A mother's instincts are incredible, and she was making full use of them by reading his eyes.

"How would you feel…if I told you I was going back to Mississippi with you?" Daniel asked with a well-rehearsed straight face.

"I'd say that'd be impossible," Susan said with a bewildered expression—even her keen senses left her clueless.

"Nothing's impossible with God. We all know that by now…I was told by my Manager to be in uniform with the Mississippi Braves by tomorrow night."

"You got called up to Double-A?" Scotty asked.

"That's correct."

After a couple of seconds to absorb the information, Susan shouts, "WELL PRAISE BE TO JESUS!"

After a time of enormous celebration, things settled down a bit. They all knew what *'the call'* meant. The Mississippi Braves were located in Jackson—about a ninety mile drive down the interstate from Meridian. Understandably, Scotty and Daniel had the most working knowledge of pro-baseball procedures. They understood that often players by-pass Triple-A ball altogether, getting the promotion to Atlanta straight from Double-A. Daniel was now technically just one phone call away from Atlanta.

And He hadn't turned twenty-years-old yet.

The seriously injured teenager, who'd been in a coma one year earlier, was the teenager who'd retrained himself to walk. Now, Daniel was the teenager of faith who was technically just one step away from fulfilling his big league dream.

Chapter 52

Daniel had spent half the night securing all his things in the back of his truck. After getting less than three hours of sleep, he was ready to drive away from his apartment of only one month. His roommates were still asleep, and he wasn't about to wake them. Instead he left a note on the coffee table. He had wished them well and hoped to see them in Jackson before long. Anyway, Daniel had spent quality time with Jeff and Bruce through the night as both volunteered in helping Daniel pack and load. He would miss the laughter they often shared, and even offered to continue paying his share of the rent until a replacement could be persuaded, but they dismissed Daniel's offer.

The trip had already been planned and calculated to precision. Daniel would arrive at the hotel, and then follow the old family vehicle across the South. Once in Meridian, Daniel intended to stop at the farm for a thirty minute breather, and then get back on Interstate-20 for the short trek to Jackson. If they left Myrtle Beach by 8:00, he would make it to Jackson by 7:00 that evening, barring the unexpected—game time was 7:40. With the hour time change going in his favor, Daniel should be in uniform before first pitch. It'd be a very long day for sure, but the drive would be much less dreaded with *Ms. Candy Stripe* seated on his passenger's side. The final leg of his trip, Daniel would be on his on.

* * *

It was 7:30 on a calm Myrtle Beach morning, and Daniel walked into the Cancer Institute carrying the same bat in which he'd hit his game-winner the night before. He stepped into the elevator and punched 2. The doors soon spread and Daniel stepped onto the second floor and meanders quickly passed the nurses station, shielding his lumber from any potential suspicious eyes. He arrived at Drew's door and tapped lightly.

"Come in." It was Andy's voice.

Daniel walked in with the bat out in front. Drew was sound asleep and his father was speechless at what he was witnessing. Daniel eases over and softly places his hand on Drew's shoulder. "Drew," Daniel calmly says. "It's time to wake up. I have a present for you."

Drew blinks a few times and weakly opens his eyes. He rubs the sleepy out and in obvious pain said, "Daniel, it's you...you came back." Drew's body looked like a skeleton, and the remaining patches of hair over his ears were gone. He appeared to be on death's door.

"Of course it's me. I told you we were friends didn't I? Look here, I brought you something." Daniel handed the bat to Drew. "This is the bat I used to hit the home run last night." He had written words on the barrel:

Drew, that one was for you
Our God is a Big God
Keep PRAYING.

Drew attempts to hold the bat up for a better view, but its weight was too much. He strains and shakes and finally manages to weld it unassisted. It was like someone had given him the greatest treasure of his life. Tears were rolling down Andy and Nancy's faces.

"Drew my friend...I want you to listen to me. I have to go play for the Mississippi Braves. I'm leaving Myrtle Beach this morning, but I want to make you a promise. We will stay in contact with each other. Every time you look at this bat...be reminded that I'm praying for you."

"You mean you won't be playing for the Pelicans no more?" Drew asked with a sad continence.

"This is the way God has planned it. Listen, I can't stay long, but I'll get in-touch with you in a couple of days. Remember, you pray for me. I pray for you." Daniel leans over the bed and gives Drew a warm hug.

Drew sobbingly said, "I can't wait until you get to the Majors, then I'll watch you on TV playing with the Atlanta Braves."

"If that's God's will...then it will happen. If not, we'll still be satisfied, because we know that God loves us both...right?"

"Right," Drew affirmed.

Daniel walked to Andy and Nancy who were still in tears, and hands what appeared to be a folded check, placing it in Andy's hand.

"Listen Andy, I got to looking at my bank account, and I noticed that there's more in it than I know what to do with."

Andy hesitates while gazing befuddled at Daniel, then glances briefly into his wife's moist eyes, and unfolds the check for a look.

It was a check made out to: *The Drew Robinson Medical Expense Account* in the amount of *$50,000*.

"Maybe this will lessen the financial burden for awhile. I'm getting a substantial bonus in a couple of days. I'll send more at the first opportunity. I still plan on organizing some fundraisers so hang tight. And by the way, there's no official '*Drew Robinson Medical Expense Account*' just yet, but there will be by the end of the week. I'll notify you when everything is set."

"Daniel…I don't know what to say."

"Just thank the Good Lord. This is His love gift."

"But—"

"Just give Glory to God."

With those words, Daniel turned to Drew and displays two-thumbs-up, smiles wide, and then leaves the room.

* * *

Daniel exited the hospital, walked across the parking lot and reached his tarp-draped truck. He opened the door, but before climbing in, he turned, looking toward the second floor window of Drew Robinson. He stares, and as anticipated, the wind of the Atlantic began to gust. It blew West-ward, in the direction of Mississippi. The wind blows through his hair, tossing it back, still West-ward. It felt good on his face.

For he knew it was the Wind of Almighty God—

Epilogue - Five Years Later

It was a comfortable, crisp November afternoon in Philadelphia, Mississippi, and more than three hundred people had arrived to witness the special dedication ceremony. The ribbon-cutting ceremony was about to begin and the Mayor of Philadelphia was in the process of making a few appropriate comments.

The outdoor platform was positioned strategically in front of the newly constructed, state of the arts two story building. The red ribbon was already pulled tight by members of the City Council. Everyone had broad smiles on their faces.

It was a day to be remembered, a day to truly be thankful.

Behind the Mayor stood Atlanta Braves All-Star third baseman Daniel Patton, along with his wife of three years, Brook. She held within her arms their six-month-old girl, Denise. The infant was wrapped in a blanket with a large red *Braves Tomahawk* pointed perfectly for the viewing pleasure of the assembled crowd.

Standing on the other side of Daniel was sixteen-year-old Drew Robinson and his Mom and Dad. He was healthy and beaming with life. The family had flown into Meridian that morning and was driven by limousine to Philadelphia for the dedication ceremony. The trip hadn't cost them a penny. All expense had been paid by Daniel.

The only other person on the stage was Alfred Thompson, son of Eugene Thompson. He seemed the most proud to be apart of *the Miracle.* His face quivered with emotion as the Mayor made his concluding remarks; "So let it be said on this 8th day of November that Philadelphia is honored to be the location of this blessing. The construction is finally over. The ministry underneath its roof will begin at dawn tomorrow morning. May it benefit countless of children in need of compassionate cancer treatment without the burden of mounting medical bills. And may thousands of children come here to these holy grounds and find love, hope and professional treatment from the finest team that can be found anywhere in America…We have on this stage a young man named Drew Robinson who won his battle. Diagnosed with a brain tumor when he was eleven, his parents Andy and Nancy Robinson soon became heavily burdened with mounting medical debt. Thanks to the Daniel Patton Children's Cancer Foundation, every single bill was paid, and they received the finest care available. Ten's of thousands of individuals from every corner of this globe have contributed to this Foundation, and that number is growing by the day…That began five years ago, and is what brings us together today. Also on the stage is a face very familiar to everyone in Philadelphia. Doctor Alfred Thompson has been treating the people of Philadelphia with integrity for sometime now. It's outstanding that Doctor Alfred Thompson has been named the Chief Medical Coordinator, and Director, of this wonderful Institute. You have all likely read the print, and I don't have the time required to repeat the circumstances of what brought Daniel Patton and Doctor Thompson together. All that can be said about the matter is…Astonishing. Thank you all for coming and with that I turn the podium over to Major league player…and the visionary founder of the Daniel Patton Children's Cancer Foundation, our very own Daniel Patton!"

Daniel moves toward the podium and waits for the applause to completely stop. He glanced in the direction of Susan, Scotty, and his sisters who sat in metal chairs on the front row. Keith Millard, Brook's dad was there also. Big Jeff had given the invocation and he sat beside Mr. and Mrs. Harper. There were dozens of Oak Grove Church members in attendance who sat scattered throughout the crowd. They all felt blessed to take part in *God's Purpose.*

Daniel clears his throat to the side of the microphone and speaks humbly, and slowly: "Thank you Mayor and thanks to all who have come to these grounds as a sign of support for this effort. I know it's tempting to look at me and give me credit for this project. But I don't deserve any praise or glory. All Glory must go to my personal Lord and Savior, Jesus Christ. It was by his Spirit that made this day possible. No brick would have been laid, and no funds would have been raised without the love of God moving on the hearts of his people just like each of you. It all started with the prayers of a warrior by the name of Eugene Thompson, who from his lonely prison cell called out to our loving Heavenly Father…And then the blessings came in abundance. It was because of the prayers of Eugene and the Grace of God that I personally have witnessed one miracle after another. I have a wonderful stepfather because of the faithful prayers of Eugene. My life was saved from the jaws of death because of Eugene's spiritual insight on the power of forgiveness. I have a wife and a child I love dearly because of Eugene's prayer. Doctor Thompson is the official Director of this Cancer Institute, who I know is so proud of his father this day. I am also proud of my dad who is in Heaven right now, and I know he is so very pleased with what has transpired. All I can say is, our God is a Good God. Romans 8:28 tells us that *all things work together for good to them that love God, to them who are the called according to his purpose.*" Who can doubt those words today? With that I think it is time to now cut the ribbon, and go to work on behalf of children who deserve to be treated with the best medical care possible, regardless of their financial situation."

After everyone is in place, a pair of over-sized plastic scissors are handed to Daniel. A host of photographers are in position to capture the moment.

The ribbon is cut and falls to the ground. A small shred of the red ribbon breaks free and is caught up by the wind.

It floats upward further.

No one in attendance noticed the piece of ribbon, except Doctor Alfred Thompson. The ribbon hovers mysteriously just in front of the institute's name. Alfred's sight goes just beyond the ribbon to the front portion of the building. The large bold letters included the name of his Mother. He missed her too, so Alfred reads the sign silently, and prayer-fully.

ELOISE-THOMPSON-CANCER-INSTITUE-FOR-CHILDREN

A Word From The Author

—

If this book has blessed and inspired you, I ask you to share it with family and friends as a gift of encouragement. You may even want to hand or ship a copy to someone you don't know that well. The book is available online or through your local bookstore.

If you are a business owner, consider placing a few copies of *Mississippi Wind* for retail purchase.

Introduce the book online to your social network, such as *facebook, myspace,* and other outlets. Tell how you were inspired, and then let them make their own discovery. Consider posting a link on your webpage to direct traffic to the book's webpage.

Consider writing an online review, or for your local newspaper.

If you are a *coach*, consider giving the book as gifts to your players. You may find them playing with a greater sense of *purpose.*

If you work in *prison ministry*, you may desire giving prisoners a copy. The message might change their perspective.

If you are a *pastor or church leader*, you may recommend this novel to your fellowship for inspiration and encouragement.

Let's get this message of God's Grace and life-changing power out to the broader public. Feel free to send me a note concerning your thoughts about *Mississippi Wind.* My prayer is that our Lord will empower you to accomplish awesome things for Him, as well.

dennispatterson@windstream.net

Made in the USA
Charleston, SC
29 November 2015